CHRIST
THE CASE OF

CHRISTOPHER BUSH was born ᴜᴜ̣

in Norfolk in 1885. His father was a farm labour

and his mother a milliner. In the early years of his

childhood he lived with his aunt and uncle in London

before returning to Norfolk aged seven, later winning a

scholarship to Thetford Grammar School.

As an adult, Bush worked as a schoolmaster for 27 years, pausing only to fight in World War One, until retiring aged 46 in 1931 to be a full-time novelist. His first novel featuring the eccentric Ludovic Travers was published in 1926, and was followed by 62 additional Travers mysteries. These are all to be republished by Dean Street Press.

Christopher Bush fought again in World War Two, and was elected a member of the prestigious Detection Club. He died in 1973.

THE LUDOVIC TRAVERS MYSTERIES
Available from Dean Street Press

CHRISTOPHER BUSH

THE CASE OF THE HAVEN HOTEL

With an introduction
by Curtis Evans

DEAN STREET PRESS

Published by Dean Street Press 2019

First published in 1948 by MacDonald & Co.

Cover by DSP

ISBN 978 1 913054 01 4

www.deanstreetpress.co.uk

INTRODUCTION

Labouring under Suspicion
Christopher Bush's Crime Fiction in the
Postwar Years, 1946-1952

SEVEN YEARS after the end of the Second World War, Christopher Bush published, under his "Michael Home" pseudonym, *The Brackenford Story* (1952), a mainstream novel in which a onetime country house boots boy, having risen for some time now to the lofty position of butler, laments the passing of traditional English rural life in the new postwar order, as signified by the years in which the left-wing Labour party held sway in the United Kingdom (1945-51). The jacket description of the American edition of *The Brackenford Story* reads, in part:

> *The Brackenford Story* is the story of a changing England. William saw the political enemies of the Hall gradually successful, whittling away the privilege it stood for. He saw squire begin to sell his land, the taxes increase, the great Hall sold, the beautiful trees along the drive cut down. And then with a Second World War, nationalization, rationing, pre-fabricated houses and queuing. William recalled with gratitude the kindness of his masters and their sense of responsibility for others. He saw that the bad old days of Toryism were not so bad after all. And he never lost his sense of outrage at the loss of something he felt was worthy of preservation.

A few years earlier, in July 1949, Anthony Boucher, the postwar dean of American crime fiction reviewers and a highly socially conscious liberal (small "l"), wrote with genial bemusement of the conservatism of British crime writers like Christopher Bush, in his review of Bush's latest crime opus, *The Case of the Housekeeper's Hair* (1948), making topical mention of a certain anti-Utopian novel penned by a distinguished dying tubercular English writer, which had just been published in June. "However much George Orwell, in *Nineteen Eighty-Four*, may foresee the forcible suppression of 'crimethink' under 'Ingsoc,' English socialism in 1949 takes pleasure in exporting mystery novels which disapprove of the Government and everything about it," Boucher observed with wry irony. "Like most of his colleagues, Christopher Bush is tartly critical of the regime; and an understanding of his unreconstructed Tory attitude is necessary if you're to hope to understand the motivations of this novel."

In both the detective novels and mainstream fiction which Christopher Bush published between 1946 and 1952, Bush, like many other distinguished mystery writers of the Golden Age generation (including Agatha Christie, Dorothy L. Sayers, Georgette Heyer, John Dickson Carr, Edmund Crispin, E.R. Punshon, Henry Wade and John Street), indeed was critical of the Labor government and increasingly nostalgic about a past that grew ever more golden in blissful, if perhaps partially chimerical, remembrance. Yet keeping Bush's distinct anti-left bias in mind, fans of classic crime fiction will find between the covers of the author's crime novels from these years--*The Case of the Second Chance* (1946), *The Case of the Curious Client* (1947), *The Case of the Haven Hotel* (1948), *The Case of the Housekeeper's Hair* (1948), *The Case of the Seven Bells* (1949), *The Case of the Purloined Picture* (1949), *The Case of the Happy Warrior* (1950), *The Case of the Corner Cottage* (1951), *The Case of the Fourth Detective* (1951) and *The Case of the Happy Medium* (1952)--fascinating observation of postwar social malaise in the age of British imperial decay and domestic austerity, as well as details about the rise of rationing, restriction and regulation, the burgeoning black market and, withal, that ubiquitous flashily-dressed criminal figure from Forties and Fifties Britain: the spiv (dealer in illicit goods).

Puzzle-minded mystery readers also will find some corking good no-nonsense "fair play" mysteries. "Few writers can equal Christopher Bush in handling a complicated plot while giving the reader a fair chance to solve the riddle himself," avowed the American blurb to *The Case of the Corner Cottage*, while Anthony Boucher applauded Bush's belated return to the American fiction lists after the Second World War, declaring: "It's good to have Mr. Bush back after too long an absence . . . he presents the simon-pure jigsaw-puzzle detective story with unobtrusive competence." Concurrently in the United Kingdom, author Rupert Croft-Cooke, who himself wrote fine detective fiction as "Leo Bruce," pointedly praised Bush's "urbane and intelligent way of dealing with mystery which makes his work much more attractive than the stampeding sensationalism of some of his rivals."

In the pages which follow this introduction by all means attempt, dear readers, to match your keen wits against those of that ever-percipient gentleman sleuth, Ludovic Travers. Frequently in tandem with his old friend Superintendent George Wharton and with occasional input from his smart and sophisticated wife Bernice Haire, the former classical dancer, Ludo continues to hunt, in his capacity as a sort of special consultant to Scotland Yard (or "unofficial expert," as he puts it), more not-quite-canny-enough crooks. Additionally Ludo, a confirmed fan of American crime films like *The Blue Dahlia* (1946) and *Call Northside 777* (1948), comes to find himself in ownership of the Broad Street Detective Agency, perhaps the finest firm of private inquiry agents in London. In these old and new capacities in the postwar world Ludo confronts his greatest cornucopia of daring and dastardly crimes yet.

THE CASE OF THE HAVEN HOTEL

And so to dinner and the cinema. The second house began at half-past eight, so Worne and I had heaps of time. It was a good show too—*The Blue Dahlia*—a whodunit of the slick American type. . . . Even Worne had to admit that it had been pretty good.

"It doesn't make you itch to write something of the same kind?"

"Devil a bit," he said. "I prefer to remain the only serious novelist in England who's never attempted a detective story."

Detective novelists, some of them arguably based on Christopher's Bush's prickly and eccentric Detection Club colleague Anthony Berkeley, had appeared before in Bush's Ludovic "Ludo" Travers detective saga—see *The Case of the 100% Alibis* (1934), *The Case of the Monday Murders* (1936) and *The Case of the Missing Men* (1946)—but in *The Case of the Haven Hotel* (1948), a vacationing Ludo encounters, and to a degree befriends, an esteemed "serious" novelist, Jeffrey Worne, author of the highly-praised *Scarlet May*, who snobbishly disclaims all interest in murder stories. Worne's smug rejection of detective fiction, made ironic by the fact that Christopher Bush himself was the author not only of esteemed mysteries but of highly acclaimed mainstream novels about English rural life such as *Return/God* and *The Rabbit* (the latter books under the pseudonym "Michael Home"), is only one of the amusing threads in the colorful tapestry of death that constitutes *The Case of the Haven Hotel*--one of Bush's most beguiling tales, despite the presence of much genteel mayhem, including two murders and two attempted murders along with assorted cases of malfeasance and misalliance.

In tone the novel, which is set in the summer of 1946, rather resembles Agatha Christie's Miss Marple masterwork *A Murder Is Announced* (1950), as well as two brightly written contemporary seaside mysteries, Miles Burton's *Something to Hide* (1953) and Christianna Brand's *Tour de Force* (1955). Sorting through the varied shenanigans, criminal and otherwise, of the people at Sandbeach's Haven Hotel—besides Travers, his Scotland Yard friend George Wharton and Jeffrey Worne there are the status-conscious owners of the establishment, Mr. and Mrs. Havelock-Rowse (pronounced Rose, mind you); raffish ex-Commando Major Brian Huffe; vicarial Mr. Peckenham

("A most distinguished-looking old chap . . . Used to be in the Church."); lovely Barbara Channard (who, though unaccompanied by a husband, sports an obvious wedding ring); elderly and confiding Mrs. Smyth ("quite a charming if slightly obvious person"); the seemingly mismatched Major and Mrs. Youngs; Winnie, Ludo's ingratiating blonde waitress; Peggy, a pert and provokingly prying maid; and an utterly egregious young boy named Gerald—will take a most perspicacious reader.

The novel is also reminiscent of another of Agatha Christie's Miss Marple novels, *At Bertram's Hotel* (1965), in that the titular lodgment offers its guests a happy haven indeed, in the case of the earlier novel from the stringent government mandated food rationing which had proven so desperately irksome to a British populace that had staunchly weathered the privations of war and now understandably wanted finally to reap some of the rightful benefits of peace. Utter weariness with rationing among the country's citizenry helped propel the return to political power in 1951 of Winston Churchill and the Conservative Party. In the meantime, Bush's legion of postwar readers could fantasize about the feasts which Ludo Travers and George Wharton enjoy at the Haven Hotel, as deliciously related by Ludo:

> There was roast duck and green peas—and generous helpings at that—followed by an exquisite strawberry flan. George, who has trouble with his dentures, always avoids pips, but Winnie made no bones about bringing him biscuits and butter and cheese.
>
> "They don't skimp you on the butter," George whispered as he began a thick spread.
>
> He might have said the same about the sugar, for he fairly shoveled it into his cup. . . .

Indeed, had it not been for those nasty murders, a perfect holiday might have been had by all the guests at the Haven Hotel that summer. Or nearly perfect, anyway. There would still have been the unfortunate matter of the utterly egregious young Gerald.

Curtis Evans

SANDBEACH
(Scale 6" to the Mile)

CARBURY

THE MOUTH

CARBURY CHINE

PIER

HIGH STREET

MEMORIAL

HAVEN

SANDBEACH CHINE

(ROUGH MOOR-LIKE COUNTRY HERE
WITH BRACKEN AND UNDERGROWTH)

N
S
W
E

PART I

Chapter I
BRIEF INTRODUCTIONS

A PROLOGUE can be an irritating thing. It is like being forced to stand in the queue and listen to mediocre buskers when one might be in one's comfortable seat and enjoying the show. I have tried to avoid it but I don't see how I can, since halting a story for the sake of explanation or harking back to account for something else seems to me more irritating still. But this prologue shall be brief, which ought to be something of a consolation.

Long before you've finished this story—if you ever do—you may think that introductions were unnecessary after all. You'll ask yourself why I didn't begin dramatically at the night when the car appeared at the back door, or the day when a ledge in the face of the cliff saved one murder. Or you may think the story should have begun with the somewhat salacious episode of the lady's bedroom door, or, indeed, at the strange circumstances of the original murder.

But whatever you may come to think, I'm still of the opinion that I'm sparing you trouble. Regard the events at Sandbeach as an anticipated meal. You would hate to be interrupted when half-way through the soup or called away in the middle of the meat course. In other words, the purpose of these three brief sections of introduction is to enable you to begin your meal and—if so disposed—to finish it without interruption.

Or look at it in another way. You are invited to a strange hotel to have dinner with people you've never met. It is a sea-side hotel and the receptionist asks you to wait for a moment or two in the lounge while she verifies the dinner and the situation of your table. While waiting you notice two people who strike you as mildly interesting or even unusual. You also take a good look out of the window at a beach that you've never seen before and the woods that hide the steep slope of the chines. Then you are escorted to your table, and you find that two of your fellow guests are the men you saw in the lounge.

A

I am Ludovic Travers. I am six-foot-three in height, lean in build and I wear horn-rimmed spectacles. All that, with attenuating hair that persists in rumpling at the back, gives me—according to George Wharton—the look of a bemused or slightly dissipated secretary bird. Once I was regarded, and indeed, was content to accept myself as an intellectual, whatever that may mean. Now, in my maturer years, I'm no longer interested in the things I used to imagine I knew. What I know now is what many a better man has come to discover—that he knows precious little and that the unknown is far more fascinating than the known. Moreover, long years in the company of George Wharton have made both my speech and general habits highly unintellectual. Not that I didn't always have a detestation of snobbery, and intellectual arrogance which is its smug relative.

My first association with George Wharton changed both myself and the current of my life. In those days I was regarded as something of an expert in social economics and as such was called in for consultation with the Yard. Something must have gone right by accident for I was called in again. Soon I became assigned to George Wharton on general murder cases, and in less than no time we were as inseparable as mustard and cress, and not wholly dissimilar.

I should here add, if only in fairness to George, that we contrived to do pretty well as a team, and maybe because that in most things we are so much unlike. I am not unpardonably rude, by the way, in introducing George after myself. What I am trying to do is to give George a big build-up. He is the professional, the maestro, and sometimes the whole cast and orchestra, and his should be any applause when this rigmarole about myself is over and the curtain goes up. I am only an electrician or stagehand. What I know, he taught me, and were he no longer there, Scotland Yard would never see me again.

As far as concerns our partnership I make no claim to amazing gifts of deduction. All I have is an alert, active and often far too impish brain; the kind, for instance, that revels in abstruse crosswords. If you are a crossword fan you will be aware of a peculiar experience that often comes to us. A clue baffles us overnight, shall we say, and when we wake in the morning the answer presents itself of its own accord. The sub-conscious has worked the problem out while we slept, at least that's what I've been told. But that same uncanny sort of thing often happens to me when I'm on a case with George. For days we may be harassed with clues and evidence, illusory and contradictory and generally muddling, and then all at once I see a flash of light. I can't explain it, but there it is. And naturally I take no credit.

Perhaps I might add too that I abominate loose ends and the apparently inexplicable. An unsolved problem gnaws at me like a nagging tooth. It follows that as a part of the same mental make-up I have a morbid curiosity. Even my hobby is an interest in every kind of my fellow men. I like to identify their dialects. I like to hear their unprompted views. I look for queer glimpses of motive or character, and enjoy an unexpected irony or an unforced humour.

My age is no one's business, though I can safely state that I am far from senile. If I admit that I soldiered in the last two wars, that should give you a clue. I am married and have a flat in St. Martin's Chambers, which is so near to Trafalgar Square that an opened window is at once taken advantage of by the pigeons. It is also remarkably handy for the Embankment and Scotland Yard. It was on a morning at the end of June that I dropped in there at George's room. So far it had been the filthiest summer on record—the year, of course, was 1946—and I wasn't too happy about holiday prospects.

In strict confidence I should say that George and I had manoeuvred a fortnight's holiday together, and I use that verb because experience has taught us that it is bad policy to let absent wives suspect that their absence means hilarious freedom. But George's daughter was having her first baby, which meant that Jane Wharton would be in Cumberland for at least a month. My

wife had a permit for Switzerland where her sister had been ma-
rooned during the war. That left us to kick up our heels, though
the impression we had tried to convey was that we might con-
trive with difficulty to manage in our wives' absence. If things
got too boring, and a chance presented itself, we might even slip
away for a short holiday. At least that is what I said, and to show
the depths of depravity to which association with George has
brought me, at the very time I said it I had in my pocket reserva-
tions for the two rooms at the Haven Hotel, Sandbeach, for the
first fortnight in July.

B

It would be an error to apply to George Wharton the old tag
of "once seen never forgotten", even if that tag seems the very
perfection of aptness. For the question would still remain—
which particular George Wharton was for the moment under
consideration.

Superintendent Wharton, *alias* the Old General, could never
have become the important figure he was except by absolute
merit. As a product of the old school and his own long experience, he hated short cuts and pinned his faith to sheer hard
logic, the importance of motive, and the eliminatory in method.
Not that he scorned modern detective science, though just a bit
apt to regard it as a parvenu. His personal assets were a vast
amount of common sense, a prodigious memory and a remarkable insight into human nature and motives. It was his boast, for
instance, that he could detect a liar at a mile range. Women were
specially vulnerable to what I may call his methods in inquisi-
torial attack. So much, briefly, for Wharton of the Big Four: in
public a dignified or menacing figure according to which side of
the law the interested party happened to be on.

But all that was only one small side of George Wharton. By
rights he should have been a character actor—a combination,
say, of Bransby Williams, Will Fyffe and a few others with all
their roles and some more of his own. So multifarious in fact
were his little acts and moods that there were times when he

could deceive even himself. George, in short, though never buffoon or mountebank, was a first-class showman, and acting was the blood of his veins.

In height he was just over six feet and his back was a barn end, but only in his dignified moments or his rages—real or simulated—would he pull himself up to his full height. The deceptive, artistic stoop of the shoulders, the vast walrus moustache, the ancient overcoat with the blue velvet collar, and the antiquated spectacles over whose tops he would peer—all those were intended to convey a harmless, slightly downtrodden father of a family in whom was never a suspicion of guile: an Edwardian survival who liked his pipe and his pint, and whose portrait by Belcher would have been an Academy sensation.

George loved the dramatic, and every time he blew his nose it would be with a studied difference. When in his eyes the means justified the end, he could be anything to anyone. He could lie like a virtuoso, wheedle, flatter, hobnob, be aloof or scowlingly suspicious, rage to the point of apoplexy, snort indignantly, be pathetically upbraiding, chuckle with false mirth or wrinkle up his eyes in synthetic grief or pain. Up his sleeve were always more cards than appeared in his hand, and though I had worked with him for best part of twenty years, I was constantly aware of some new stratagem or hypocrisy. Often he could exasperate me to the point of fury, mild-mannered though I claim to be, and my only consolation would be that at times I could be just as infuriating as himself. And yet all these things were what made George Wharton the intensely human and likeable personality that he was. My wife, who simply adored him, once said that if ever he died—which she doubted—she'd love to have him stuffed.

But that morning when I entered his room at the Yard, I couldn't quite identify his mood. There was something vaguely apologetic—or was it pathetic?—in his welcome. He actually helped me off with my wet overcoat.

"A hell of a day, George," I said. "Not much fun at Sandbeach if it's going to be like this. We'll be spending our time playing darts in low pubs."

He gave an asseverating shake of the head, wiped back his moustache with a handkerchief that looked as if it had been the last word in chic in his grandfather's day, and then lumbered back to his desk. Then he adjusted those antiquated spectacles, and I knew at once that something was coming.

"Don't think it's going to make much difference to me," he said. "I look like being stuck here for the best part of next week."

"My God, no!" I said blasphemously.

He shrugged his shoulders.

"Might manage it towards the end of the week. Fodman's mother's seriously ill and not likely to recover, so they've asked me to take over till he gets back."

"And what about the booked room?"

"That's all right," he told me, and the quick crafty look might have included a wink. "That'll come under the heading of justifiable expense."

Then as if ashamed of that brief relapse into frivolity, he gave me a glare.

"That reminds me. All this morning I've been trying to get you. Where the devil do you get to these days?"

"Here and there," I said flippantly. "Still, I'm here, and you've given me the bad news, so what else?" Then I thought of something. "Fodman's on black market stuff, isn't he?"

Then he was staging an ersatz tantrum. Didn't I know he was. And why did things always happen to George Wharton. Nothing but a damn Jack-of-all-trades, that's what he was. And why couldn't Fodman's mother live in London instead of Scotland.

"What's doing specially in the black market line?" I asked him.

He glared again.

"Dammit, don't you ever read the papers! You go to that damn club of yours and instead of informing your mind, what do you do. Drink cocktails and talk politics with a lot of your Oxford and Cambridge pals."

"Oxford and Cambridge is good, George," I told him. "I might say it's really good. But you tell me what was in the papers."

He muttered away for a bit, and then said there'd been two big jobs pulled off the previous night—two lorries at St. Albans and a warehouse job in Camden Town.

"Food or what?"

"Sugar, butter and marge on the lorries," he told me. "The other job dried fruits and jam and the devil knows what."

"I've got an idea," I said, and he raised expostulatory hands. George being ironical is rather like a bear doing a minuet.

"No, no. Not another of your goddam theories! I've got enough worries without that."

I should say that I'm very much of a theorist. When there's a problem to be solved I have no trouble in finding a likely answer and probably I'm right once in three times, which is an amazingly good average. George throws in my teeth the two occasions when I'm wrong. As for the good guess, he casts original scorn on that too, but when it turns out right, calmly appropriates the idea as his own.

"I know it's like teaching grannie to suck eggs," I said, "but what about all these robberies of food-stuffs. It seems to me—as an outsider—that you concentrate too much on the jobs themselves. Why not do a bit more concentrating on the receiving end? The big hotels that buy the stuff."

"Why not?" he told me. "You can settle the whole thing yourself."

That was more of his sarcasm and I didn't see the point.

"Going to Sandbeach, aren't you? Where all the nobs go. They pay through the nose, don't they, and they jolly well expect something better than rations? There's your chance, then."

The buzzer went and he grabbed the receiver. A couple of minutes and he was putting on his waterproof.

"Let's leave things like this," he said. "If I can I'll pop along to your place tomorrow night. If I can't, I'll give you a ring. You carry on as arranged and I'll be at Sandbeach as soon as I can."

He did ring me, late on the Friday night. Fodman's mother had died the previous day, he said, so he expected to get away on the Thursday at the latest.

"Something else might interest you," he said. "Remember that nice little chap, name of Fry, who gave evidence in the Hunt Case? He's at Sandbeach, they tell me, in case you'd like to look him up."

I said I certainly would, even if it meant mixing business and pleasure. Fry was an inspector of the very latest type, and it says a good deal for his likeableness that George had thought him quite a decent fellow. Then before he hung up he mentioned that the gang—the black market lads, he meant—were trying a wholly new technique. If I'd been more interested I'd have asked him what he meant.

C

Facing this chapter is a rough map of Sandbeach, and that, by the way, is not its real name. I think it essential that you should run a quick eye over it while you read these few notes. Houses and hotels, except the Haven and the hotels round Carbury Chine above The Mouth, are not indicated.

Sandbeach is in the South, and you may recognise it when I say it is one of the last seaside strongholds of what were once known as the upper classes. There by the sea they still have their decorous holidays with their children and their nannies. On the excellent course west of the town they play golf in spite of the now abundant presence of the *hoi polloi*, and they lounge in chairs on hotel lawns or on the beach beneath umbrellas with their women-folk or take an occasional swim. They are more subdued and less sure of themselves than before the war, and no wonder after the wringing that Comrade Dalton has given them.

But even Sandbeach is being encroached on by the same *hoi polloi*, among whom I ought to include George and myself, in whose ancestry there's precious little blue blood. From the pier to The Mouth and beyond it to the suburb of Carbury there has been a successful invasion of the non-elect, and there you can hear good cockney and the accents of the Midlands and North. Women paddle there with skirts held high, and there are cafés and kiosks on the beach, and loudspeakers that seem to be always blaring the emetical programmes of the B.B.C., and there is also a monstrous dance hall.

The whole of the beach lies beneath an arc of lofty cliff that rises to as much as four hundred feet. Beneath the cliff then, is the beach, and a hard road, and there are five ways down from the town. The chief is a road—a series of hairpin bends—which is the only vehicular connection. Then there are steep steps between the pier and the Haven Hotel, and by the Hotel itself there are steps for the use of the residents of the west and superior hotels. Then there is a fairly easy descent at Carbury Chine. The one at Sandbeach Chine is more elaborate, with gardens and a waterfall, and there is a charge of sixpence to those who use it.

From the pier to the Haven the beach is comparatively quiet. It is true there are bathing boxes, and donkeys for rides for children, and deck chairs and sun umbrellas for hire, but it might be a wholly different resort compared with the east end. Everywhere the sands are magnificent, and the bathing, even at high tide, is excellent for children, with the sea no more than a couple of feet deep at twenty yards out.

The line of cliff protects the whole beach from north winds. All along its top are gay gardens, cunningly placed shelters and open seats with superb views across the Channel. Just back are a long line of hotels, and still further behind is the town itself. Its population is about six thousand, and with its innumerable trees, immaculately kept streets and its really good shops is as attractive a place as one could wish, crowded though the High Street always seems to be. There is a theatre with a repertory company, a handsome modern cinema, and at the Pavilion on the recently repaired pier, is a pierrot company. A fleet of motor coaches with headquarters at the railway station connect with Carbury, and are available for trips along the coast and inland.

And so to the chines. My dictionary describes a chine as merely a ravine, but there is more to it than that. A chine begins well back from the cliff, cuts sheer through it, and then ends at the sea. In its descent the sides, too, fall gently away, and these are generally hidden by woods and undergrowth. Within a few hundred yards the drop may be as steep as one in two, and if there are paths down, they are hair-pinned.

It is to Carbury Chine that I would particularly call your attention. Its woods and undergrowth descend to that narrow inlet which is known as The Mouth, and on the Sandbeach side the undergrowth at high tide covers the water's edge. But there is another peculiarity. Towards Sandbeach the side of the chine slopes only gradually away. On the Carbury side it practically disappears and long before it reaches the beach it is merged into the shore. But what I want you to deduce is this. All round Carbury Chine are hotels. If you are on the lawn of an hotel on the Sandbeach side, the cliff is still so high that The Mouth is invisible and Carbury is the first thing you see. If you are on the lawn of an hotel on the Carbury side, you can see the whole of The Mouth and even back up the chine. I should add that at high tide bathing in The Mouth is dangerous for children since the water is very deep. Only at the very lowest tide can one cross on foot.

The Haven Hotel is classed as select, even if smaller than most. I chose it because I despaired, so late in the year, of getting anywhere at all. Every hotel in every resort seemed to be booked up, and then an acquaintance of mine happened to remark that his brother-in-law, Havelock-Rowse, owned the Haven Hotel at Sandbeach and something might be wangled. I thought he was talking hot air, but wangle something he did, even if the terms seemed a trifle steep. Twelve guineas a week plus ten per cent for staff seemed to me to demand a high standard of comfort in return, and I doubted if George and I would get it. Neither of us is financially embarrassed, but an outlay of fourteen pounds a week for the sole pleasure of being numbered among what George calls the Nobs or the Big Bugs, didn't strike me as an attractive proposition.

But, as I said, we were only too glad to take anything, and there'd be time enough to holler when occasion arose. On the Saturday morning then—June 29th, 1946—I set off for Sandbeach, and I had George's big bag with my own luggage in the boot. I left the main road early and had lunch at Arundel, then lingered the afternoon away and had tea at Brockenhurst, and it was after six o'clock when I got to Sandbeach. Then I was wrongly directed and it was a quarter-past when I arrived at the Hotel.

I believe that if Shakespeare hadn't used it first in *Macbeth*, I'd have told myself that the hotel had a pleasant seat and that its air did sweetly recommend itself to my senses. Certainly I liked the spot at my very first sight of it—its long smooth lawn overlooking the sea, its background of the chine wood, its own shady trees and the unobtrusive beauty of its gardens. But like Duncan, I wasn't anticipating anything remotely resembling murder, and certainly not the murder of myself. I wasn't anticipating anything but dinner, and the man who took the luggage told me that it was at seven o'clock sharp. He also found a place for my car in the garage annexe, and showed me the room where I'd find Havelock-Rowse, the proprietor.

Which brings us at last to Sandbeach. The introductions are over, the cackle has been cut and we're at the horses. But just a final word of warning. You'll be troubled by no more descriptions—no beauties of nature or exquisite sunsets. Conversations there will be, but you'll make a mistake if you take them for aimless chatter. From now on there'll be never a word of padding. The least bit of what seems chit-chat will probably contain a clue, and everything will have its real significance. And between ourselves, you are lucky to have the Sandbeach happenings pruned and edited. I only wish I'd known at the time what was important and what was not. But that sounds like more cackle, so we'll get back to the moment when I heard a "Come in!" as I knocked at the door of Havelock-Rowse's office.

CHAPTER II
FIRST CONTACTS

HAVELOCK-ROWSE—he pronounced it Rose—was a man of about fifty, of medium height and running to fat. His weather-beaten face had purplish veins and he looked the kind who can take a tot at any time of the day or night and get up in the morning ready to begin all over again. There was a general air of the sporting, man-of-the-world about him, and he had a heartiness which was obviously meant to convey to all his guests that they were in a home from home. He spoke well, if a trifle slangily, and though he began by calling me *sir*, it was *old boy* before our little chat had ended. But I definitely didn't like the sudden pause in the flow of geniality and the wary look when I mentioned that my friend mightn't be down yet, but as soon as I gave assurances that it would make no difference to the payment, and gave him my ration book and Wharton's as well, the heartiness was on top again.

He hadn't the least notion who Wharton was, nor had I the faintest intention of informing him. When he began putting subtle leading questions about myself, I suddenly had one of my cussed, ironical moments and I divulged that I was not wholly unconnected with the Exchequer—a statement not quite devoid of truth considering the sums in which I am yearly mulcted by Comrade Dalton. But I hate a snob, and Rowse was obviously a snob of the first water. Maybe he had to be, but as my old nurse used to tell me—those who ask no questions will hear no lies. Rowse—he was soon telling me to drop the Havelock—was good enough to say he'd known me for a Civil Servant as soon as I'd entered his office.

"You weren't at R—, were you?" he said, mentioning a famous public school.

I said I was at H—, which is much lower down in the hierarchy.

"Both my brother and I were at R—," he said. "Poor chap, he was killed in the last war. Irish Guards, at Loos."

I could have mentioned that that was where I got a D.S.M. as a sergeant of common-or-garden infantry, but I didn't.

"He was a lean sort of cove, like yourself," he was going on. "They used to call us the two Roes. He was the Hard Roe and I was the Soft Roe. Damn good—what?"

I forced a Whartonian chuckle and said it certainly was.

But being at H— had made me one of the elect and he began telling me about my fellow guests. As there were only twenty bedrooms, with Wharton and myself having two, it didn't take long to enumerate the more important. A Brigadier and his family were mentioned first.

"Then there's Jeffrey Worne," he said. "He's staying here for the whole season. He's actually writing a book at the moment."

The name had recalled something, and I had frowned. Then I remembered.

"I've got him," I said. "He writes what one might call domestic drama. Let me see now. What have I read of his. Didn't he write a book called *Scarlet May*?"

"That's right," he said. "Don't get time for reading myself—you know how it is, old boy—but my lady gulps down everything of his she can lay her hands on. Everybody's thrilled of course about him writing a book down here. All wondering if they're going to be in it. I think, by the way, you'll find him very much up your alley."

The list went on with a colonel and his family—this war vintage—and a Major Huffe, who'd arrived only that morning. Then there was a Mr. Peckenham who'd arrived at tea-time.

"A most distinguished-looking old chap," Rowse said. "Used to be in the Church. I think he'll be right up your alley, too."

Those were all the guests he mentioned by name but he added that the children were remarkably well behaved and never bothered a soul.

"Perhaps you'd like to know the routine," he said, and I'd advise you to remember his exact words. "The best hotels here have come to a working arrangement with the theatre and cinema and Pier Pavilion. Dinner is at seven sharp, and the shows start their second houses at eight or half-past, which is very convenient. Lunch is at one sharp and breakfast at nine. Tea's at four but we like to be told at lunch whether or not you'll be in for it. That helps the staff. You know what things are like nowadays, old boy."

I said I knew only too well.

"You'll soon find your way about," he went on, and waved back at the window. "You go down the steps and you're on the beach in a couple of jiffs. We've two boats of our own, by the way, for the use of guests, but you're not supposed to hog them for long at a time. Share 'em all round, if you get me, old boy."

He glanced at the clock and got hurriedly to his feet.

"Getting a bit late. I'll just show you the layout, and then perhaps you'd like to go up to your room. No dressing for dinner, by the way."

I liked the lounge with its verandah overlooking the sea. It had two or three immense chesterfields and lots of easy chairs. There were illustrateds and newspapers and a handsome wireless set, and above all there was a notice which said that children and dogs were not allowed in. Beyond the lounge was an annexe writing-room, and beyond that the dining-room. Rowse said there was a large play-room for children downstairs and a sitting-room for nannies. The lounge, by the way, was deserted, but I could see guests already assembling on the lawn as if waiting for the gong.

I liked both my own room and Wharton's but I didn't like the look of the chambermaid. It wasn't because in my eclectic days I like them young and pretty, for she wasn't much over thirty and she had a certain flashy kind of prettiness. But the lipstick only accentuated the hard lines of mouth, the eyes had a shifty look, the manner was too assured and even pert, and I always did dislike sharp noses. She looked, too, as if she could tell me a considerable deal about the facts of life, and I didn't like the quick peevish look of disappointment when I said I'd do my own unpacking.

"What's your name?" I asked her.

"Peggy, sir."

"I think that's all then, Peggy. Thank you very much."

"Thank *you*, sir," she told me and there was something in the tone that made me wonder just what the devil she meant.

The bathroom was just across from Wharton's room and mine, and there was a handy lavatory. By the time I'd made a quick toilet it was nearly seven o'clock, so I had a peep out of my window which overlooked the lawn and sea. About a dozen people were out there, and obviously waiting for the gong, however indifferent their attitudes might be. Most of the women were seated and the men were standing around. An obvious nannie was collecting costumes and towels from the shrubs on which they'd been hung to dry.

It had been the sunniest day for weeks and it was a perfect evening with a sky that promised well. I gave my glasses a good polish and amused myself by trying from Rowse's descriptions to identify some of the guests. I actually did spot Peckenham. He was a shortish, plump man with a face like a stage bishop's. He was standing apart, chatting with what I guessed—and rightly—was the Brigadier, for he had one of those desert-rat moustaches. I loved the way old Peckenham stood, his plump legs well apart and his hands grasping the lapels of his jacket. If he'd suddenly announced, "Dearly beloved brethren," or looked up at me and called, "Zacchaeus, come down!" I don't think I'd have been much surprised. I was chuckling at the sight of him when the dinner gong suddenly went.

I delayed my entry so as to seem neither too eager nor too diffident. But you know what an ordeal it can be to enter an hotel dining-room for the first time, and the eyes that sum you up and dismiss you, and the heads that crane round as you pass. But this crowd was far too well-bred and never a head was turned. As I was steered across to the very far window, a perfectly charming and handsome woman actually gave me a smile, which was far from bad for a start, and at once I felt that we were going to be a non-cliquish, friendly sort of crowd.

The table for two was in that window recess, and I chose the seat that faced the room. The twenty or so guests looked a normal collection with the younger married generation predominating. The men were in lounge suits and the women had no startling creations, and there was a general air of comfort and quiet good humour. One table of four was actually being jolly in a none too noisy way, and of the old hands everybody seemed friendly with everyone else. Those old hands were easy to spot with tanned arms and faces. Others were pinkish, and some were not even that. The nickname for newcomers was, I was told, the Palefaces. I was definitely a Paleface.

Soup arrived and then a latecomer entered, and I was telling myself that he simply must be Jeffrey Worne. For all his air of apology, his was a studied entrance and—uncharitably perhaps—I thought his pose that of a certain kind of author who imagines he ought to resemble what the public ought to think an author should be. He looked at least forty, and to make him that I allowed for the little side-whiskers that came just below his ears. He was clean-shaven and his face rather sallow, but he looked sturdy enough in spite of the scholarly stoop of the shoulders. His longish hair was brushed well back and he wore tortoiseshell glasses even larger than my own.

He bowed and smiled at this one and that as he made his almost mincing way to the window opposite my own, and then a table hid him from my view and I got on with my meal. The second course was a most excellent boiled fowl, and I was telling myself that it looked as if I'd dropped on my feet, for the soup had been uncommonly good. A few moments later a voice caught my ear and with just a slight turn I could see old Peckenham holding forth to the elderly woman who shared his table. His voice was startling because it was such an epitome of himself—deliberate, curiously prim and even unctuous. I distinctly heard the words: "The Chinese, my dear lady, are an admirable people," and I was wishing he would speak more loudly, for there was something peculiar about his accent. Australian was the nearest I could come at it.

Raspberry and red currant tart arrived, with mock cream, and it was followed by some excellent coffee. Over my cigarette I felt at peace with the world and almost anticipating the next day's meals. I sat on, in fact, till the room was almost empty. From snatches of conversation I gathered that most of the guests were going to various shows. At any rate, when I entered the lounge there were only three people in it, and one was Peckenham.

I took a corner seat by myself and had a look round. The charming lady who had smiled at me came to fetch an illustrated, and remarked what a lovely day it had been. Then she dropped into a chair alongside me and we began discussing the weather. She wore a wedding-ring and looked about thirty, and she was as attractive a brunette as—thirty years ago—I'd have wished to meet. Her manner was just a bit kittenish but she certainly had both looks and an attractive voice. I couldn't help wondering where she had got the gossamer stockings that adorned her shapely legs.

"My only pair," she suddenly said, and I must have blushed up to the eyes.

"A bit hard to come by nowadays," I said, and I didn't notice that she had taken a cigarette from her case.

"May I give you a light?"

The third member of the party was offering his lighter—a gold one at that. He was a tallish, well-built fellow in the early thirties, with a head of hair of what I might call a reddish auburn shade. But there was something the least bit raffish about him; maybe because his manners seemed just a bit too good.

The lady smiled dazzlingly and the cigarette was lighted. Then he was offering me his case—a gold one.

"I've only just arrived here," he told us. "My name's Huffe, by the way."

"I'm Barbara Channard," the lady said, and her eyes lifted enquiringly to mine.

"I'm Travers," I said. "I arrived only this evening."

"That your Bentley in the garage annexe?" Huffe asked, and before I could answer, there was another voice.

"Permit me to introduce myself too. My name's Peckenham." He gave a curious little bow. "I trust I don't intrude."

"Not at all, sir," Huffe told him. He had a Rowse-like heartiness and I was finding it hard to place him. His voice and manner said he was public-school and possibly Army, and then I remembered that Rowse had referred to him as Major Huffe. But old Peckenham was addressing me direct.

"Did I understand, my boy, that your name was Travers?"

I gulped down the subtle flattery of age and somehow we became divided into two pairs. Huffe drew up a chair near Barbara Channard's, and Peckenham and I had a chesterfield in one of the bay windows. He was telling me that he had known a Colonial bishop of the name of Travers and I was admitting with due regret, that he was no relative of mine.

"You're from London, my boy?" Maybe he saw my reactions to that far from apt address. "You'll pardon the familiarity, but I imagine I'm old enough to be at least your father."

"That's all right, sir," I told him, and I couldn't help noticing how primly he sat in his corner, podgy legs well apart and fingertips together.

"You were asking about London," I said. "As a matter of fact I spend most of my time there."

"The Great Wen," he said slowly and raised his eyes to the ceiling. "I often wonder what Cobbett would think of it now." Then he let out a sigh. "It's a city that I haven't really seen for years. In my youth I spent some months there, but since then—" and he gave a slow wave of the hand for the rest.

"A cigarette, sir?" I said.

"Thank you, my boy—no," he said. "The weed and I have been at cross purposes for many years. When I first took up missionary work in China. . . ."

I wish I could play you a record of that slow, fruity voice with its touches of clerical intonation and stilted vocabulary. To me it was a sheer joy to be listening to someone straight out of Dickens, and someone who could talk convincingly and not pester with questions. Now and again I could also catch the faint voices or little gurgles of laughter from across the room. Major Huffe and Barbara Channard seemed to have taken to each other from the word go.

"And you've now retired, sir?" I asked Peckenham.

He pursed his lips reflectively.

"Not retired—no. It was the parting of the ways. I felt a loss of sympathy with my vocation. There were serious doubts about fundamentals, if I may put it that way. I felt it time that the Church and myself went our separate ways." He hesitated for a moment. "I trust you don't regard me as one who set his hand to the plough and then turned back?"

"Not at all," I said piously. "One ought to respect every man's principles."

He gave me a little bow at that. He had fortunately not been without means, he said, and now in his declining years was allowing himself to partake of a little leisure.

Barbara Channard and Major Huffe were just leaving the room. The door was actually closing behind Huffe when I saw them.

"A remarkably attractive woman, if I may say so," Peckenham observed, eyes still on the door. "She reminds me of the wife of a certain Dean of my acquaintance far too many years ago. *Eheu fugaces labuntur anni.*"

He gave me an almost whimsical look out of the corner of his eye, and I took the challenge up.

"True enough, sir. The years certainly do gallop away."

He gave a little chuckle.

"A classical scholar, I perceive. But about the lady. A widow, I understand."

"Genuine or grass?" I asked him.

He chuckled again, but before he could answer, in came the elderly woman with whom he'd shared a table at dinner. He introduced her as Mrs. Smyth, and she seemed quite a charming if slightly obvious person.

"Would you mind if I had the wireless on?" she asked us. "There's a play on about Florence Nightingale, and I do so like Gladys Young."

"My dear lady, of course not," Peckenham assured her. "In fact I'd like to hear the play myself."

"I have to go now in any case," I told them, and smiled a good-bye and left.

As I came rather absentmindedly to the junction of the two corridors just short of the front entrance, I barged into a man. It was Jeffrey Worne, and we were going the same way. Each hastened to apologise to the other, and then we introduced ourselves.

"You're an author, aren't you?" I said.

He seemed a bit taken aback by the abruptness of the question, and I knew it would have been more tactful to have said *famous* author.

"As a matter of fact I am," he told me. "An indifferent one, I fear."

"You're too modest," I said, and I saw him perk up at once. It was still short of nine o'clock and almost as good as broad daylight, and now I was seeing him closely, there was something vaguely familiar about him.

"Do you know, I think we've met before," I said.

He looked quite startled, then gave a nervous little laugh.

"Probably at some reception or other." He gave me another cautious look. "You're literary, are you?"

He had a rather querulous voice and an unfortunately patronising manner. I could have said that I'd done some writing myself but I preferred at the moment to keep that side of me dark.

"I subscribe to a lending library," I said with what was meant to be humour. "But invitations to receptions for literary lions like yourself never come my way."

I threw in that bit about the lions because I guessed it would please him, but I was more sure than ever that I'd met him somewhere, and in that forgotten context my mind was refusing to associate him with Jeffrey Worne. I had in fact seen the man but I didn't recall the name.

"Are you going anywhere in particular?" he asked me, for we were well past the main entrance.

"Just taking a casual stroll," I said. "Trying to get the lie of the land here. I'm an absolute stranger."

"I always take a walk about this time," he said. "I happen to be writing a book, and that can be pretty tiring work. I find a late walk makes all the difference next morning." He led the way left along the cliff gardens and he began telling me about the town. The paths went up and down, and often fairly steeply, and soon I was noticing something. When one goes steeply up, the tendency is to throw the body forward. That should have been easier for him with his scholarly stoop than for me, but what I noticed was that when we came to the top of a rise and we naturally straightened ourselves, he forgot once or twice to reassume that scholarly stoop.

"You're a Londoner?" I happened to ask him.

"No," he said slowly. "I can't say that I am. If it didn't sound egotistic, I'd call myself a citizen of the world. I like moving from place to place. Staying here a few months and then there." He waved a hand at the steps in front of us. "Like to go down to the sea?"

I waved him on and he went first down the steep steps, a hand always on the rail. The setting sun caught us dazzlingly as we turned west on the open face of the cliff, and then as it came sideways I noticed something else. I almost missed a step and my eyes were hardly a foot from his hatless head, so I couldn't have made a mistake. I even contrived to look again and at as close a range, and there was never a doubt about it. Worne's hair was dyed. At the roots I could see the newer growth and it was either blonde or grey against the dyed black hair.

That didn't give me any feeling of superiority or contempt. Authors can be queer fish, and if he thought it necessary and a duty to his public to remain forever young—assuming, that is, that the new hair was really grey—that was his business and far from mine. But again it stirred something in my memory, and I was trying to imagine him with greying hair, and then we were on the last steps down and at the beach road. The tide was out. People were strolling along the sands and a belated bather or two was swimming far out where the water was more deep.

Soon we were nearing the Carbury end. The front was more crowded and music was coming from the dance hall, and I had almost caught what it was that I was trying to remember. So near did it seem that at any moment it might flash into my mind, and then tantalisingly it went altogether again. It was Worne's profile that I recalled. The chin had a forward jut and was heavily dimpled, and the nose had the faintest hook. That may sound trivial, but part of my job has had to be the study of faces. Somehow they stick in my mind, and I knew that somewhere I had seen that profile of Worne's.

It was too crowded and noisy to talk or even move in comfort so we turned back and took the steep hairpinned road to the cliff top and the town. He must have been pretty fit for he was hardly panting at all, whereas I had had quite enough at the end of the three hundred-foot ascent. Then he suggested we should walk back to the Hotel by the High Street so that I could get my bearings. I suggested a drink at a pub, but the only two we came to were closed for lack of supplies. Then he suggested coffee instead but the cafés all seemed crowded, so we gave the idea a miss. Soon we were passing the cinema, and I saw that one could book for the second evening show, so I made a note to get a seat for the following week's thriller which had been specially well reviewed.

"I suppose you've never tried your hand at a murder story?" I asked him.

He gave me a quick look. Perhaps it *had* been rather an insult.

"Not much in my line," he told me, and his lips pursed in quick contempt. "Do you like that sort of thing yourself?"

"When it's well done—yes."

We left it at that. Another minute and we were passing the theatre. The announcement for the following week was a comedy—*Ginger for Pluck*.

"What's the company like?" I asked him.

He shrugged his shoulders.

"Not too bad."

"And not too good?"

"That about hits it," he said. "Still, it's one way of clearing your mind. And it passes a couple of hours after dinner. The leading man's quite a decent chap."

We left the High Street then and turned into a quiet road that brought us in another three minutes to the Hotel. From the lounge was coming the sound of the broadcast play. Worne looked at his watch and said it was nearly ten, and he'd do a spot of work and then turn in. I took a garden chair to the entrance end of the lawn and lighted my pipe.

It was a clear still night with a green afterglow along the horizon, and from quite near was coming the heavy, nostalgic scent of pinks. A baby cried somewhere in the hotel and then the crying ceased and the night seemed even more quiet again. The broadcast play could scarcely be heard and fainter still was the dim music from the dance hall, and—a background for the quiet—below me was the endless lapping of the sea. I lighted a second pipe and suddenly felt deliciously alone. I even felt that Worne was not such a bad sort when one got to know him better. I even forgot the teasing question of whether or not I'd seen him before.

Dusk had gone and soon a young moon would be in the sky. I lighted another pipe and then there were voices. Various residents were coming home from the various shows and so still was everything that I could hear each word they said as they passed my unseen self and made their way along the gravelled drive. My watch said five minutes to eleven, and I was just thinking of bed when I heard steps somewhere among the shrubs behind me.

Later I was to use that short cut through the shrubbery and by the garage to the cliff gardens but at that moment I didn't know that I had heard the steps because they had suddenly left the grass for the concrete of the car park, or its continuation that curved round to the back premises of the Hotel. But when there was a little laugh, I guessed that it was Barbara Channard and Major Huffe who were coming home by some sort of path behind my chair. Then the steps ceased. Before I could cough or get to my feet, there was a voice. I sat tight. It was too late then to do a thing about it, nor could I guess what was coming.

"We'd better say good night here." That was the lady.

Huffe said something but what I couldn't catch.

"No," she said, and "No!" again. "Not tonight—really!"

There was a rustling noise and I caught the sound of a kiss.

"Good night, darling. Mind you dream about *me*."

She gave a little laugh.

"Don't you believe it. I'm going to dream about silk stockings."

"Sh!" he said, but he was too late. I saw her for a moment as she slipped across the lawn, and then he came into sight, and he was humming cheerfully to himself. I stayed motionless. Then I let out a sigh. Huffe, I thought, was an exceedingly fast worker. I also thought what a thing it was to be young. I also thought what a hell of a thing it was to be getting old.

Then I gently knocked out my pipe. Everyone in the Hotel seemed to have gone to bed for there was no light in the lounge, but as I passed the corridor junction I did catch sight of a couple of people. Curious as ever, I had a quick look. Huffe and Rowse had their heads together in earnest conversation. They were facing the office door and so intent that neither noticed me, and so quietly were they talking that I caught not even one whispered word.

I moved on and then I did catch something. A key turned in the office door.

"Let's get down to it in here," Rowse said.

I moved on, waited, and then came back, but the office door was closed.

CHAPTER III

THESE YELLOW SANDS

I woke soon after seven that Sunday morning, remembered that I had forgotten to order early tea, decided that I didn't need it after all, and finally got up just short of eight. It was a magnificent morning and I was just in time for the weather forecast which I switched on in the lounge. It said, continuing fine in the South.

I asked my waitress about Sunday papers and she told me of a shop in the High Street, though I'd probably have to join a queue. I like my own papers for the sake of the crosswords, so I made my way to the town. By half-past eight I had secured one paper—strict rationing was on—and as I was dressed for breakfast I decided to take a walk. For a change I went on past the railway station and as far as Carbury Chine. I stood for a few moments on the cliffs above the chine on the Sandbeach side and then turned for home, keeping to the paths of the cliff gardens. By the time I was back at the Hotel I had five minutes still in hand, and I thought it might be a good idea, if the weather continued fine, to make that pre-breakfast walk a regular one.

Breakfast was pretty good, with the only snag a stinting of marmalade, and that marmalade wasn't too good in quality. The butter was cunningly blended with margarine, but one has got used to that. But the toast was beautifully done, the milk showed more than traces of cream and the eggs were real eggs. The coffee was exceptionally fine and there was abundance of sugar. I like my coffee sweet, and I thought it would be good news for George Wharton who likes even his tea as a saccharine solution.

It was about ten o'clock when I went out to the lawn, and the scene was what is known as animated. Peckenham waved a pontific hand at me, Barbara Channard smiled and one or two other people mentioned the weather. Mothers were sitting about waiting for their children, or there were nannies with children waiting for mothers. It was rather noisy, but one expects that, and the noise was under control. Children—I quote my old nurse again—are like dogs. Well-mannered they can be a joy and bad-mannered a pest. The lawn that morning had only one pest, a boy of about nine or ten named Gerald. He was indulging in a bout of exhibitionism, and one word from either of his parents was enough to make him worse. He pushed over a charming little girl and made her cry, he crawled on hands and knees, whooping all the time, among people's legs, and one could only smile bleakly and hope that that morning he might be carried away by the tide.

When part of the beach procession began moving off, I judged it was time for me too, so I went up to my room, put on my bathing costume—heavily repaired—a wrap, my ancient *espadrilles*, and took a towel. It was just about two minutes' downward climb to the beach, and there I hired a deck chair and placed it well in the sun, and then I began mustering my courage for a first dip. The beach was nicely sprinkled with sun umbrellas and I spotted one or two of the Hotel guests. I also noticed the two boats belonging to the Haven, and principally because the unutterable Gerald was amusing himself by banging one with one of its oars. Suddenly a shadow crossed my chair and I looked up to see Huffe. He was wearing flannel bags with his bathing costume as a kind of slip.

"Not going in yet?" I asked him.

"Going to do a spot of rowing first," he told me.

"Pretty good at it, are you?"

"I don't know," he told me diffidently. "I did do rather a lot at Cambridge."

"At Cambridge, were you? So was I. At Cranmer."

I was at Latimer," he said. "Had to come down pretty early. My father died unexpectedly and that rather bitched everything up."

He had squatted in the sand by my chair. The sun made gold glints in that reddish auburn hair of his and I thought what a good-looking chap he was. I'd thought him just a bit raffish at first, but now I decided that what just spoiled him was a slightly dissipated look. Maybe he'd been giving himself too good a time on his gratuity. He'd certainly bought himself a car, for he told me he'd been involved in an accident, which was why he'd had to come to Sandbeach by train.

"Bad luck," I said, referring to his leaving Cambridge early. "What did you have to do? Take a job?"

"That's right," he said. "It may sound dam' silly but I actually went into a publisher's office with the idea of starting on the ground floor and working my way up. I was doing rather well too, and then the war came. That's strictly between ourselves, by the way."

"Where'd you do your soldiering?"

"Most places," he said. "Libya, Italy and then Normandy. Commando work the last part of the time."

"A pretty tough mob?"

"I'll say we were. Then I got a Hun bullet in the ribs and that finished things. Got demobbed just over a year and a half ago."

"And now you're finding things pretty slow?"

"I don't know," he said, and as he got to his feet he was smiling ironically to himself. "Plenty of exciting stuff going if you know where to get it."

"You've got a job?"

"Oh yes," he said, and then suddenly his voice lowered. "Who's that nasty bit of work just on our right? Isn't he at the Hotel?"

Worne must have been sitting all that time within earshot of us, and I hadn't seen him because he was hunched down in his chair ostensibly doing a spot of writing. Although under a huge sun umbrella he was wearing a hat as big as a sombrero.

"That's our author, Jeffrey Worne," I said, or whispered. "How come you haven't spotted him before?"

"I thought I had seen him," he said. "The trouble is I can't see a thing from my table. I've got my back to the room."

He took another quick look.

"So that's Jeffrey Worne. Pederson's publish him, don't they?"

"You're still well up in publishing news, then?"

"It's just a kind of hangover," he told me. "I still take an interest especially in any of the authors I used to know in the old days. I was with Howlett and Holmes."

"Quite a good firm," I said, and noticed that he was having yet another look.

"Curious," he said frowningly. "I'm sure I've met him somewhere. Must have been in the old days." He closed his eyes and frowned. "Funny, you know. The name doesn't convey much to me."

I had a sudden malicious idea.

"Hallo, Worne!" I called. "Come over and meet Major Huffe."

"Why, hallo!" called Worne, as if he hadn't known I'd been there all the time. He hoisted himself from the chair. Huffe whispered hurriedly.

"Keep it dark about me and the publishing business. I'd rather no one knew."

Worne came over and I introduced Huffe.

"I've read some of your books, sir," Huffe told him. "Grand stuff, if I may say so."

"That's very nice of you," Worne told him. "An author's only human. It's all poppycock to think we don't like a little flattery."

But he too was giving Huffe a curiously searching glance or two.

"Well, I must slip off now," Huffe was saying. "Going to do a spot of rowing."

He smiled a good-bye at me.

"We'll be seeing each other, Mr. Worne. Good bathing."

A cheery wave of the hand and off he went. At least he went two yards, and then looked back.

"I think we're all going to have a dam' good time down here, don't you?"

A somewhat impish grin and he moved off. Worne stood there watching him, and then turned at last to me.

"What *is* this chap Huffe?"

"Just a demobbed officer," I said. "Why? Did you think you recognised him?"

He simulated a smile.

"Not at all. He did faintly resemble someone I used to know years ago. Not the same chap, of course."

Then he was changing the subject abruptly. Was I going in? He himself always bathed at about that time and then spent the morning on the beach collecting ideas. I welcomed that stimulant to my moral courage and said I was ready if he was.

The tide was coming in, though still a goodish way out. We discarded our shoes at a safe distance and I noticed that he put his glasses in one of his shoes. Whatever the discomfort of wet glasses I always wear my own, for without them I'm as blind as a bat. Worne then walked steadily on, and when he was up to his waist he took a dive under and that was that. To me the water was damnably cold, and I hate to be hurried, so I took advantage of my height and walked much further out in order to screw my courage to the sticking point of a plunge. The water was like ice and when at last I emerged from my first dive, I gasped at the cold.

In a minute or two I was enjoying it. Worne was swimming about and diving like a porpoise, and he wouldn't be doing the same kind of stroke two minutes together. He was certainly an extraordinarily good swimmer. I was merely a paddler by comparison, with the good old breast stroke a stand-by, and little else to follow. When we were touching bottom and were having a breather, I noticed something red coming down the steps.

"Who's that?" I asked him, for the lady was vaguely familiar.

"Looks like our Merry Widow," he said. "I may be wrong, though. Can't see much without my glasses."

Barbara Channard it was, and a fetching figure she looked. Her rig-out was a warm red, with the bathing cap a perfect foil for the wisps of black hair. She also had scarlet pantie arrangements and a scanty kind of brassiere, and the whole was finished off with scarlet shoes.

"Why lads leave home," I commented flippantly.

"She's certainly easy on the eyes, as they say." He shrugged his shoulders. "My time for that sort of thing's over, though. And the particular lady is just a bit too over-sexed for my liking."

That was carrying flippancy too far but he had turned his back to the shore and was doing a crawl stroke out to sea. I ambled round a bit more and then noticed the boat. Huffe was rowing and Barbara Channard was his passenger. He could certainly handle the oars and that boat shot between me and Worne at what seemed to me the very devil of a lick. Barbara waved at me with a shriek of enjoyment. Huffe hollered that they were bound for Carbury Chine and back.

I was feeling just a bit cold so I made my way to my chair. I had dried myself and wrung out my costume and was basking in the sun when Worne at last came in. We agreed that the swim had been a tonic. When he too was ready for a bask, he was asking what I was going to do. I said I'd sit on for a bit and then go to the town and book seats at the theatre and the cinema. They are open for bookings on Sunday mornings.

"Would you book a theatre seat for me?" he said. "Tomorrow night if it's all the same to you." He smiled apologetically. "Sorry. I was taking it too much for granted that we might be going together."

"Why not?" I said. "Tomorrow night it shall be. What about the cinema?"

"Well," he said, "gangster stuff doesn't really interest me but I think I'd like to give it another chance. Wednesday night suit you?"

I said it would suit me fine. I had a friend coming on the Thursday, I hoped, and it might be as well to leave that night free. And that ended our talk. He settled to his scribbling again and I lit a pipe and watched things generally. The children were a joy, especially the youngest, and it was fun to watch the dare-devils who rushed towards the sea and then ran back like blazes at the sight of an oncoming wave. So absorbed did I get in their antics that when I looked at my watch I saw it was half-past eleven.

I made my way back to the hotel at once and got into walking clothes. I wondered if I should or should not wear a tie with the sports shirt and when I decided on one and opened the drawer, it seemed to me that that drawer had been disturbed. I opened another drawer where there was a letter or two that I had brought down to answer. One of those letters had been put back too hurriedly into its envelope. A photograph of my wife which I'd uxoriously brought with me had a finger mark at its bottom corner, and suddenly I was feeling very annoyed. Peggy, I realised, must be a snooper, and yet there didn't seem anything I could do about it. If I challenged her, she'd deny it. If I reported her to Rowse, she might leave, and that would do me no good with Rowse.

What made me forget the whole thing was a sudden realisation of where I'd seen Worne—or someone remarkably like him—about a year before. So clearly did everything come back that I made my way down to the beach again. One of the Hotel residents was talking to him, so I waited till she'd gone, though I couldn't help hearing something of the conversation for she was rather strident voiced.

"It's positively thrilling to hear all that, Mr. Worne! And you really think everything out, as you call it, before you actually write a word?"

Another minute and she'd moved on.

"These people can be a blasted nuisance," Worne told me with a synthetic annoyance, and it rather recalled for me the occasion when a film star visiting England complained of the crowds besieging his hotel, with his publicity manager rubbing his hands in the background.

"You can't be a celebrity without paying for it," I told him ironically. "But I've thought of something that might interest you. Remember how I said last night that I felt I'd met you somewhere before? I've thought of when it was. Thought of it just now when I happened to remember barging into you last night at the door."

"Really?" His eyes seemed rather anxiously on mine.

"You'll remember it," I said. "I live in St. Martins Chambers and I was walking along St. Martin's Lane. Round about last Christmas twelve-month it'd be. You were carrying a portable typewriter and I was mooning along in my usual way and barged full into you."

"Sorry," he said, and smiled. "When did you say it was?"

I told him again.

"You may believe it or you may not," he said, "but I haven't set foot east of Trafalgar Square for years. All that December and January I was at Buxton. I actually wrote a book there."

"Then what an extraordinary resemblance," I said. Then he was frowning.

"Wait a moment, though." Then he shook his head. "It couldn't be. Stretching the long arm of coincidence a bit too far." He looked up again. "Just what was this chap like—the man you barged into?"

"Like you, obviously, or I shouldn't have made the mistake."

"Did he have fair hair?"

"As a matter of fact he did," I said. "Or I think he did." Then I knew I'd dropped some sort of brick and I gave a laugh. "Of course it couldn't have been you!"

"Do you know it might have been a cousin of mine?" he said. "Henry's very much like me, but for the hair. Well, superficially he's like me. We'll leave it like that. But he had a flat in Long

Acre. And he's a free-lance journalist. That'd account for the portable typewriter."

"That must be it," I said portentously. He roused himself in his chair.

"I'll bet that's it. Henry's working in Edinburgh now but I'll drop him a line if I can find his address. Extraordinary, isn't it? If I'd put anything like that in a book, every critic would have jumped on me."

So much for that. I left him at his scribbling and made my way to the steps again. Then I thought I'd invest sixpence and go up the chine. It was a poor investment except for a lover of the postcard sort of prettiness. It is true there was a miniature waterfall and patches of rock-garden and flowering shrubs that had ceased flowering—except the buddleias—and intermittent seats shaded by bowers of rambler roses, but there were also the interminable upward steps that twisted and wound till I was puffing like a walrus. Then I came to where side paths led off, so I took one to the right, thinking it might be a shorter cut to the town. It was then that I saw Peckenham.

Luckily he didn't see me, and I dodged behind a tree, and ultimately behind some shrubs and so away. He was occupying a seat by himself well off the main path, and in his hand he held what looked to me a pair of powerful glasses, and from where I stood I could judge that through an adventitious gap he had the whole beach that fronted the hotel well beneath his eye. But the staggering thing was that he was smoking! And he wasn't doing things by halves. He was smoking a pipe and the smoke was round his head like a busted halo.

I heard again that voice of the previous evening. The weed and Peckenham had parted company years ago. When he was a missionary in China, in fact. And when I remembered that, I almost laughed aloud, and my belly shook with, the chuckle. Peckenham was a humbug! And when humbugs are not dangerous, there can be few more delightful people, at least for one like myself who likes collecting human specimens as some collect curios or stamps. So I took another look at Peckenham, chuckled to myself again, and then made my secretive way on up that cursed slope.

It was a very good lunch. Usually I have no use for plaice but the fillets I had were excellent; so was the sauce and the new potatoes that went with them. The pudding was a lemon sponge, and not too bad.

"Like your pudding, sir?" asked Winnie, my little blonde waitress. It was evidently a favourite of her own.

"I like good treacle duff," I said.

"Ah, but what about the treacle?" she asked me.

I said, well, what about it, and all I got was something to do with points.

"But never you mind, sir," she told me consolingly. "Perhaps there'll be some before you go."

I took my crossword out to the lawn and dug myself well in with a chair that had an awning. What I hadn't accounted for was the assembling of the afternoon's beach parade, and the awful Gerald. He took possession of a smaller boy's ball and was hurling it in all directions. One effort caught my paper clean in the back.

"Gerald, darling, you really must be more careful!" his mother told him petulantly.

Then the owner of the ball began yelling for it, with Gerald yelling, "Shan't! Shan't! Shan't!" in return. Then I remembered something and as I got up to go to my room, the two children collided with my legs. I trod heavily and deliberately on Gerald's toe, and with that left the stricken field.

When I came down the lawn was deserted except for Peckenham who was sleeping peacefully and rather noisily in a deck chair under a tree. He looked so bland and innocent that I could have imprinted a chaste kiss on his forehead and tiptoed gently away. But I left him to his slumbers and made my way to the local police-station, and asked the constable on duty if he would give me Inspector Fry's private address. He asked if I wanted him on business or privately, not that it mattered as it so turned out, for the Inspector was in his office on the second floor. I gave my name and the constable pressed the buzzer.

Fry was waiting for me at the top of the stairs.

Good lord, sir!" he said. "I couldn't believe it when he said who you were."

"I expected you'd be spending your Sabbath at home," I said as we shook hands. It was nice to see him again, and I told him so. He was a clever, unassuming fellow, who'd go pretty far.

"And how are you, sir?" he said.

"In great form," I told him.

"And the Old General?" I noticed that he smiled as he used the nickname.

We had a yarn about things generally and I asked if he'd have dinner with us one night at the Haven. Then X wondered if I might ring George up. He waved at the phone for me to help myself.

I took a chance and guessed that George would never be getting his own lunch at home, and I backed a winner for there he was at the Yard. We had a good six minutes at Government expense. He said it was a stone certainty that he'd be down on the Thursday by the train that got in at six, and I said I'd meet him. Then I asked if he'd like a word with Fry, and Fry was grinning all over his face as he took the receiver.

"Never a dull moment when he's around, sir," he told me when he'd hung up again.

"You're right," I said. "But what about yourself? Isn't Sandbeach pretty dull?"

"I wouldn't say that," he said. "It's restful. And that's not a bad thing for a change."

"No crime?"

"Plenty," he said, and grinned again. "Desperadoes riding without lights and a drunk or two."

"No black marketeers?"

There was a curious look on his face.

"Why'd you ask that, sir?"

"Oh, I don't know," I said airily. "The black market's pretty omnipresent, you know."

"I suppose it is," he said, and was even looking a bit worried. "What's on your mind?"

"I don't know that anything is," he told me, still hedging.

"The subject not popular with your superiors?"

He stared as if I'd hit a nail clean on the head. Then he gave a wry shake of the head.

"I'd rather not talk about the black market, sir."

"Drop that *sir* business," I said, "and open up a bit. Get things off your chest."

"Well," he said reluctantly, "I thought I was on to something a week or two back, and then I was told to lay off."

"Who by? Not your Chief Constable?"

"I'd rather not say," he told me. "Keep this to yourself, though. The Chairman of the Watch Committee owns the two largest hotels in the town."

"Does he, by God!" I said. "That's awkward. It's damnably awkward."

"All the same, sir," he told me, "if it has to come to a show-down, I'll take my chance. I've got a thing or two up my sleeve and I'm waiting to see which way the cat jumps."

"Jolly good luck to you," I said. "And now I'll tell you something. You've a good forgetfulness?"

He stared, then got it.

"I think so. I think I can forget to remember."

"And if anything arises you'll keep me out of it?"

"I'll forget I ever knew you," he told me.

"Right," I said. "Then I think I know someone in this town who may be interested in the black market."

"Name?" he said at once, and out came his pencil.

"That's a hell of a way to forget," I told him. "I haven't much to go on, at the moment, but I know he's promised a certain lady some sheer silk stockings. I think if he's not one of the smart lads himself, then he knows who some of them are."

"And his name is what?"

"He's a feller-me-lad at the Haven Hotel," I said. "A guest of the name of Huffe. Major Brian Huffe."

"Major—Brian—Huffe." He wrote it down. "Regiment?"

"Commando."

"A tough lad, eh?"

"Maybe," I said. "All this is in private, though, and without prejudice. Only one thing I'd like. If you keep an eye on him, let me know anything you happen to find out."

"I will that, sir," he said, and slipped his note-book back. Then he frowned. "Hadn't better call him by his name, though. If I happen to ring you at the Haven, he'll be our friend Jones."

"Personally I don't think you'll get much," I said. "With a chap like that it's not himself that matters so much as the people he can buy stuff from. Now if we knew where he's getting those stockings from, we'd be going places."

"You leave it to me, sir," he told me dourly. "All sorts of things might happen. You never know your luck."

But as I strolled back towards the Hotel I was thinking that Fry, for all his dourness, could do precious little about Huffe. He couldn't open his correspondence or listen to his telephone conversations. Those seemed the only approach, for I doubted if any of Huffe's black market pals were in the town.

Besides, there was the question whether I had been precipitate in assuming that Huffe was connected with the black market racket at all. I had mentioned the matter to Fry on the spur of the moment, and perhaps because Wharton had been in my mind. Then Fry's strange acceptance of the remark had led on and on, till I had mentioned Huffe. But what had I to go on besides a considerable experience of judging character? Only a matter of the silk stockings, a gold lighter and cigarette case, and a late interview with Rowse. But those three things were good evidence, added to my judgment of Huffe himself. And suddenly it struck me that in a day or two I might have other evidence handed to me on a silver salver, as it were, and in addition to anything that Fry might happen to collect.

It was just before tea-time when I got back to the hotel and I glanced over at the corner where Peckenham had been sleeping, but he was no longer there. And then something else struck me.

I had thought of him as a delightful old humbug, but what was I myself? I was at the Haven for rest and comfort, and the more I got of both, the better I'd be pleased. Should I, in my present capacity of private citizen, refuse to eat black market extras? Never a bit of it. I'd already had boiled fowl that had probably cost Rowse a packet. And the more extras and abundance there were, the better I'd be pleased. In other words, I was in the game like a lot of other people, and as much a humbug as any.

Then I told myself that I was having those ideas because it was a Sunday, and that I was getting introspective in my old age. Then I chuckled to myself as I wondered how George Wharton would see things. Would he refuse righteously to eat fowl and honest-to-God eggs, or heap the sugar into his tea? I very much doubted it, but it might be interesting to see.

Chapter IV
COMPLICATIONS

I was up early that Monday morning but when I arrived at the newsagent's, the queue was forty yards long, and I thought my chance of getting *The Times* was a pretty slight one. As it happened I got the very last copy, but I made up my mind that in future I'd be up earlier still.

It was a grand morning and the view from the top of Carbury Chine was magnificent. As I turned back to the cliff path I suddenly heard a "Hallo, there!" It was Worne.

"I didn't know you were an early bird," I said.

"Oh yes," he said. "I always take a walk of some sort before breakfast, if it's fine. If it isn't, I do a bit of work."

The mention of work started us talking about books, and once he got off the subject of himself, he was quite an informative chap. When we came to the road that led down to the beach I suggested taking it, so we walked along the front till we came to the Hotel steps. I let him go ahead for that allowed me to get as near to him as I wanted, and what I saw was that his hair had

had a recent application of dye, for never a trace of a lighter colour showed at the scalp beneath.

On that Monday morning it seemed as if I knew everybody in the Hotel. If you met people on the stairs or in corridors or on the lawn, they were friendly and spoke, or you might happen to speak first. I didn't know names but I knew faces, though everybody seemed to know my name. I even knew the layout of the rooms on the west side of the first floor. The east side, I should say, was occupied by parents or nannies with children. This is a rough plan:

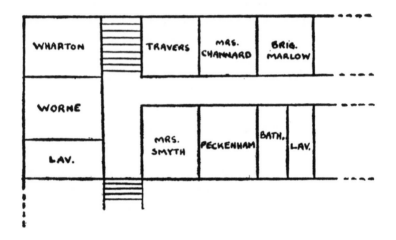

Of the other people I knew, Gerald and his parents were somewhere on the other side of that first floor, but as there were two staircases, I never saw them at my end. Huffe was somewhere on the floor above, and at my end, for he used the same staircase.

I'd woke that morning with an idea in my mind, and after breakfast I made my way to the post-office. To telephone from the Hotel seemed too risky, and, as luck would have it, I wasn't too long in getting my trunk call. It was my old friend Bill Ellice of the Broad Street Detective Agency, whom I was calling, and I got him first time. Things were pretty slack and he said he'd have ample time to make the enquiries I wanted about Huffe.

I suggested two things only: a verification of his having been at Latimer College, Cambridge, and his record in the publishing firm of Howlett and Holmes.

"Tremendous discretion, if you don't mind, Bill," I said. "I've got nothing on this chap at all. Just following a hunch."

"You leave it to us, Mr. Travers," he told me. "We'll get what you want, and in the right way."

It was well after ten o'clock when I went up to my room to change for bathing, and both hotel and lawn seemed deserted. I had a minor disaster as I was undressing, and when I was ready for the beach I had a look round for Peggy. Then I noticed that the door of Peckenham's room was open so I tapped and there she was.

"I've dropped my only back collar-stud on the floor somewhere, Peggy," I said, "and I can't find it. Put it on the dressing table, will you, if you run across it."

She said she'd have a look. I'd come right into the room to speak to her, for she was dusting in the far corner, and I noticed two things. One was that Peckenham was a subscriber to the American *National Geographic Magazine,* for the June copy was on his side table. I'd already seen that copy, and it struck me that the *National Geographic* was just the magazine for old Peckenham to take, with its information and news about the lesser-known places of the world. For Peckenham it would be at times like making contact again with old friends.

The other thing I noticed was really two—a couple of photographs, each of what used to be called cabinet size, and each in a silver, standing frame. One was of Peckenham himself in clerical garb, and the other was of the late Archbishop, Lord Lang, and this was autographed. What it said I hadn't a chance to see, but at the time it pulled me up with rather a jerk. I'd been assessing Peckenham as an interesting, if somewhat windy raconteur, and an amiable old humbug, but that photograph took me considerably aback. I decided that Peckenham would need re-assessing.

It was very curious that when I was half-way down the steps to the beach, I overtook him. Where he had been I didn't know, though I did know that he hadn't been in a chair on the lawn, but now he was making his careful way down. He greeted me with obvious pleasure. I tried a gentle leg-pull. "What's happened to your costume, sir?"

His smile was mournful.

"The machinery clanks too heavily, my boy. There was a time—you'll pardon the boastfulness?—when I could swim with the best. Now the heart is my master instead of my servant. It just won't stand it."

I hope I was duly sympathetic. I say that I hoped, because while I was offering condolences, I was wondering how a man with a tricky heart could make his way up those infernal steps of the chine. Peckenham might have come *down* to where I had spotted him with his pipe and his field glasses, but that didn't alter the fact that ultimately he'd have to go *up* again. And all that was highly puzzling. I'd decided that he required re-assessing, and immediately afterwards he was back where I'd had him before.

I didn't feel like more Worne that morning. He was on the beach ostensibly at work, but with a couple of lady fans occupying chairs alongside him, so I took chairs for Peckenham and myself and planted them well away. I also noticed the awful Gerald being taught to swim by his father, and yelling like mad when immersed to his chin.

"You get on with your bathe, my boy," Peckenham told me. "I shall sit here and ruminate. I should have said *meditate*, but, as the Bard remarks, the word is somewhat over-worn."

I made my way to the sea and caught sight of Huffe and Barbara Channard. She waved to me and I joined them.

"What's the sea like?" I said, delaying my submersion.

"Marvellous," she told me, and after that I had to go under. Huffe was floating lazily around. I'd expected him to be a phenomenal swimmer, but he was only in my class, and Worne could have made rings round us both. Barbara was little more than a paddler with a few breast-stroke yards as her swimming limit. But with her figure, she didn't need to worry.

Gerald and his father came by us in one of the Hotel boats.

"Don't I hate that child!" Barbara told me. "I could even hope the little beast would drown."

"Speak the word, lady, and it can be managed," Huffe told her flippantly. "All part of the Huffe service."

"You call his bluff," I advised her, but she only laughed.

My insulation of fat is very meagre and ten minutes in the sea is my comfortable limit, so I left them to it and rejoined Peckenham. Already my skin was turning pink and as I sat in the chair with legs outstretched, my shins had an ominous itch. I offered Peckenham my cigarette case, then apologised. He waved his pudgy hand and smiled an acceptance of the apology. He even admitted that he liked the smell of tobacco, though he'd long given up its use.

It was deliciously warm and peaceful. I happened to mention that that week the Americans were making the atom bomb test at Bikini, and to my surprise he said he knew the atoll remarkably well. He mentioned a certain chief by name, and he seemed personally distressed at the natives having to leave their homes. He'd actually officiated at burials in one of the cemeteries that would have to be abandoned.

So interested was he in his reminiscences that he didn't appear to notice when a man came up, smiled, and put something into my hand. I knew what it was and slipped the paper into the pocket of my bath-robe. Perhaps I had better explain.

On the front opposite the pier entrance a firm of beach photographers had their headquarters. Two of the firm would work the beach and the methods of approach were subtly different for the two ends. At the popular end the photographer would accost a likely group and proffer for inspection enlargements of photographs already taken on previous days, and, of course, of other people. That might bring new business, and when he snapped the group he'd collect a preliminary fee and give a receipt card authorising collection the following day. But for the Haven end the method was very different. There he would snap likely people or groups—unless they were aware and objected—and then present a card which said that your photograph had been taken and finished photographs would be available at such and such a time at the Pier Studios the following day.

But, as I said, Peckenham was so interested in his reminiscences that he didn't notice the presentation of that card, and, if he did, he probably wasn't aware what it meant. Maybe he thought it some sort of bill for the chairs, though I'd already paid. At any rate he went on with his flow of talk, and then Barbara Channard and Huffe went by us on their way back to the Hotel.

"No sun-bathing?" I said.

"Not this morning," she told me. "A little shopping, perhaps."

"Including ices?"

"Maybe," she said, and gave Huffe a suggestive grimace.

"What a thing it is to be young," remarked Peckenham tritely when they'd gone. Then he was giving me a whimsical look. "But I think I've mentioned that before."

Then he was hoisting himself to his feet.

"But that mention of shopping reminds me. There's a purchase or two I wish to make myself. Pray don't disturb yourself, my boy. I can manage by myself."

I watched him making a slow way up the steps, and then I was alternately frowning and chuckling to myself as I sat on in the sun. And this was the reason.

I'd read that copy of the *National Geographic Magazine*, to which I happen to be a subscriber. In it was an article on the evacuation of Bikini. There were superb photographs as usual, and they included the chief whom Peckenham had mentioned and the cemetery at which he had officiated. So there was the problem. Was Peckenham a subscriber, or had he bought that copy because of the interest of that particular article? Had he read the article and then unloaded its contents on me? In other words, was he a consummate and artistic liar, who'd never been near Bikini? And why was he trying to make an impression, not only on me but doubtless on any other guests to whom he talked? Was it mere vanity? Was he still only a delightful, specious, champion humbug, or was there far more to it than that? I didn't know, and the more I thought, the less I knew.

*　*　*　*　*

It was not till very much later that anything happened that had a bearing on this story. After dinner I was inveigled into a game of bridge by Colonel Grant and his wife, and who should offer to make a fourth but Peckenham. I'm supposed to be pretty good but he was streets ahead of the three of us. Everything quiet, mind you, and nothing showy, but both in attack and defence he had the real master's touch. At the very beginning of the game I noticed a peculiar thing.

A cricketer goes to the wicket and from almost the first twiddle of his bat you can tell what sort of a bat he is. I and Peckenham cut together and he dealt, and the way he handled the cards showed more than a long familiarity. And then, before he'd dealt a dozen cards, he lost the fluency and tempo and acquired a certain clumsiness for which he was apologising.

"I'm afraid I'm just a bit awkward nowadays," he told us with a sigh. "In my unregenerate days—but there, we don't want to talk about that."

I made no comment, but I did think that in those far off unregenerate days there'd been no contract bridge; in fact, there'd been no bridge at all. And then later there was a remark that he made when we'd lost a game. We couldn't have saved it, even if the four hands had been exposed.

"I'm afraid I'm very rusty, partner," he told me. "I ought to have led a diamond."

There was no question, by the way, of his trying to appear a novice for the purpose of making a killing at our expense, for it was family bridge at a penny a hundred, and when it ended just short of eleven o'clock, nobody had lost more than a shilling, and Peckenham himself was a loser. But something else happened during that game.

At about ten o'clock Barbara Channard came into the lounge. I'm almost sure she'd been somewhere with Huffe, but there was no sign of him. She had a look at us, owned that she didn't understand the game, and then took a seat by the wireless and turned it quietly on. A few moments later I happened to be dummy, so I slipped out to the lavatory.

At the downstair one I was just in time to hear the bolt click, so I went on up the stairs. The carpet was thick and I could hardly have made a sound, and as soon as my head rose to the level of the landing floor, I stepped a stair down again. For Peggy was at Worne's door, ear well against the keyhole!

I backed carefully down and then gave an artistic cough. When I came up again there was no sign of Peggy. But I went very slowly past Worne's room, wondering if she had been listening for any special purpose. No sound was coming from it that I could hear, and then I was wondering if Peggy had not been misjudged. Perhaps it was part of her duties to make sure that guests were in their rooms, and then report to Rowse who could lock up for the night. And then again I thought that ten o'clock, or soon after, was a bit too early for that sort of inspection.

It was well after eleven when I went up to bed. Huffe was in the hall as I went by, humming cheerfully to himself and consulting the list of local amusements that hung on the letter board.

"Thinking of kicking your heels up?" I asked him.

"Hallo, sir," he said, a bit surprised at the sudden sight of me. "You been to the Pavilion yet?"

I said I hadn't had the opportunity.

"You ought to go," he said. "It's quite good. A bit on the short side; that's the only thing against it."

I was gathering that he'd been there with Barbara Channard, but he changed the conversation as we went up the stairs together by wishing he was on that first floor instead of the second. He had a good look in at my room and admitted that his own was as good.

"How're you enjoying it here?" he asked me.

I said I was having a great time.

"Quite a good spot," he said. "I'm doing myself no harm either."

"Combining business with pleasure?"

"We've got to live," he told me with a grin. "You can't lose the chance of making a bit on the side."

It was a pity he said that from the door, just before he said good night, or I might have drawn him out a bit more. I don't know why, but he seemed as if he liked confiding in me—to his own certain extent. But as I got ready for bed I was wondering how Fry was coming along with his enquiries, and somehow I didn't see him getting very far. I also had the uneasy feeling that I'd be several kinds of a fool if everything about Huffe turned out to be open and above-board after all.

The Tuesday was fine and clear again. I got up still earlier and managed quite comfortably to get *The Times*. That morning, too, I stood rather longer than usual admiring the view from the cliffs above Carbury Chine and I was hurrying back to the Hotel when I saw Worne ahead of me, and going at a rare pace. He had come up from the beach road; I gave him a call and he waited for me. On a sudden impulse I told him about Peggy. He was furious.

"What time was this?" he wanted to know.

I said about a quarter past ten.

"Then I was sound asleep," he said. "I'd been working rather hard and I turned in early. But it's pretty damnable. What the devil was she listening for?"

"Heaven knows," I said. "Maybe she listens at all the doors in turn. Picks up a bit of gossip or scandal."

Then he was talking about going straight to Rowse, and then as quickly he was changing his mind. That would bring me in as witness. I said it would mean her getting the sack and that might put us both in bad with Rowse and perhaps the staff. I told him about her having been through the things in my drawers and said we oughtn't to take it too seriously. The danger would be if she were dishonest. If I missed anything, for instance, I should go straight to Rowse, and meanwhile I'd keep a check on my bedroom belongings.

"Perhaps you're right," he said, and then we began discussing arrangements for that evening's visit to the theatre. The show began at eight and we decided to leave the Haven at ten minutes to.

The next happening was after lunch and it was by chance that I was still in the Hotel. Rowse found me in the lounge doing my crossword and said I was wanted on the telephone. "Hallo?" I said, and waited.

"I'm talking about our friend Jones," came Fry's voice. "That is Mr. Travers, isn't it?"

I said it was, and then somehow I didn't like talking over the telephone. I didn't know if Rowse was able to listen in, but he struck me as the sort who wouldn't scruple to do so if he thought he had reason.

"Any chance of seeing you in the next few minutes?" I said. "What about the foot of the beach road?"

He said he'd be there at once; in fact he was waiting when I got there. We adjourned to a shelter nearby.

"Something peculiar has happened," he told me. "But first of all about this Major Huffe. I've got a man I can trust and he was picked up soon after lunch yesterday. What do you think he did with his afternoon?"

"No idea," I said.

"Well, he called on the two biggest hotels this side of Carbury Chine. One's got a hundred bedrooms and the other one eighty, so they're pretty big for Sandbeach. He spent the best part of an hour at the Regal and over half an hour at the Ocean. On his way back he called at the Royal. That's not far from the Haven."

"Just a minute," I said. "Do those three hotels include the couple in which your Watch Committee Chairman has an interest?"

"They don't," he said. "As far as I'm concerned they break new ground."

"You think the idea is that Huffe's a kind of commercial traveller for a black market gang?"

"That's what it looks like to me," he said. "But there's a check we can make. If he's done business, then there'll be deliveries. Once a lorry's collared, then we'll have something." If Fry had been George Wharton I might have indulged in that most irritating of reminders—"I told you so!" All I could say was that he looked like getting somewhere. Wharton would be down on the Thursday and might suggest some sort of unofficial help from the Yard. But all the time I was puzzling my wits about something else.

Huffe had said to me, only the previous night, that he was making a bit on the side. Now if he was in Sandbeach—just before the beginning of the climax of the season, by the way—to get orders for black market stuff, *then that was his job*. What did he mean by making a bit *on the side*? Was that just blether to conceal his real activities? Was he *selling* those silk stockings to Mrs. Channard, and establishing a small connection with her as agent? I didn't know. I couldn't even guess with any feeling of certainty.

"But this other business," Fry was saying. "Do you know a shortish, fattish man, clean-shaven, who looks like a parson? He's staying at your hotel."

"Peckenham!" I said.

He made a note of the name.

"You listen to this," he said, "and tell me what it means. My man, as I told you, kept the Regal under observation while Huffe was in it. When Huffe came out he got on his tail again. Then he noticed this Peckenham. Just noticed him, if you know what I mean. Then Huffe went to the Ocean, and when he came out my man noticed this Peckenham again. He thought it rather funny, so he dropped back a bit and this Peckenham seemed to be tailing Huffe! When Huffe went into the Royal, Peckenham took a seat nearby, got well behind a newspaper, and then followed Huffe back to the Haven when he came out. He took good care Huffe didn't see him."

"It's got me beat," I said, and it had. For once in my life I couldn't find a theory at the end of my tongue. Then I did suggest something.

"Huffe can't be muscling in on another gang's territory?"

"You mean Peckenham might be an agent for this original gang?"

"Something of the sort," I said.

"Don't know," he said. "That's one of the things I've got to find out." He gave a wry shake of the head. "I'd like to know a lot more about this Peckenham."

"Wait a minute," I told him. "Sit tight here for a minute or two. I might be able to help."

A couple of minutes and I was in the photographer's office, showing the slip I'd been given on the beach. Everything was well organised.

"Number 7753," the assistant said. "Here we are, sir. Just ready."

"And the price?"

It was four shillings for six prints, with a special price for postcard-size enlargements. I said I'd take the prints and I'd probably be giving him a supplementary order later. Then I hurried back to Fry.

It was a very fine photograph, at least in the sense that both Peckenham and I were clear and well defined. Had the moment been a less bewildering one, I must have laughed, for Peckenham had been caught in the act of holding up a pontifical hand while he told me about Bikini. It was like a cardinal giving his blessing.

"So this is Peckenham," Fry said. "It's curious, sir, but I seem to know the face."

"Probably from your choirboy days," I said flippantly.

"There's something about it I ought to know," he told me dourly. "Mind if I keep one or two of these?"

I told him to take all but one which I'd like for a keepsake.

"Let's hope it turns out a Rogues' Gallery," Fry told me. "But I'll get a couple of these to a friend of mine in Birmingham. They've been having the devil of a lot of black market trouble there. The other two I'll hang on to, if you don't mind."

When he'd gone I sat on for a bit and I was thinking hard. A few minutes later I was making my way back to the Hotel for tea, and I still hadn't an answer to the questions of who, or what, and why, was Peckenham.

CHAPTER V
MURDER EVE

PERMIT ME to offer some very brief explanations or apologies. All the happenings that follow may seem to you disjointed, isolated and unconnected. But they have been picked out from a mass of happenings and the irrelevant ones discarded, and it should not be long before you discern a clear pattern. I was too close to things, and too hemmed round with irrelevancies, to see anything of a pattern, at least till the very last minute. But you may even have discerned something of a pattern already. You may be pretty sure of who it was that was due to be murdered, which is something of which I had not the faintest conception at the time. For me, nothing was more remote from Sandbeach than murder.

So much for that. Tea ended and I went down to the beach and sat in a deck chair in the sun. Slowly things came back to me. I knew now that Peckenham had chosen that seat where I had seen him smoking, because it had the beach under observation. He was watching Huffe, and was ready to tail him when he came back to the Hotel and left again. I remembered that very morning, and how when Huffe and Barbara Channard had gone back from the beach to the Hotel, Peckenham had shortly afterwards announced that he, too, had shopping to do in the town.

Another strange thing struck me. So many people had seemed to remember other people! I thought I had seen Worne before, and apparently I had been wrong. Huffe thought he too had seen Worne before. Fry thought he had seen Peckenham. Three happenings of the same kind, and that seemed to me far too many. And just then I happened to catch sight of Huffe. He was coming down the steps from the Hotel and mopping his forehead with his handkerchief as if he had been doing a spot of work. The sun was very hot in spite of the slight sea mist, and he had on a lounge suit.

He saw me waving and came across, grabbing a vacant deck chair as he came.

"Been walking?" I said.

"Got to walk on account of that damn car of mine getting smashed up," he told me, and then changed the conversation as if he'd already said too much. "Something I meant to ask you. What a weird old boy that Peckenham is! Has he ever been a parson?"

I told him what Peckenham had divulged to me about himself, and I was feeling just a bit uneasy, wondering as I was if Huffe had become aware of the interest Peckenham was taking in his movements. Then it struck me that I was worrying about nothing.

"That explains it," he said with a laugh. "He looks a damn boring old cuss, though."

"By the way," I said, "do you remember the other day when you first saw Worne and wondered if you'd seen him before? Did you ever remember where?"

"Good lord, yes!" he said. "It was at some reception or other those publishers gave that I was with. He didn't wear glasses in those days. That's what puzzled me."

"What do you think of him?"

"In himself, you mean?" He gave that little contemptuous pout of the lips. "Not a bad chap in his way. Too top-heavy, of course. Likes to be the great Jeffrey Worne."

"Isn't that rather an over-assessment?" I said. "There *is* a Jeffrey Worne but he's a hell of a way from great."

"Exactly what I mean," he told me, and was getting to his feet. "Think I'll have a splash before dinner. I feel too damn sticky for words."

After dinner, Worne and I went to the theatre. The place was packed to the roof and the show didn't look likely to freeze for lack of an appreciative audience. When I go to a comedy show in town I like to have a good dinner inside me and one or two good drinks. I'd had a good dinner but not the drinks, for the Haven was unlicensed, and maybe that was why I was feeling on the pessimistic side. I should say that I'm far from a bigoted highbrow. Anything goes with me, provided it's good, from the Shavian to the Rabelaisian.

But *Ginger for Pluck* bored me stiff, and what made it worse was that the audience seemed to like it. It was in fact like one of the average B.B.C. variety broadcasts, where an audience of picked morons roar their heads off at jokes and situations that had had their day when I was in the nursery. The cast was good enough—surprisingly so—but they were just working themselves to a frazzle over something that had never been worth while.

Even the bare story dated from my youth: the supposed-to-be married nephew, the irascible uncle, the bedroom complications, the friend impersonating the bride, the heavy butler and the over-drawn cockney maid. Usually at a boring show I yawn aloud and my wife digs me angrily in the ribs. I deported myself much better that night. Perhaps something of the holiday spirit kept me from too open a show of boredom. Indeed, Worne seemed far more restless than I. Before the end of the first act he nudged me and whispered: "My dear fellow, this is simply dreadful!"

The show began at eight and fortunately it was over at a quarter past ten. We got separated in the crowd on the way out and I hung around to look for him. Then I realised that he, like myself, had had a choice of two doors and more than two ways back to the Hotel. I also saw along the High Street people going into an open café, so I went to explore. I found that I could get coffee, so as I was abominably thirsty I had a couple of cups. It was getting on for eleven when I got back to the Haven. Worne was promenading up and down the drive, smoking a cigarette.

"Thought I'd lost you for good," he said. "Where on earth did you get to?"

I told him and then he was telling me what had happened to himself. He'd got outside and then remembered that he'd left his hat under the seat. Which, as I told him, was what came of wearing a hat at a holiday resort.

He went up to bed but I wasn't feeling like sleep. It was a wonderful night, for one thing, with a moon that made the lawn look like white paper. I sat at my bedroom window with no light on, admiring beneath and beyond me a nocturne in silver and shadow, and sniffing appreciatively at the heavy scent of the pinks. Once more the faint sounds of traffic or of music from the dance hall was a not unpleasant background, and deep against it all was that eternal lapping of the waves.

In the Hotel it was quiet as death itself, and then suddenly I heard a sound. It was like a grunt or a smothered exclamation, and it came from the corridor outside. I went to my door and found I had left it ajar. A dim light was showing as usual in the centre of that corridor and as I happened to glance through the slit of my door, I saw Huffe. With infinite care he was turning the knob of Barbara Channard's door. A quick look each way and he was inside, and the closing door made never a sound behind him.

"Well, well," I said to myself, and I almost left it at that. I've told you, and maybe shown, that I have an almost morbid curiosity, but it didn't go so far as making me jam my ear against the wall that separated me from Barbara Channard's room. Thank God I'm no moralist, even if I do use the word *suggestive in its better sense. Barbara Channard and Huffe were certainly of an age to please themselves, and what was suggestive about what I had seen was just a mere idea. I was wondering about those silk stockings and if Huffe had arranged a not unpleasant method of payment.

But it was an unusual situation. I now wanted to go to sleep and yet I couldn't. At the back of my mind were those two people just through the wall which was not a yard from my recumbent head. Then instinctively I was listening for the closing of the door when Huffe emerged again—I couldn't imagine his taking the risk of spending the whole night there—or the sound of an exclamation when he once more stubbed his toe against a stair. I even had the queerest thought, or perhaps preposterous is the word. Had Worne ever entertained a lady in his room? And was that why Peggy had listened at his keyhole?

When one o'clock struck somewhere in the town, I was cursing the whole business. Wide-awake as ever I got out of bed and lighted a cigarette, and then I slipped on a dressing-gown and once more sat at the window. Ten minutes went by, and just when I was deciding that I might give sleep another chance, I heard another sound. This time it was a car. A large saloon of the type of an old-fashioned Daimler appeared and turned in at the car-park. It forked left and slowly moved along the concreted track to the back premises of the Hotel.

A minute or two later I was in the lavatory just beyond Peckenham's room. Very carefully I raised the window till I could get my head out, and there was the car below me to the right. Three men were removing what looked like boxes and heavy packages from the back, and one of the men was definitely Rowse. And then came another sound that made my blood run suddenly cold. Someone was rattling the handle of the lavatory door.

I stood motionless and hardly dared breathe. The door stopped rattling and there was silence again. But I had seen enough, and all I wanted was to get unobserved to my room. So I let a minute or so pass and then pulled the chain. The noise of the flush drowned the closing of the door and I nipped across to my room. But quickly as I went, I noticed something. Peckenham's door must have been just ajar, and as I went by, it was gently closed.

It was well into the Wednesday morning when I at last fell asleep, and yet I woke at much the usual time. If anything I was a bit earlier, for there weren't thirty people in the newspaper queue, and it was only ten past eight when I was away with my *Times*. I decided to use the extra time by a quick exploring of the country immediately to the north of the town so I took a road that went almost at once beneath the low embankment of the railway and then petered out to a rough track. Soon it became a wide path that curved a way between gorse and bracken and brambles across the moor-like sweep of rising land. But there was too much dew for my liking and I cut back along another path and ultimately found myself on the Sandbeach side of the chine.

I was almost back at the Hotel when I saw Worne. He was on one of the cliff garden seats, just in earshot of the Haven gong.

"Had a good walk?" I asked him.

"Not far this morning," he said. "Perhaps it was that show last night that did it, but I overslept a bit."

He was walking with me then, and twenty yards or so on, he stopped.

"What's going on between Huffe and that Channard woman?"

The question took me a bit aback. I wondered just how much he knew.

"You should know," I said. "A novelist and all that. Student of psychology, and so on."

"That's just it," he said unblushingly. "It's just because I do happen to be interested in people that I can't quite make the situation out."

"In what way?" I asked guilefully.

"Well, they seemed to be thick as thieves, if you know what I mean. Old Mrs. Smyth was actually hinting to me about a possible marriage—you know how women talk. Then last night, just before you turned up, I happened to hear the tail of a first-class row. I naturally didn't listen more than I could help; in fact, I sheered off."

"Interesting," I said. "Who was quarrelling with whom?"

"I think he must have overstepped the mark," he told me. "She was telling him that if he dared do something, she'd kill him. Mere hot air, of course. *Killing*, in those circumstances, is always a figure of speech."

"Ah well," I said. "Maybe they'll make it up again today. It ought to be interesting to see."

So much for that. The gong went and I was well at the head of the procession. I didn't notice anything different about the breakfast table till Winnie, my waitress, drew my attention to something as she took the plate that had held my kipper.

"Real butter!" she whispered as she stooped.

I could only raise my eyebrows knowingly, but real butter it certainly was. And the marmalade was more plentiful and very different. The sort we'd been having had been all treacle and no shreds, but this was good honest chunky marmalade. And I was telling myself that if Fry had been watching the Regal and Ocean and Royal, then he'd had his eye on the wrong hotels.

After the meal I went to the letter rack and there were two letters for me. My wife's had been forwarded as arranged, by the post-office people, and the other was from Bill Ellice. I took it out to the lawn and read it in a deck chair under a secluded tree.

DEAR MR. TRAVERS,

A little advance information which I think you may like. I don't expect the complete report before the end of the week. You asked for diplomatic handling and that means slow work.

But the party in whom you are interested *was* where he claims apparently to have been. Your covering letter, which reached me yesterday, gives certain reasons for his leaving. They are incorrect. He was sent down—I think that's the term—for smuggling a woman into his rooms. There's also an as yet unverified rumour about some scandal to do with defrauding a fellow student of a considerable sum of money.

Hope you are having a good time.

Yours as ever,

BILL.

I read that letter a second time, then put it in my small wallet and carefully buttoned the pocket. When I looked up, Worne was coming towards me, waving a letter.

"This might interest you," he said. "Only the first paragraph. The rest is more or less private.

He folded the letter accordingly and gave it to me to read.

DEAR JEFF,

What a remarkable coincidence, as you say. I remember the occasion perfectly. The bloke didn't give me his name, but he was tall and dreamy-looking and he wore horn-rimmed glasses, and had what you might call a patrician sort of face. A quite decent sort of chap and I'm not surprised that you like him. . . .

"Patrician kind of face is a bit flattering," I said as I handed the letter back. "But it *was* a coincidence. Not that I think, mind you, that many coincidences are such at all. It's the wrong word to use."

That led to a discussion, or the beginnings of one, for all at once there was the most horrible din. The beach parade was assembling and there was the awful Gerald, a beach spade over his shoulder like a rifle, marching round and shouting at the top of his lungs that he was a soldier. His parents watched with besotted eyes, and soon he was giving an imitation of a machine gun, and pointing the spade at this person and that. When he reached me and put the wretched weapon within an inch of my nose, I got to my feet and ostentatiously left the lawn.

While I was dressing for the beach I was thinking over that extraordinary quarrel that Worne had heard the previous night. I call it extraordinary because of the strangeness of the sequel—a couple quarrelling at half-past ten, and then indulging in amorous dalliance an hour or two later. It didn't make sense, unless, of course, the quarrel had been made up in the Hotel after the two had passed out of earshot of Worne. But when I went down to the beach I was at once on the look-out for the couple. I didn't see them because I didn't look in the right place. In fact I was actually swimming when I saw them by one of the Hotel boats. Huffe was chasing Gerald, who, I imagined had been using the boat as a wigwam or pirate's lair. Then the boat was pushed out. Barbara got in and Huffe followed.

A minute later it came by. Barbara called something laughingly and Huffe gave a grin, but the interesting thing was that no couple could have seemed happier. Never a twinge of conscience for the dalliance of the night, and the quarrel had gone like a forgotten dream. I wondered what Worne was thinking of it all, but when I made my way to my deck chair again, there was never a sign of him on the beach. There was also no sign of Peckenham, and suddenly I had a feeling of uneasiness. It was almost certainly he who had tried to use the lavatory in the early morning hours. And why? For a relief of nature or for the same reason that found me in it? And did he know that it had been I who was inside? And might he suspect my real reasons for going there?

The best way to handle a perplexity is to face up to it. I made my way back to the hotel and, when I'd dressed, had a look round for Peckenham. What I was intending was to get into conversation, and so use my judgment about what he knew or suspected. I even had a look along the cliff gardens, but there was never a sign of him, so I went back to the Hotel and wrote a quick note for Bill Ellice. When I came out to the lawn again, there was Huffe, dressed as if for the town.

"You've been pretty spry this morning," I told him.

"Having a swim this afternoon," he said. "Just going down the town. What about joining us for an ice?"

"Hardly in my line," I said. "Now if you'd said a pint of iced shandy-gaff. . . ."

Barbara Channard was coming towards us.

"I was asking Travers to join us for an ice," Huffe told her. "He turned me down."

There was a moment or two of kittenish badinage before they left. She was a damned attractive woman, as I've said before, and that morning she was looking better than ever. Maybe the new sheer silk stockings had something to do with it.

A minute or two after she'd gone I had a sudden idea, old Peckenham was really keeping Huffe under observation, then where Huffe went, Peckenham ought to go too. So I followed on Huffe's heels, taking care to keep reasonably out of sight. Then I spotted what I thought was Fry's man. He must have been waiting quite near the Haven and there he was, mooching along a few yards behind the unconscious pair. Then the four of us came to the High Street. Huffe and Barbara Channard made for a dainty-looking tea-shop. Fry's man took up his stance against a wall a few yards back and pulled a newspaper from his pocket. I waited for Peckenham to appear. I waited, in fact, for a good ten minutes but there was never a sight of him.

So I turned back and made for the police-station. Fry was out and the man on duty didn't know where. And that virtually concluded my morning except that about five minutes before the lunch gong went I was fetched to the telephone. It was Fry.

"Heard you'd called round," he said. "Anything special?"

"This was the hole you should have watched," I said, taking a chance, and hoping he'd understand. "But what about our friend Jones?"

"More visits yesterday afternoon," he said. "Something queerer still about the Reverend, though. I've been with him this morning and he's paid calls on Jones's friends. You get me?"

I said I did. I also asked if he thought the two were in cahoots, and he said he didn't know. But he did add that he'd be remarkably glad when our other friend arrived the next day.

I hung up as bewildered as Fry had been. If I had interpreted rightly what he told me, then Peckenham had spent his morning in calling at the Regal, the Ocean and the Royal. That he was in some sort of partnership with Huffe seemed as good a guess as any, and yet I felt as sure, when I thought back, that Huffe had been genuine enough when he had made enquiries from me about Peckenham.

Still, there was one thing of which I was pretty sure, that what I had witnessed in the small hours of that morning had been a black market delivery. I had confirmation at lunch, for Winnie grinned at me as she brought my pudding. It was a treacle sponge with heaps of treacle!

And something really funny happened. Winnie actually manoeuvred me a second helping. I wasn't wise to what she was up to, and when she brought it I protested that I'd already had pudding. She gave me a surreptitious kick, but it was too late.

"Of course you have, sir," she said. "I'm very sorry."

"Oh no, you don't!" I told her as she made as if to take it away again, but everybody laughed. When I came out to the lawn after that meal, the Brigadier wanted to know if I was going to spend the afternoon in a comatose state, and that was when he saw me loosen a button or two when I'd sunk into my chair.

And so to dinner and the cinema. The second house began at half-past eight, so Worne and I had heaps of time. It was a good show too—*The Blue Dahlia*—a whodunit of the slick American type; good cinema while you watched it, however much the machinery creaked when it was over and you looked back. Even Worne had to admit that it had been pretty good.

"It doesn't make you itch to write something of the same kind?"

"Devil a bit," he said. "I prefer to remain the only serious novelist in England who's never attempted a detective story."

He went straight up to bed and I followed him a few minutes later. I took out a final cigarette and then found my lighter not working, and I hadn't a match. So I tapped at Worne's door but there was no reply. I thought he might be in the lavatory, so I waited. Then I tried the door of the nearest one, and the door opened. I looked at the downstair one and that was free too. I came up again and again tapped at Worne's door, and there was no reply. After that I gave up the idea of a cigarette and had a bath instead. And that night I slept like a dormouse.

It was Murder Eve, and I was the last person in Sandbeach to suspect it. The next morning—in fact before I'd been awake much more than an hour—someone was to be murdered, and in a most peculiar way. Who that someone was you may have already surmised. If you have not, you are due for at least one disappointment, for it wasn't the abominable Gerald.

PART II

CHAPTER VI
MURDER?

THE THURSDAY dawned superbly, and it was a joy to be out before breakfast. After getting my *Times* I took the usual walk to Carbury Chine, but that morning something happened. By chance I took a careful note of the time.

It was at about one minute before half-past eight when I caught sight of Huffe, and his boat was then almost at The Mouth. I wondered what the devil he could be doing, rowing before breakfast, for mid-morning had been his usual time and with Barbara Channard as a passenger. Then—and that was just as those cliffs on the Sandbeach side hid him from view—I thought I knew the answer. In just over a week's time there was to be a local regatta. Nothing spectacular, of course, like yacht racing at Cowes, but a jolly, friendly affair solely for the benefit of visitors. Pleasure boats, with or without a mainsail, and canoes figured largely, and there were rowing races for both men and women, with and without crew. Huffe doubtless intended to enter for a race—if that's what one calls it—and rowing alone. That was why he was getting in some practice. Maybe he was timing himself to see what chance he'd stand, though when I'd seen him he hadn't been rowing very fast.

I thought no more about it, at least till the breakfast gong went, and then I naturally guessed that he'd be late. I'd also seen no sign of Worne that morning, not that I thought much about that, for on at least two mornings previously, I'd only run across him by luck. Even if we both did visit Carbury Chine before breakfast, there was always the choice of various ways back.

We were in the middle of breakfast. Suddenly the door opened, and Rowse appeared. I thought he was looking for somebody.

"Ladies and gentlemen. . . .

"I regret I have some bad news. Mr. Worne just telephoned to say that Major Huffe was drowned this morning. He was out rowing and his boat sank for some reason or other. He got into difficulties, and his body hasn't been recovered. Mr. Worne himself happened to see the accident and tried to save him." He paused dramatically. "That's all, ladies and gentlemen. I'm sorry to disturb you like this, but you were bound to know sooner or later. I thought sooner would be best. Perhaps we shall know more when Mr. Worne gets back."

He gave a little bow and went out again, and at once there was a babble of shocked voices. I looked round in time to see Barbara Channard leaving the room. Others were leaving too, for it was the end of the meal for those who had been served earlier than myself. I picked up mechanically my last piece of toast, and somehow I couldn't believe it true. Accidents like that do happen, but never so near to one's self. And there was Huffe whom I'd seen not an hour before. Huffe—alive, strong, driving that boat through the water. Little mannerisms came back to me; the scornful way he'd puff out his lips, his impudent grin and the way he had of looking away at nothing when he was talking to you. Then suddenly I didn't feel like more toast, and out I went to the lawn.

A local taxi drew in at the drive and Worne was in it. He looked an extraordinary sight with his sodden clothes and disordered hair. I was practically touching him as he got out.

"Better sprint up and get those clothes off," I told him, but I was too late. The Brigadier—he ought to have had better sense—was there among others and all asking questions at once. Worne—never the one to lose a second's publicity—began telling what had happened.

He had been taking his usual walk and had gone down to the Carbury side of the chine. He was just turning back when he caught sight of Huffe. Huffe was wearing slacks, he thought, and a bathing costume, as he always did when rowing. Then things happened very quickly. The boat seemed suddenly to fill. Huffe was standing up and then he fell and his head appeared to strike against the side of the sinking boat. Then both boat and Huffe disappeared.

"I waited a bit," Worne said, "thinking he'd come up, but he didn't. I didn't know what the devil to do. You know how it is. Then I went in after him. Another man came in too: in fact he was in first. Other people on the Carbury side had seen it happen." He shook his head. "And that's all I really know. We dived and swam around but there wasn't a sign of him. Someone had rung the police and I made a preliminary statement, and that's all."

He went on to his room. I was shaking my head dismally when Winnie came running out and told me I was wanted on the telephone. For a moment I wondered who on earth it could be. Wharton, perhaps, and something gone wrong again with his holiday. Then I thought it might be Bill Ellice, or Fry, and Fry it was. He didn't mention his name. He just asked me if I could come along at once. If I waited at the end of the road outside the Hotel, a car would be there almost at once to fetch me.

It was a police car and it dropped me at the foot of the chine on the Carbury side. There was no need to ask if anything had happened, for a constable was ordering the holidaymakers to keep their distance, and hollering that there was nothing to see. My arrival seemed to cause a new sensation.

There were two witnesses standing with Fry on the beach at the edge of The Mouth. The tide was just going out and the water had fallen slightly below the undergrowth on the Sandbeach side, and I hadn't time to notice anything else, for Fry was introducing the two witnesses. I noticed he didn't mention my name.

Salt was a Cockney of about forty; a short, sturdy man wearing sodden flannel bags and as sodden a shirt. It was he who had dived and swum with Worne with the hope of getting Huffe to the surface. He was a modest sort of chap. "The other gent," as he called Worne, had done just as much as he had, if not more.

Filey was the other man; a Staffordshire man of about thirty-five, and recently demobbed. He'd been reading his newspaper on the lawn in front of his boarding house when he'd noticed Huffe standing for a moment in the boat. He'd run to help but he was not much of a swimmer. Later he'd rung the police.

"That's all for now, gentlemen," Fry told them. "We're very grateful to you, and we shan't bother you more than we can help."

"We'll get back to the station, Mr. Travers," he told me. "Nothing we can do here."

"What about the body?" I said. "Any chance of recovery?"

"Not in The Mouth," he said. "The local fishermen say the backwash would take it out to sea and along the coast. The last two persons drowned here came ashore at Whitesands shoal. That's about fifteen miles west."

"What about the boat?"

"We've got the boat," he said. "Salt went down and got a rope on it. It was only in ten or twelve feet of water. I had it taken to the station on a truck. We'd only have been pestered with people if we'd left it here."

That was the first thing I wanted to see, for unless that boat had stoved its ribs in against some extraordinary and unsuspected obstruction, I couldn't understand why it should have sunk. Then as soon as I saw it I was even more surprised, for in its centre bottom was a hole. It was a hole of about the size of a barrel bung-hole, and it certainly wasn't new.

"It's one of the Hotel boats?" Fry was asking me.

I said I thought it was.

"As a matter of fact, it *is*," he told me. "I just wanted your confirmation, that's all. And now about this hole."

Once more he was quoting the local experts and from the old oil round the hole and various marks underneath, I could follow what he said. A previous owner had bored the hole, and another through the central seat, so as to rig a light mast to carry a sail. The hole was plugged with a stout cork firmly driven in, but to remove it, it was only necessary to turn the boat up and punch with a piece of wood of the same bore, and a mallet.

"But was the boat safe?" I wanted to know.

"Absolutely," he said. "The cork was well oiled or tarred and driven home, and it was flush with the bottom of the boat. No sea pressure could possibly shift it."

He gave me a peculiar look as he said it.

"You mean that it must have been eased before Huffe took the boat out?"

He shrugged his shoulders.

"That's one of the things we've got to go into. But just one other little thing. Was the boat ever on its side, or upside down, when it was on the Haven beach?"

I couldn't say. I did seem to remember seeing one of the two Hotel boats upside down, but I wasn't sure. But there was something else that I did suddenly wonder.

"About that cork," I said. "Or should we call it a plug. It either popped suddenly out or else it loosened gradually. If it came out gradually, then surely Huffe must have noticed the boat beginning to fill. On the other hand—"

"Wait a minute," he said. "Let's settle one thing first. Suppose, as you say, she gradually filled. Huffe must have seen the water or felt it against his feet and ankles. He ought to have seen the actual cork floating, so he could have jammed it in again. Maybe he did. And then what should he have done?"

"I'm no boatman," I said. "You tell me."

"Well, if there was more water than he thought safe, then he should surely have pulled in-shore."

"Perhaps he thought he could make the end of The Mouth and beach it there." Then I thought of something else. "Perhaps he was timing himself from the Hotel to the far end of The Mouth. That's why he went on too long."

"You're thinking of the regatta," he said.

"Damn you, Fry," I told him. "Never saw such a fellow as you are. You think of everything."

"Don't you believe it, sir." He gave his shy, deprecatory smile as he shook his head. "But about that other thing you were going to mention—the plug coming out suddenly."

"All I was going to ask was, just how quickly would the boat fill, or sink."

"That's what I thought we'd try out," he told me. "She's still here on the truck and I know a nice quiet little spot. Parker can go with us and be extra evidence."

Parker was the man who'd been tailing Huffe. Fry drove the truck and we must have gone ten miles before we turned off the lane to a track that led down to a little cove between the cliffs. A family was having a picnic there, but they were mildly interested and no more—at least, till the boat sank.

We had put a home-made plug in her and Fry was in bathing clothes. We didn't need more than three feet of water, so she was about twenty yards out. Fry pulled out the plug and Parker did the timing. In almost exactly two minutes she went down. Fry tried it again when we'd emptied and righted her, and the timing was the same.

"What's all this going to lead to?" I asked Fry with a humorous exasperation when we were on our way back, for he hadn't been talking about the boat at all. He'd been interested in that car delivery that I'd seen in the early hours at the Haven Hotel.

"You may not think so," he said, "but I'm damned if I can say. What I will do is lay you five to one that the inquest verdict is death by misadventure."

"Take the evidence we've got," he went on. "Mr. Worne saw everything, and so did Salt and Filey, and they corroborate each other. Everything was what might be called a natural sequence."

"Wait a minute," I said. "*Will there be an inquest?"

"You mean the body," he said, "but that'll turn up. The local experts say so. There've been two deaths from drowning in The Mouth in the last five years, as I was telling you—both soldiers, by the way—and in each case the bodies came ashore at White-sands shoal, which is fifteen miles west of here."

"Right," I said. "There'll be a verdict of death by misadventure. What's wrong with that?"

He gave me an almost startled look—the look, say, of a schoolmaster whose favourite prize pupil has made some idiotic blunder. I had to smile.

"I know I'm a fool," I said. "But you go on taking that for granted and tell me what's in your mind."

"Sometimes I can't make you out, sir," he told me. "Still, here're a few things. Why should it be Huffe who's dead? The one man in all Sandbeach you mentioned to me by name. The man we were beginning to get something on. The man we might have got something out of if we'd caught him in an act. The man we never will get anything out of now."

"Carry on," I told him, and waited.

"Well, it was someone's interest to get him out of the way."

"Whose?"

"Some other gang—if he was trying to cut in on their terri-tory. Peckenham, for instance. He's never been explained yet."

"Very well," I said, and I'm afraid it was a bit resignedly. "We've got to begin somewhere so we start off from the assump-tion that he was murdered. The initial theory is that he was killed by a rival gang. A tough mob, shall I say, who'd stick at nothing. See anything wrong about that?"

"Ought I to?"

"Don't know," I said, "but it doesn't hang together—not as I see it. A tough mob would have done a tough murder. Huffe would have been stabbed or shot or cracked on the head. This murder's too subtle, too lady-like."

"It *was* subtle," he said. "It was murder made to look exactly like an accident. Stab a man or shoot him or smash his skull in, and you're for the long drop if you're caught. In this case it's got to be proved first of all that it *was* murder and wasn't an accident, and against tremendous odds."

"Very well then," I said. "We'll accept all that. It was a subtle murder. A murder planned to look like an accident. The motive is that he was handling his end of the black market job so crudely that he was bound to be caught, and likely to blab. He was killed by loosening the plug in the bottom of the boat."

Then I pulled up short and said I still didn't like it. "Why?"

"There's something wrong," I said. "The chances against his being drowned were simply enormous. After that water had entered the boat we'll allow half a minute for him to have noticed it. We'll allow another half minute while he made up his mind. He still had another half minute to have turned the boat aside into safe water. It was a very few yards away."

"Could he have manoeuvred a waterlogged boat?"

"That'll be for you to test," I said. "I don't see why not. While she was afloat he could row her. But he didn't."

Then suddenly it struck me that there was the crux of the problem. Why did he let the boat almost fill before taking action? Fry thought the same thing at the same time.

"That's what puzzles me," he said. "Since we made that test it's been puzzling me still more."

"There's our real starting point," I said. "We've got to find an answer to the question of why he was such a fool as to go on rowing a boat that was obviously filling damnably fast."

"Wait a minute!" he said. "I think I've got it. He was a stranger here. He didn't know The Mouth was so deep. Why should he worry about a boat sinking when it'd be in only about three feet of water."

"Maybe that's it," I said. "It's got to be it. The question of why he was in the boat at all is tied up with the regatta. There I think you might question a Mrs. Channard with whom he was friendly. He might have mentioned the matter to her." He took a note of the name, then gave me a shrewd look.

"Why shouldn't he have been combining business with pleasure? If he was merely practising for the regatta he ought to have turned before he got to The Mouth. But why shouldn't he have had an appointment before breakfast with one of those hotels? The Regal and the Ocean, for instance. He could have walked up to either from the foot of the chine."

We went on talking and arguing until we decided that some sort of undercover enquiry would have to be begun, and prior to the recovery of Huffe's body. There was the chance, for instance, that he might have been shot by a gun with a silencer from the shelter of the undergrowth as he entered The Mouth. Only a post-mortem could tell that, but meanwhile it would be folly not to anticipate. If it was murder, then the murderer mustn't be allowed several days' start to cover his tracks. But any enquiry would have to be discreet. Fry would have to be making an enquiry into what was obviously an accident. And it would hardly have to be an enquiry, but merely apparently a tying-up of loose ends in readiness for the inquest.

We made out a list of things it was highly advisable to do. Questions should be asked of:

(a) Barbara Channard and other residents as to whether or not Haifa had mentioned the regatta, and above all if he had mentioned that morning's pre-break-fast row.

(b) The chambermaid to see if he had mentioned rising earlier.

(c) Rowse about the plug. (That would give Fry the chance of running his eye over Rowse.)

(d) Barbara Channard about the plug. Were she and Huffe aware of it? Had they discussed it from the angle of safety?

That would be a start. Meanwhile Huffe's finger-prints could be obtained from his bedroom and sent to the Yard in case he had a record. Above all, Fry must make an immediate search of Huffe's belongings, if only on the plea that he wanted to get in touch with relatives. He should also get from Rowse the address from which Huffe had written to the Hotel. Enquiries might then be made there which ought to reveal something about Huffe's business and connections.

Fry dashed off in his car. I left the station by the back way, and on foot. The last thing I wanted was to be connected with the local police, and, as a blind, I was going to the Hotel where Fry would catch sight of me, ask Rowse who I was and then ostensibly ask me a few questions. After that I thought of going down to the beach for a swim before lunch, and I hoped to hear Peckenham's views on the tragedy. They, as I told myself, ought to be highly interesting for what they would have to conceal.

But I wasn't at all elated, and that was a strange thing. Murders are right up my alley, and here was the chance for surreptitious enquiry and the ironic satisfaction of being, in the eyes of those watched or questioned, wholly unconnected with the law. But I knew just why I wasn't being gratified at the prospect. In the first place, as I'd tried to show Fry, the whole thing was too tenuous and vague. If it was murder, then, frankly, it was a dam'-silly one. If, as the available evidence showed, it was an accident, then I wasn't interested. What I was interested in, as I had been from the first, were people themselves—the dead Huffe and that queer bird Peckenham, and, to a lesser extent, Barbara Channard and even the beefy Rowse.

As I came in at the Hotel entrance I saw Rowse and Fry with their heads together. Rowse hailed me and duly introduced me, and he would have sheered off if Fry had not asked him to stay. I answered the pre-arranged questions and then went up to my room, and it was just about midday when I got down to the beach. I caught sight of Worne in a deck chair, and he wasn't even pretending to work.

"How're you feeling?" I asked him.

"Think I've got the most damnable cold coming on," he told me. "I've got three aspirins inside me and I thought I'd get out here in the sun."

"Well, it was a pretty heroic bit of work you put in this morning," I said.

"That be damned for a tale," he told me, and so irascibly that it was as if I'd been suddenly savaged by a pet rabbit. "That kind of publicity is what I hate. It was that chap Salt who did the real work. He was actually in the water before I was."

"You're too modest," I told him, and then moved on. From my vantage of height I was looking for Peckenham, and when I did see him, I was almost startled, for he was reclining at ease in a deck chair, hands folded across his ample belly, and to whom should he be talking but that awful child Gerald! Gerald was standing on one leg and idly twisting round on the other, but his eyes were intent on Peckenham's face. Peckenham, I guessed, was spinning him some yarn about cannibals, and then Peckenham caught sight of me. He hoisted himself slightly up in his chair, felt in his pocket and produced what must have been a coin. Gerald made no bones about taking it. Peckenham dismissed him with an avuncular smile and a waft of the hand, and off he made in the direction of the ice-cream stand.

"Going to have your bathe?" he asked me.

"Straightaway," I said. "I've been catching up with arrears of correspondence. Also I didn't feel so much like bathing this morning. I don't know why, unless it was on account of that poor devil Huffe."

He gave a heavy sigh.

"Most untimely. A grievous tragedy indeed, my boy. Cut off, as one says, in his virgin prime."

Virgin, I thought, was hardly the word, and then Peckenham was taking a brighter view.

"Still, the ways of Providence are inscrutable. Who are we to question the Purpose? For all we know, everything may have been for the best."

There wasn't anything I could very well add to that. Chadband himself could hardly have expressed it better. But Peckenham was looking up at me, and in his eye was either a quizzical or an ironical look.

"Do I understand that this unfortunate affair occurred because of a loose cork, or something similar, in the bottom of the boat?"

I did some very quick thinking.

"I've heard gossip to that effect," I said.

"Sit down a minute, my boy," he told me with a curious gentleness, and I'm damned if I didn't squat by his chair on the sand as if I'd been ten years old and he was an uncle.

"My old brain," he began, "is not as spry as it once was. Nevertheless I have my moments. Between ourselves—this is strictly confidential, by the way—I was highly disturbed at the thought of that cork, and the tragic consequences that ensued."

Then he was swivelling on me an eye that suddenly seemed far from whimsical.

"You have never been in any way connected with the police?"

I hope my face didn't flush, but I felt hot and cold, wondering just how much he knew.

"As a criminal?" I asked with a simulated flippancy.

"In any way, my boy," he told me. Then he heaved a sigh. "In my days out East I had often to be a detective, as they call it, and magistrate, and even—on one unhappy occasion—a public executioner. That was why I have just yielded to a regrettable impulse to make some private enquiries of my own."

My eyes bulged. I knew what a fool I'd been to overlook that one thing.

"Gerald," I said. "That blasted Gerald!"

Then I was hastily begging Peckenham's pardon. Perhaps I shouldn't have called the boy that.

"Don't apologise, my boy," he told me piously. "There are times when I too have been tempted to reprimand that unhappy child."

"It was he who loosened that plug—or cork, or whatever it was?"

"Sh!" he said, and peered solemnly round. "In these matters it is best never to commit one's self. If this deplorable mischief was brought home, think of the distress to his perfectly inno-cent—if misguided—parents. And the shadow that might be cast across the future of the boy himself."

He raised a pontifical hand and then resumed.

"Also in these matters, there is an old adage that could serve one remarkably well. Never keep a dog, my boy, and then bark for yourself. The police are public servants, paid for by the taxes of people like you and me. Let us leave them to their duties."

His pudgy hand went out and he gently patted my shoulder.

"Let us say no more about it. We will, in fact, forget it. That is understood?"

"Perfectly, sir," I said lamely and stiltedly. Then I was adding that if I didn't have my swim I shouldn't get one at all.

But I didn't enjoy my swim in the least, and not because I am naturally a gregarious person who missed the company of Huffe and Barbara Channard. It was a grand morning, the sea was fine and the sky unclouded, and yet my brain felt suddenly as heavy as lead. And that, as I soon realised, was due to old Peckenham. It was Gerald who had loosened that plug. I could see him ham-mering at it with a piece of driftwood and one of the unnumer-able half-bricks that lay by the sea wall. Peckenham was sure of it, and he had prised out the information in some specious way of his own. But he didn't want the information to go further.

And why not? Never for a moment did I believe all that humbug uttered so smugly about the boy's parents or the cloud across the wretched Gerald's life. What I thought was something very different: something that to you may seem very far-fetched. I thought that in some inscrutable way of his own, Peckenham had discovered who I was, and he had passed the information on to me, knowing that almost certainly I should pass it on to the police.

That led to some more furious thinking. My name might have aroused a train of thought and a memory in Peckenham's mind, for on a good many occasions I have had to give evidence at murder trials, where I have been designated a consulting expert at the Yard. More than once I have been honoured by a picture, if only in the Sunday papers of what I might call the what-the-butler-saw type. And yet that shouldn't have caused any uneasiness. Why should I care a cuss if Peckenham knew as much about me as, say, George Wharton himself. But the trouble was that I *was* caring. There was even an alarm and a vague ridiculous fear, and that was something to puzzle me more than ever. Peckenham inspired that uneasiness and that fear. And yet why should he? But he *did*. . . . and so my thoughts went on and on round that uneasy circle.

I went up to my room and changed, and I wasn't feeling any better. There were fillets of sole for lunch and a delicious blackcurrant tart but they took Peckenham only for a little while from my mind. What, in fact, finally gave me a certain ease was the remembering that at six o'clock I should be meeting George Wharton.

CHAPTER VII
NO MOURNING FOR ELECTRA

AFTER LUNCH I didn't fed like joining the beach parade on the lawn, especially when I heard the noisy shouting of the unspeakable Gerald, so I did my crossword in my room. But I made a poor hand of it and after a few moments I laid it aside. Hearing that wretched urchin had brought on a train of thought and I knew I'd have no mental peace till I'd followed it to some logical end.

If Gerald, for instance, had loosened the plug, then the situation had very much altered. But that was now seeming a very big *if*. Doubtless among Gerald's other accomplishments was the art of fluent lying, and what he had told Peckenham I didn't know. Maybe Peckenham had been wrong in his approach. Suppose he'd said something like this: "You tell me how you got the plug out of the boat and I'll give you sixpence for a big ice." My own idea of Gerald was that he'd have owned up to any enormity if he'd only felt certain of the sixpence.

In fact, my idea now was that Peckenham hadn't been talking to Gerald about the plug at all. That had been a yam for my benefit. Why shouldn't Peckenham have done the loosening himself?

And that loosening was what I had to consider. It didn't matter for the moment who did the loosening, provided it was done with the intent and the hope that Huffe's boat might sink. The deed itself then: the actual loosening with intent: what did it amount to? Little more, surely, than a highly dangerous practical joke. Huffe could swim well enough, and if he couldn't get the boat into shallow water in time, then he'd get a soaking and no more. But the usual course—the sensible, straight course, in feet—that I'd always seen him take, was never in water deep enough to drown him even if he could swim hardly a stroke. The only deep water was in The Mouth, and The Mouth was the focal point of all argument.

It seemed therefore logical to look at the affair from two points of view. If only a practical joke was intended, then there had been no murder. But because of the unfortunate consequences of the joke, the joker would never come forward. On the other hand, if in some very subtle way the loosening of the plug had had murder in view, then that murder must have been connected with The Mouth. But I was inclined to regard the loosening of the plug—or rather the consequent flooding of the boat as incidental. It just happened to occur at the time of Huffe's death. That might have been from a heart attack. It was far more likely to have been from a shot fired from the undergrowth round The Mouth. In fact I was prepared to wager that when Huffe's body was recovered, it would be found that shooting was the cause of death.

Everything suddenly seemed very quiet outside and I realised that the beach parade had moved off. But one chair was still occupied, and by someone with her back to me. I gave my glasses a polish and saw that it was Barbara Channard.

At once I began thinking again. She and Huffe were virtually inseparables. Why hadn't she accompanied him in the boat? Because he was rowing a trial? Because, as I'd gathered, she wasn't fond of early rising? And then I left all that when I thought of something else—that quarrel that Worne had overheard.

Now if anything was utterly illogical, it was that quarrel. What went before it I didn't know, but I knew what came immediately after it, and it just didn't make sense. There had even been the mention of *killing*. She had said she would kill him if he did something. That something couldn't have been coming to her bedroom that night, for that was precisely what he did. And *killing*, as Worne himself had hastened to point out, was an absurd word in her mouth. A violent exaggeration, or a figure of speech if you like, but even then absurd. And then I suddenly had an inspiration.

She *had* talked about killing. She *had* said she would kill Huffe if he did something, and I had to laugh when I knew the reason. She and Huffe had also been to *The Blue Dahlia*, and they'd been discussing the picture. The whole thing had been hypothetical and concerned with the merits of or justification for murder. That's why she had said, "If you did so-and-so, I'd most certainly kill you." That's what Worne had heard. The argument had been a bit vivid, perhaps, and might even have led to a slight display of temper, but what happened later that night was proof that it was nothing more.

I always get a thrill when I hit on a theory that pleases me, and rarely have I found one that pleased me more. I took off my glasses and gave them a polish—a trick I have, usually when at some mental loss or on the edge of discovery—and then I had a good look at myself in the glass and made my way down to the lawn.

Barbara Channard was lying in that deck chair in the shade and doing nothing else. But she wasn't asleep. She didn't hear me come across the grass. When I looked down at her, smiled, and said, "Hallo?" she gave a little start.

"Hallo?" she said, and smiled back.

I reached for another chair.

"Not feeling like bathing?" I said.

"Not today," she said, but there was nothing like a break in the voice, and only an implied regret.

"A bad business," I said. "It's cast a gloom over everything. He was such a lively, friendly sort of chap."

There was no comment. She smiled, I thought, and no more.

"I was actually questioned by the police this morning," I told her more briskly. "Nothing exciting. Just a few stock questions which they have to ask on account of the inquest. I suppose they haven't questioned you?"

"But they have," she said, and sat up in her chair.

"What did they ask you? Do tell me."

"Well, they wanted to know if Bri . . . Major Huffe knew about the regatta. I said he'd just mentioned it and no more. I knew nothing about him going out this morning."

"Just what they asked me," I said glibly. "Do go on."

"Well, they asked me about that awful cork thing in the bottom of one of the boats. I only went in that boat once, and it was perfectly safe. You couldn't move the cork thing if you tried." She smiled. "Isn't it funny how you remember things? I remember Major Huffe and I had an argument about it and we were talking at cross purposes. I was talking about a cork and he was talking about caulk. You know—C-a-u-l-k."

"Of course," I said. "Something you press into a hole in a boat to make it watertight. And that was all the police wanted to know?"

"I think it was," she said. "Oh, no. They asked if we'd always gone as far as The Mouth. I said we always did. We went as far as we could and then turned back. Major Huffe said he liked to get value for money. Just one of his jokes."

"That's just about the kind of thing the police asked me," I said. "Something else, too. If he'd mentioned his parents or any relatives. I said he'd never mentioned a thing."

Then she was telling me what Huffe had led her to understand. Most of it, as his reasons for leaving Cambridge, I'd heard, but he'd told her that he was now without a single relative in the world, for his widowed mother and only sister had been killed in a London air-raid. He'd said that he now had a good job with a London firm of shipping agents. The export drive was doing him a lot of good.

I listened patiently and, I hope, sympathetically. Then I was giving one of my paternal smiles.

"You mustn't be annoyed with me at what I'm going to say. After all, I'm old enough to be your father."

"Flatterer," she told me archly.

"But it's true," I said. "You're still short of thirty and I—well, we won't go into that. But what I was going to say is this. You and Huffe were pals—we'll put it like that . . ."

I was watching her closely at that last phrase but she never turned a hair. Maybe she didn't catch the innuendo.

"But what I was going to say," I went on, "was that you mustn't let this get you down. Just do as you did before. If the worse comes to the worst"—I was as arch as I could make it—"I'll even bathe with you of mornings myself."

"That would be lovely," she told me, and at once I began to hedge.

"Get about a bit," I said. "Which reminds me. Have you seen *The Blue Dahlia*?"

"I loved it," she said. "I thought it was awfully thrilling. I simply adore Alan Ladd. And I'll bet you like Veronica Lake."

There followed a certain amount of badinage and then I glanced at my wrist-watch.

"It's after three," I said. "What about going out to tea somewhere in the town. Know anywhere good?"

"The Regal's the best place," she said, and was getting to her feet. "I'll just warn Winnie and powder my nose and then I'll be down."

The lady was just a philanderer, I decided. I even flattered myself that an artistic and sustained attack of a very few days might lead to a loss of what remained of the lady's virtue. I even found myself humming cheerfully to myself, and that had been a habit with Huffe.

I hardly know how to describe the Regal, but maybe you've met hotels like it yourself. In the long-gone palmy days it catered for what I have termed the elect, when the elect still had money. Now its residents had merely the money. There were some of what we used to call profiteers, but there certainly was money, for the lowest terms were ten guineas a week, which is pretty big for a caravanserai. Moreover a resident had to spend money, for it was licensed, and had a cocktail bar and a ball-room, and what else, heaven knows.

Barbara and I had tea on the terrace overlooking Carbury Chine, and we were looked after by a waiter who wasn't the least enthusiastic about the tip I thought it proper to bestow.

Then we walked down the private steps to the shore, and they were steps so steep that more than once I held her arm to steady her. And I was thinking Huffe must have been for her no more than a few days of highly satisfying romance, or she could never have come on that afternoon of all afternoons to within a few yards of where he had died.

I was thinking too of what Fry had suggested, that Huffe might have gone out that morning in the boat to kill two birds with one stone, the more important being an appointment with the management of either the Regal or Ocean or both. I noticed, now the tide was well out, that there was a stone jetty slight-ly concealed by the overhanging trees, at the very foot of those steep steps from the Regal, and at that very moment Barbara happened to say something.

"I thought that manager was awfully rude."

I didn't get it at all.

"Who was the manager?" I said. "That little cove who looked like an Italian?"

"That's him," she said. "I forget his name, but it's foreign. But I've been twice to the Regal with Mr. Huffe, and the last time the manager was almost effusive. Today he went right by our table and didn't say a word, and he must have noticed me."

As I steered her to the left where a path led at low tide round The Mouth, I didn't make any comment, except to tell her to forget it. Sporelli was the manager's name—I'd seen that on a menu card—and doubtless he had his own reasons for disso-ciating himself from any friend of Huffe. And then by the time we were up at the cliff path again I was feeling rather tired of Barbara Channard.

"Gosh!" I said. "I've just remembered something. I'm meeting a friend at the station. He's coming to the Hotel. What about finding you a taxi?"

She said she'd much rather walk back. It'd be good for her figure. More badinage, of course, and some of it rather roguish, and we were going our different ways.

I let out a breath of relief and then made for the railway station at the double. It wasn't because Wharton's train was due, for it was only a quarter past five. I wanted to ring the police-station to see if Fry was in, and he was. Five minutes later I was in his room.

He hadn't a lot of news. I let him tell me what I'd already heard from Barbara Channard, and the versions were the same. He'd seen the chambermaid who'd said that Huffe had said nothing to her about being up early and not wanting his usual cup of tea. She'd taken it to his room only to find him up and gone.

So that was where Worne was when I went to his room, and then waited—though I didn't mention that to Fry. Nor did I tell Fry what I already knew about Huffe. I asked about Peckenham instead, and if there was any news from Birmingham. Fry said his pal had rung that very afternoon. He'd received the photographs but the sight of Peckenham had brought nothing back to him.

It was ten minutes to six so I hurriedly left, and we arranged for a meeting next day with Wharton. Then when I got to the railway station I was told that the train was running a bit late, so I sat down on a hard station seat and waited. On a seat nearby a clergyman of some kind was waiting too, and the sight of him turned my thoughts to Peckenham.

Peckenham was a super liar, that was one thing of which I was convinced, and maybe it was the only one. It seemed to me too that at some time he had been a cleric and missionary, as he claimed, and I could quite conceive of his having been of some importance, for he had what with no disrespect I might call the gift of the gab and the tricks of the trade. I was fairly certain too that he had lived for some time in Australia. At one time too he must have been a card game addict, even if that hardly went with the cloth. I felt too in my very bones—though less than when in his actual company—that in spite of his bland smugness he could if necessary be a mightily dangerous customer. There was a chill look that would come to those usually twinkling eyes: the look I had seen when he had asked for my silence about Gerald, and had mentioned the police.

Could he then, for all Huffe's pretence of ignorance, have been an associate of Huffe? I thought it very possible. Maybe he had been a sort of follow-up man. Huffe went to a hotel and when he came out he gave some prearranged sign—unnoticed by the trailing Parker—so that Peckenham knew that everything was all right. Later on Peckenham would also go to that hotel, perhaps to make final arrangements about deliveries or receive some cash in advance.

That's what I was thinking, and then I became aware that the train was drawing in. Another minute and there was George in the crowd that was surging my way.

George, I thought, was looking a bit tired, but otherwise there'd been a transformation. He was wearing, for instance, a smart grey suit and soft hat, and he'd actually trimmed the ends of his moustache. I nearly suggested that he'd gone over them with a pair of shears.

I had a car waiting and I'd told the driver to go the High Street way and take it steady. It was a lovely evening, but for a slight sea mist, and George was very much struck by the town. When the car was slowing up, he didn't seem unduly disturbed by the news that the Haven was unlicensed. He likes his pint when so disposed, but better still he likes a cup of tea.

I took him along to Rowse's office. To Rowse, George at once was *sir*, and it rather amused me that never once did he get down to the familiar *old boy*, and the reason was that George was looking his most dignified and gracious best. Another thing was that Rowse didn't try to impress him with the names and titles of residents. He did tell him—through me—that certain guests were leaving the next morning; the Brigadier and family, for instance, and the Plummer-Hedges. He saw that the latter hadn't conveyed very much to me.

"The boy Gerald and his parents," he told me with a suggestive look, and I said there ought to be congratulations all round.

I had a cigarette in George's room while he washed and brushed up. He liked his room; he liked its being on the first floor and he liked the view.

"That Rowse doesn't seem a bad sort of chap," he told me, and I agreed. Now I had come to think things over, I hadn't any intention of immediately involving George in the various happenings at Sandbeach. What I intended was to let him arrive at them gradually, so to speak, and with the hope that he might first of all notice things for himself. As for his being recognised at the Hotel as one of the Big Four, there seemed to me not one chance in a million of his privacy being disturbed. Ask yourself the question whether you would recognise one of the Big Four yourself. In fact it's only on rare occasions that one sees photographs of even the most important of what are supposed to be public figures great scientists, doctors, authors, artists, shall we say unless they are needed in the *Radio Times*.

"By the way, George," I said, "how did you leave the black market?"

"Thank God that's no longer in my line," he said. "But I did give them a new idea which Fodman's already working on."

"Really?"

"Yes," said George, squinting at himself in the glass, and giving his hair another dab. "As I told him, there'd been too much work done at the wrong end. There's got to be a receiving end—that's what I told him. Concentrate more on hotels and stores that get the stuff."

I was so flabbergasted I hardly knew what to say. George, as I told you, often appropriates my theories, but hardly so blatantly.

"Not that we're worrying our heads about the black market now we're down here," he went on. Then he was looking at his watch. "Another quarter of an hour before dinner. What about a little look round?"

I don't know if I'm patting myself on the back when I claim to have a keen sense of irony, but it did strike me as not unamusing that George might soon be enjoying the produce of the black market. There was the first thing I was going to let him discover for himself, and then I hoped for more amusement in watching his reactions. Someone, and certainly Fry, was bound also to tell him about Huffe, for George is the gregarious sort who likes getting into conversations. But I'd already warned Fry to be as discreet as he could about myself. I didn't want George upbraiding me for not letting him know what had been happening.

"You take all the credit," I had told Fry. "Don't mention the black market in connection with the Haven at all. Tell Wharton all you like, provided you add that you didn't tell me. Say you didn't want to disturb my holiday."

George and I went round the garage to the cliff gardens.

"We had rather an unfortunate accident here yesterday, by the way," I began, and then, merely from the point of view of a Haven resident, began telling him about Huffe. He didn't seem too interested. To him it was merely an accident.

"Fry seems to have the idea that there's something behind it," I said casually. "Nothing like murder, of course, but I rather think he's of the opinion that the plug in the boat was tampered with."

Even that didn't seem to interest him much. But he did prick up his ears when I mentioned Worne as one of the Hotel's star residents who'd happened to play a part in the tragedy.

"Jeffrey Worne," he said. "I've got him. Jane read a book of his that she liked and she got me to read it too. Not a bad book at all. What was the name of it?"

"*Scarlet May*?"

"That's it," he said. "Quite a good book. In fact, I've read many a worse."

We were nearing the Hotel on our way back and suddenly the gong went. As we came in at the entrance gates I caught sight of Peckenham. He heard our steps on the gravel and looked round. I called to him and then introduced Mr. Wharton. Peckenham beamed as he held out a pudgy hand.

"You are about to become a resident here, sir?"

George was a bit taken aback. He did manage to say something about hoping to stay for some days. I had somehow got just ahead and the two moved slowly up the steps together. Peckenham's suave chatter just reached me and no more. But he must have buttonholed George, for I'd been at our table a good couple of minutes before the two entered the dining-room.

"An interesting old gentleman," George told me sotto voce. "Been in the Church, so he was telling me."

I almost said he'd be just up George's alley. What I did say was that he'd had some remarkable experiences—as at Bikini, for instance—and he and George ought to get along fine.

Friday seemed the usual day for guests to leave and a new batch to arrive, and certainly the dinner on the Thursday seemed designed to send them away in the best of humours, for it was easily the finest we'd had. There was roast duck and green peas—and generous helpings at that—followed by an exquisite strawberry flan. George, who has trouble with his dentures, always avoids pips, but Winnie made no bones about bringing him biscuits and butter and cheese.

"They don't skimp you on the butter," George whispered as he began a thick spread.

He might have said the same about the sugar, for he fairly shovelled it into his cup. And as he folded his napkin after dry cleaning his moustache, he described the meal as not at all bad. In fact, if he'd paid ten bob for it in town, he'd have thought he'd had a good bargain.

Chapter VIII
WHARTON GETS INTERESTED

I deliberately lost George in the lawn beach parade after breakfast and slipped out to a telephone kiosk some two hundred yards away at the back of the cliff gardens. A taxi came into the drive as I left it, and as the Brigadier had left earlier, I guessed I was missing the departure of my friend Gerald.

I managed to get Fry. What I told him was that Wharton would almost certainly be calling on him that morning round about midday. I said I'd told him about Huffe and I was careful to add just how much I'd said.

"You may think this a lot of duplicity on my part," I said, "but it's nothing of the sort. Wharton's the kind who doesn't like to be told what to do. He likes discovering things for himself, and after that you can't hold him back."

He said he understood perfectly and he was grateful for the tip. I was asking divine aid for myself as a fluent liar as I walked back to the Hotel. The taxi had gone and there were Wharton and Barbara Channard and Peckenham having a great gossip on the lawn. George seemed in fine fettle, and why not? He had had a wonderful breakfast—eggs and bacon, and lashings of toast and butter and first-class marmalade.

I greeted the others and told George it was time for a bathe. Barbara said she was going too, but I avoided her look.

"He's a great lad, that Peckenham," George told me with a chuckle as we went up the stairs. "Seems a bit familiar too, somehow."

"My God!" I was thinking blasphemously to myself. "Not another recognition!"

"You're probably thinking of Count Fosco," was what I actually said.

"Count Fosco," said George. "Now there's a character for you. A real character." He paused to give me a glare. "Could one of you modern authors do a character like that? Not on your lives."

"Take care Jeffrey Worne doesn't hear you," I told him. I got ready for the beach and then looked in at George's room. He was almost ready.

"Something I want to say, George. Don't think I want you tied to my apron strings, or vice versa—"

He was giving me what he probably thought was a roguish look, but was really a most horrible leer.

"Got an eye on the widow?"

"Many a worse prospect than that," I said. "But seriously, George, don't you give a damn about me if you want to go anywhere on your own. I shall do the same, and if we want to go anywhere together—well, that'll be all right with me." That seemed to suit him, and down we went to the beach. Barbara Channard was just ahead of us. She looked round—did I flatter myself in guessing that she was looking for me?—and then waited for us, and the three of us went in the sea together. I had forgotten George as a swimmer, and he surprised me. The beefy type make good swimmers, and George swam like a porpoise. And he was the kind who can stay in for hours. I'd had my ration in the usual ten minutes, but George and Barbara hung on.

I caught sight of Worne as I made for our chairs. "How're you feeling now?" I asked him. I noticed, by the way, that he wasn't dressed for bathing, but was wearing a thin lounge suit. Even under the sun umbrella he must have been pretty hot.

"I think I've staved off the cold," he told me. "Going to take things easy for a day or two, though."

"You're a lucky chap. You can afford to miss a few days. I'm not here for the season."

"How long are you actually staying?"

"Till Saturday week," I said, "then back to the old grindstone. Which reminds me. Something I want to ask you. I thought of it last night in bed. That cousin of yours. Did I understand that he had a flat in Long Acre?"

"Why?" he said, as he nodded.

"Well, I'm at St. Martin's Chambers. My wife's in Switzerland at the moment with her sister, and she badly wants to get a flat or something for the sister and her husband. Naturally the nearer to us the better. I was wondering whether your cousin was still holding on to his flat or had given it up."

"He gave it up," he said. "It's re-let."

"Bad luck," I said. "I didn't know, by the way, that there were flats round that way. I suppose they're over the tops of business premises. I think I'll have a good hunt round there when I get back."

"I wouldn't waste my time if I were you."

"I know what things are like," I told him. "All the same, people do get the most extraordinary strokes of luck."

I was going to tell him a case in point but I caught sight of George and Barbara Channard emerging from the sea. George didn't look too unlike a grampus.

"My friend Wharton's a great admirer of yours," I said. "Mind if I introduce him?"

I waved at George and he was duly introduced. I left him and Worne because I wanted to dodge the lady who'd halted for a chat with some pals and was now heading our way. It was a good five minutes before George joined me. Barbara was still talking to Worne.

"Been hearing about that Major Huffe affair," he told me. I said we'd better be getting straight up to our rooms as I wanted to show him the lay-out of the town. On the way up he gave me another of his special glares.

"Been hiding your light under a bushel, haven't you?"

"In what way?"

"Well, Worne didn't know that you were an author?"

"Oh, that," I said airily, though I felt a bit annoyed at his blabbing. "If it comes to that, Worne doesn't know what you are in what I might call civil life. Besides, I thought we were to be here incognito."

"So we are," he told me placatingly. "Writing's only one of your old sidelines. But you don't make enough of yourself. Why shouldn't you be the centre of attraction as well as that chap Worne?"

I had to laugh.

"*Centre of attraction* is dam'-good, George—not that it isn't remarkably thoughtful of you. But who gave you the low-down on Worne?"

"I've got eyes, haven't I? And ears?"

"Forget it, George," I told him, and that was that.

We got into town garments—sports shirts and flannel bags—and made our way to the High Street. I had coffee and George had tea and then we arranged to get seats for the next week's theatre and cinema. The Pavilion could come later. After that it was nearly midday. I said I'd remembered something I had to do. I added that the police-station was about three minutes away, and George was at once saying, to my relief, that he thought he'd look up Fry.

The lunch gong went that morning at its usual time, but there was no sign of George. I waited on the lawn, then decided to make a start. He arrived, full of apologies, ten minutes late. If it had been I, Winnie would have given a meaning look. But George has a way with women, and she actually beamed as she brought his hors d'oeuvres.

He didn't do any talking till he'd worked off the arrears. Then he was saying that he and Fry had been yarning and the morning had gone before he was aware of it. But I was suddenly suspicious. The apologies had been too pat, and the manner too deprecating. George, I was telling myself, already had something well up his sleeve.

Barbara Channard was the last to leave the lawn after lunch and I had an idea she was waiting for me. When she had gone, and in the direction of the town, I came down.

I thought George was having an after-dinner nap in his room but apparently he'd been in the lounge, chatting with old Mrs. Smyth.

"Feel like a walk?" he asked me.

I said it would suit me if it wasn't too far, and then he was suggesting the end of the town and beach that he hadn't seen. When we came to the first steps and I asked if we should go down, he said he'd rather go on for a bit. When we came to where the road cork-screwed down to the beach, he still thought he'd go on. By then I thought I knew what was in his specious old mind. What he wanted was to see Carbury Chine and the site of the previous morning's tragedy. Fry had started him thinking and now he was anxious to prove that the Old Gent—as he would sometimes deprecatingly call himself—could still show the young 'uns the way to handle a case. As soon as he began talking about Huffe, I knew I was right.

"That Major Huffe rather took you all in at the Hotel, didn't he?"

"How do you mean?" I said.

"One of your Oxford and Cambridge men," he told me with a snort of contempt.

"What's wrong with that?"

"Didn't tell you he'd done a year for embezzlement."

That made me stare.

"Where'd you learn that?" I said.

"Fry sent his prints to the Yard. It seems he was kicked out of Cambridge, and then he had a job with a firm of publishers. Influence, I should think. Two years before the war he left them and started some sort of agency on his own and turned it into a regular swindle. He was doing time when the war broke out."

"That's interesting," I said. "But what about his war record? Is his rank genuine?"

"That remains to be seen," he told me, and by that time we were nearing the end of the cliff paths and coming to the private road that ran behind the hotels. He put on his antiquated spectacles and peered ahead; why, I don't know, for the word REGAL was in letters at least two feet deep.

"So that's the Regal," he said, and put the spectacles back in their antiquated case. "Fry says Huffe was trying to do business there. Think we might have a look?"

"Posh place," he told me when we were in the grounds.

It was only just after half-past two and I led him in the direction of the cocktail bar. It seemed to be closed.

"Too late for a drink?" I asked what looked like a resident.

"You've missed the bus," he told me. "Won't be open again till half-past six."

"Can't you get down this chine place?" George was wanting to know, so I led the way towards the steps. I don't know why I looked back, but I did, and then I was grabbing George's arm and hauling him behind a holly clump.

"What's the idea?"

"Look over there, George," I told him. "The verandah, just to your right."

Peckenham was there, and Sporelli, the manager, with him. Just as we looked, they were shaking hands and Peckenham was moving away. His back was towards me so I couldn't see the expression on his face. Sporelli stood looking after him, and then went back into the hotel. Peckenham disappeared among the shrubs that bordered the drive. George gave a grunt.

"Peckenham, eh? What's the idea?"

I told him who Sporelli was. I added guilefully that the two might be old friends.

"Looked to me as if they were shaking hands over some deal or other," George said. Then he was wanting to know what we were waiting for.

We went down the steep steps with George halting every few moments to look about him. He said it was a nice spot on a sunny day, and when we came to the little stone quay with its ring for tying up pleasure boats, he was asking what use it was, standing there high and dry. I pointed out that it was almost low tide, and that the sea would be there right enough when the tide was full in, even if the high-water mark showed that there'd be only a couple of feet of water.

"Hasn't been used much," he said, "or they'd have cleared away these bushes and things."

We went round Carbury Chine bottom by the public path, though we could have walked across the far end almost dry-shod. When we were well round on the Carbury side among the holiday-makers, George halted for a good look. The steps to the Regal were now invisible, but there was a fine view of the chine itself: the steepness of its central rise, the steady felling away of its wooded sides towards Sandbeach and its far more sudden felling away to the east. In the centre of The Mouth one could see the deep channel where in the winter and spring the rains from the cliffs still ploughed a way.

A couple of vacant chairs caught his eye and he suggested we might sit down. His eyes were at once on that deep channel, and it wasn't hard to imagine the whole Mouth at high tide.

"That Peckenham is a bit of a mystery," he suddenly said. "Did Fry tell you what he's been up to?"

That put me in rather a hole. *No* was on the tip of my tongue, but George was going on and I heard all about Parker and how Peckenham had apparently been tailing Huffe, and then calling on the very hotels that Huffe had visited.

"Rather convenient for Huffe—getting drowned," he said.

"You mean, for Peckenham."

He gave a superior sort of smile.

"What's happened to your brains? Do you think this Huffe was a fool?"

I didn't know what he was driving at. I could have said that if Huffe wasn't a fool, at least he'd been indiscreet with me. Maybe he'd taken me for an amiable fool and that was why he'd told me some of his business.

"Usually the black market boys aren't what you'd call fools," I said. "Admittedly they make mistakes like most criminals."

"Suppose Huffe knew Sandbeach was getting a bit too hot," George deigned to go on. "Suppose he knew Fry's man was tailing him, and Peckenham was wise to who he was. And something else. Suppose he'd promised marriage to the Merry Widow—"

"Who's been talking scandal?" Then I guessed. "That Mrs. Smyth?"

"Didn't you see anything for yourself?" he challenged me.

"Look, George," I said patiently. "Don't do the heavy schoolmaster act. I was—and am—down here on holiday. I don't go snooping on the Hotel residents and looking for criminals."

Just as I realised that that was just the very thing that I *had* been doing, George decided to adopt another attitude.

"Of course I'm not thinking anything of the sort," he told me largely. "What's wrong with you is you get so damned touchy. All I thought was you might have noticed something."

"Now you put it like that, I did," I said. "Huffe and Mrs. Channard were pretty close friends—I'll leave it at that."

"Well, I've heard a thing or two the short time I've been here," George said. "I'll lay a fiver he'd promised her marriage and he was after her money. Now do you begin to get me?"

I had to think a long way back to recover the context.

"Not quite," I said. "Something about Huffe's being drowned at a convenient time. Convenient time for whom?"

"For himself," George said. "He knew what a short stretch was like, and if Fry nabbed him, then he was in for a long one. Perhaps he'd already had some of Mrs. Channard's money. That's for Fry to try to find out."

"I still don't see it," I said. "Huffe might—and I only say *might*—have seen himself getting into the very devil of a hole, but a man of his aplomb and ability could have wriggled out of far worse holes than that."

"Exactly what I'm driving at," George told me blandly, and only then did I see it.

"You mean he wasn't drowned at all!"

"So you've got it at last," he told me, and then was hastening to add that he hadn't said a word to Fry.

"Huffe wasn't half a bad swimmer," he said. "All that boat business was hokum. He pulled out the plug just at the right moment. Then he went under, and how far would he have to swim under water? Not more than ten yards and he was hidden by those bushes there. All he had to do then was make his get-away. I admit he left ten pounds in his wallet at the Hotel, but that was a flea-bite. And where's he now? Somewhere in town. And Fry can't do anything about it, unless he can bring home a black market charge."

"He could have him held on a charge of causing a public mischief," I pointed out. "If the drowning was a fake, that's good enough."

"If," George told me contemptuously. "Why the *if*? I'll lay a fiver his body's never recovered."

"No takers," I said. I've been bitten before, thinking I'd read George's hand and disregarding what he had up his sleeve. All the same, I was very much tempted, and I might even then have taken him if I'd thought there was a chance of getting my money.

We started off back to the Hotel for there was not too much time if we were to be there for tea. We took the short way across the end of The Mouth and then by the beach to the hard road, and all the time I was thinking about that astounding theory that George had propounded. The more I thought about it, the more it seemed to fit in. Loth as I was to exonerate the now departed Gerald, I could see that the whole business of the plug was explained if Huffe had loosened it himself and flooded the boat at the right moment. But there was still something else missing.

"About that theory of yours, George. Didn't Fry think Peckenham was in Sandbeach for the purpose of tailing Huffe? If so, why is Peckenham still here?"

"All in good time," he told me genially. "Didn't you say we were here on a holiday? That'll be Fry's headache."

"You'll tell him about this theory of yours?" I added that it was a damn good piece of theorising.

"The Old Gent's not down and out yet," he told me smugly. "Of course I'll pass it on to him, and that's all. I've had a bellyful of black market the last few days. Let Fry earn his keep."

I hope I didn't smile. I could see George keeping his nose out of things. If I knew him he'd be closeted with Fry again that very night.

"That Peckenham," he suddenly said. "I'd rather like to have his prints. A photograph might be useful."

We happened to be within twenty yards of the photographic studio.

"Follow me, George," I said. "The Travers service at your disposal."

The same assistant was there. Two customers were in the studio and when my turn came, he recognised me.

"You haven't by chance got a print in stock of those photographs I had the other day?" I asked him.

"Let me see, sir," he said. "What was yours?"

I told him, and I had to describe Peckenham. At once he was giving me a queer sort of look.

"I'm afraid I can't let you have any more, sir."

"Why not?"

He hesitated. Then he was saying that the other gentleman had objected. Wharton stepped forward, then he went back and deliberately locked the door. Out came his Warrant Card.

"Look at that, young man, and then keep your mouth closed. If anything gets out about what we're going to say, you may be for it. Now tell us about this other gentleman. Why did he object?"

That very morning Peckenham had come to the studio. I guessed he'd done some thinking back, or he'd subsequently seen someone else handed a chit by the beach photographer.

At any rate he'd realised that his own photograph had been taken.

In the Studio he'd been very annoyed, and he'd insisted on being given the original negative. He'd also learned that I'd been there and collected half a dozen photographs.

"That's all we want to know," Wharton said. "We're grateful to you for the information. All you've got to do is keep it under your hat." He asked for a piece of paper. "Here's my telephone number. If this old gentleman comes here again, just do anything he says. Carry on normal. Then when he's gone you ring that number and say you'd like to speak to Mr. Wharton. If whoever takes the message asks who you are, don't tell them. Got that?"

He had it all right. He also said he was the only assistant, which made things easier.

As soon as we came out he was wanting to know what I'd done with the half-dozen photographs. I told him not to worry. Much as I regretted parting with my only copy, I was thinking it best to let him have it.

I gave it to him in his room just before we went down to tea. Luckily he didn't ask for two copies and I hoped Fry wouldn't let slip where the rest of the copies were.

"The next thing is to get his prints," George said. "You going to do it, or shall I?"

I volunteered and an easy job it was. Peckenham was already at tea—he gave us the blandest of smiles as we went by his table—and still on his table were a couple of cakes, each in a paper wrapper, and those wrappers were the smooth and not the crinkley kind. George and I stayed on till the very last. Winnie had begun to clear some of the tables for dinner but George attracted her attention as we went out, and both wrappers went into my pocket.

Ten minutes later George had written a covering letter and both the wrappers and the photograph were in an envelope.

"Not a word to Fry about this," George told me with a wink. "This is a little something we're doing on our own. No harm in showing these young 'uns they don't know all the tricks."

Then he was saying that he might do worse than go to the main post-office and get on the telephone to the Yard and have a word about what they were getting. He added chucklingly that my face on the photograph would make Fodman open his eyes.

"What'll you be doing with yourself?" he asked politely, and I told him I'd plenty to do. To me it was plain as the nose on his face that he was making an excuse for another pow-wow with Fry, and who was I to interfere with George's innocent pleasures. As a matter of fact I felt at rather a loose end when he'd gone. Then I thought I'd take another short walk, and it turned out to be the most startling walk I'd ever taken in my life.

CHAPTER IX
RESULTS OF A WALK

I OUGHT to have had more sense than to take a road that brought me out half-way along the High Street. Mid-morning is the time to go shopping in Sandbeach, not at half-past four when people swarm up from the beach in search of tea or ices, and a last hunt round the shops. That afternoon the High Street was seething with people, and most of them had children. Progress along the pavements was intolerably slow, and to walk in the narrow road was to ask for trouble from motor-coaches and cars. I soon threw my hand in and cut back into a side street.

In a minute or two I found myself approaching Sandbeach Chine. The sun was still blazing hot and the heat came up at one from the sticky tar of the road, and it seemed to me that the chine mightn't be too bad a spot. I had never fully explored it, and someone, as I remembered, had told me there was an exceptionally fine rock garden. So I paid my sixpence and went through the gates.

At first there was the wide asphalted path that I had taken before, and then came the first of the downward steps. Below them was what might be called a landing, and rough paths radiated from it along the slopes. So far I'd seen hardly a soul, and that led me for some reason or other to think about Peckenham. I wondered if he were by chance somewhere in the chine, and for a moment I toyed with a malicious idea—that it might be amusing if I could get another sight of him smoking his pipe. It would certainly be interesting to see his reactions if I caught him in the act. Then I chuckled to myself. Peckenham would have an adequate excuse. Maybe he'd say he was smoking medicinal herbs, and by the doctor's orders.

But I didn't keep that idea much in mind, for I was also remembering that I was hardly at the moment what might be called *persona grata*. Not that it was my fault that our photographs had been taken. Where I had gone wrong was in not mentioning the matter to Peckenham. I could think of some extraordinarily good reasons why he should not wish his photograph to come into certain hands—and that could be the only reason why he had gone to that studio and insisted on being given the negative—but that didn't excuse my own clumsy handling of matters. All the same, there was something else that ought to be interesting—to see Peckenham some time that evening and mention the photograph and apologise for the whole thing slipping my memory. It would be interesting, as I said, to see his reactions and how he would explain his own visit to the studio.

I was thinking of that when I found myself on one of the side paths. Then it struck me that it was uncommonly rough for a public path, and just ahead of me it definitely petered out. I was in the act of turning back and then I stopped, for through a gap in the overhanging boughs I was suddenly getting a perfectly marvellous view. It was something like looking through a funnel, with myself in shadow and far below me the dazzling white of the beach, and the splash of sunlight on the trees of the funnel sides. The dots in the sea were bathers and the coloured dots were sun umbrellas or bathing costumes, and on the incredible blue of the sea was a speck of white that would be the sail of a distant yacht. That was what I was thinking, and then something happened.

Something struck me, high up between the shoulders, and by some uncanny luck I slewed round as I went forward. I fell backwards and even now I remember nothing of what thoughts went through my mind in that second or two while I fell. Then I crashed and felt a pain in my side. Thin leafy branches tore at my neck and I tried to grasp them. They skinned my palms but I held on and all at once my feet were against what I saw was a stout shrub. There was a pain in my ribs that hurt me as I gave a gasp, and there for a minute I lay, flat on my back and my feet against the sturdy stem of that bush. Everything was in shadow, and suddenly I wondered if I had broken my glasses. But it was only a side-frame that had become dislodged, and I hooked it round my ear again. And, believe it or not, only then did it occur to me what had really happened.

That was when the stone came down. It was a lump of rock, and almost before I heard it coming, it hurtled past me. It took a leap over the ledge within two yards of me and I heard it thud against a tree. My ribs hurt me but I tried to wriggle into the hard ground of the slope, and there I lay listening. Somewhere below me to the left I could hear the voices of people on the steps of the chine and there was the noisy laughter of some children. Then at last I turned slowly over and looked up.

It was a young acacia tree with its dense, slender branches, that had broken my fall. That fall must have been almost twenty feet sheer, but it was what lay beneath me that was frightening. Beyond the ledge where I lay was another drop of some twenty feet, sloping perhaps, but with a jagged outcrop of rock. But for that tree above me I would have been lying down there with my skull caved in, maybe, or at the best with smashed ribs and a broken leg. Even if my glasses had smashed when I had hit that tree, I should have cut my eyes. At the best I should have been helpless for without my glasses I'm as blind as a bat.

I felt my ribs and wondered if something were broken. But the pain wasn't so bad as all that, and then I saw that the fall had played the very devil with my clothes. There was a jagged tear in the sleeve of my coat, and another down the leg of the trousers, and beneath it the blood was drying. The green of the tree was smeared across the grey of the flannel and even my shirt was tom, and then as I looked over that ledge, I was wondering how I could climb either up or down.

In a minute or two I was moving sideways, feet against a shrub or a handy rock. It took me ten minutes to reach the first tree, and I clung to a trailing branch and so to the next tree. The sounds of people were just below me now, and when there was a momentary quiet, I slithered down. When I looked at my wrist for the time, I found that my watch had gone. More people were coming down and I sat on the slope till they'd passed. It had been a kind of testing, but they'd seemed to notice nothing unusual about me, and I followed just behind them down the steps till at last we were at the end of the beach road.

There was a taxi at the stand, and on my side of the road. The driver gave a questioning look at me and another look when I asked him if he'd drive me to a doctor.

"Had an accident, sir?"

"That's right," I said. "Thought I'd do some mountaineering on the cliffs and I wasn't so good as I thought."

It wasn't his surgery hours but the doctor happened to be in. Whether he believed my yarn I don't know, but whether he did or not, he must have thought me several kinds of a fool. The ribs were badly bruised but not broken, he said, and they'd hardly hurt at all when strapped up. If I'd like an X-ray he'd arrange it. Then he dressed a cut on my leg and various abrasions, and charged me half-a-guinea for the lot. I was to use my own judgment about seeing him again. The charge, by the way, included a few pins and I was reasonably presentable when he showed me out.

I told the taxi to wait and arranged to be driven right up to the front door of the Haven. People were already on the lawn but I went through that door as quickly as I could and up to my room, and the doctor hadn't exaggerated when he'd said the strapping would ease the ribs. Then I locked the door of my room and stripped. Then I adjusted the dressing-table mirror till I could crane round and see the bruise between my shoulder blades. The skin wasn't broken, but it must have been the very devil of a wallop and it hurt me when I took a deep breath.

I went to get a clean shirt and on the top of the chest of drawers was my wrist-watch. That was a stroke of luck, even if it was a habit of mine to forget half my time to put it on. It was a quarter to seven and I was wondering when George would be back, then as I looked in the drawer, I noticed something unusual. I tried the other three drawers and then had a look at the wardrobe. There wasn't a shadow of doubt that someone had been going through my things.

That was when I heard George's voice coming up from the lawn. I slipped on a new pair of flannel bags, and was fastening my tie when I heard him coming up the stairs.

"Sure you didn't slip?" he was asking me, and I had to show him that bruise on my back.

"You couldn't have made it when you fell?"

"Listen, George," I told him patiently, "I remember that lump of rock, or whatever it was, hitting me in the back. It was as if someone had thumped me on the back."

"Then who the devil did it?"

"I'll give you two guesses," I told him.

"Peckenham," he said. "Something to do with those photographs, or my name's Robinson."

I said I thought he was right first time. Only Peckenham could have gone through my drawers, and in search of the six photographs.

"What about that Peggy you warned me about?"

"By this time," I told him, "she knows everything I've got better than I know it myself. Besides, she's got all the mornings up here by herself. This bit of searching was done since I left here after tea. Whoever knocked me down that chine was pretty sure I was down and out. He was the one who's been going through my things."

"Let's be dead sure of something," George said. "Could it by any chance have been some mischievous boy or other who hit you with that lump of rock?"

"There wasn't any mischief about that second lump of rock that came down," I told him. "It was about twice the size of a football. If it had hit me in the head I wouldn't be here."

"Tell you what," he said. "You carry on as if nothing has happened."

"I can't do that," I said. "It's put an end to my bathing. Even if the ribs didn't hurt, I'm all over cuts and scratches."

"You'll have to say you've got a cold," he told me, and then was looking as if he'd suddenly got an idea.

"Suppose this Huffe is still somewhere in the neighbourhood. Any reason why he should want to do you in?"

I said there might be. What, exactly, I couldn't say. But to think of Huffe as the one who'd tried to kill me—for that's what it amounted to—was to accept a hypothesis. But there were no ifs about Peckenham. He was alive all right.

Then the dinner gong went. We were five minutes late in coming down, and I was looking round for Peckenham. I didn't happen to catch sight of him, and probably, I thought, because there were a few new guests, and tables had been rearranged. But the lateness left George and me the last in the room.

"How're you feeling?" he said.

"Not too bad and not too good," I told him. "Tomorrow I'll be a bit stiff."

"Feel like a little trip to the chine?"

We set off at once. Everything would be downhill, which was all to the good for me, and the only snag turned out to be that the evening light was far less strong. Now it was much more gloomy in the shadows, though George was professing to see quite well.

I was supposed to think back to where I had suddenly been wool-gathering and had left the main path. It took quite a time to find it, but find it we did. A widish side path forked down to our right and a short way along it, it forked again. The downward fork was the one I'd taken, and it wasn't really a path at all. The upward one was almost at once bounded by fencing on its dangerous side and soon it was widening out and there was a rustic seat set in the face of the slope. I waited there while George went back. It was a good twenty minutes before he returned. And he'd found the very spot where I'd stood and seen the smashed boughs of the tree into which I'd fallen.

"I'll go down again," he said, "and you stay here. It shouldn't take five minutes. You look over the railings when I give a holler."

A couple of minutes and there he was, and only about fifteen feet below me. When he turned his back on me I could still see his head and shoulders perfectly plain. And he'd been standing at the very spot where that lump of rock had hit me. And all round me in the slope were plenty of rocks. In less than no time one could have collected a cartload.

"There we are then," George said. "You took the low road and your pal took the high, and you were damn near in heaven before him. Lucky for you he wasn't an even better shot than he was. I'll bet I could drop a rock from here clean on anyone's skull."

He had a good look round but that was hopeless from the start. Footprints were out of the question and there was nothing else to see, and the light there among the shadows was getting pretty bad. So we made a slow way down to the bottom of the chine. It was like a different world on the beach, full in the slowly setting sun. There was no taxi there, so we sat on a shelter seat and waited.

"What I can't quite get at is the significance of this business," George told me. "The only thing I'm sure of is that it makes that Huffe business more serious. Someone must have been in a pretty bad hole to have made that attack on you." Then he was giving me a shrewd look. "Can't you think of something? It isn't like you not to have any ideas."

I said I wasn't feeling like thinking—at least beyond what I'd already said. Peckenham was my favourite for the job, and because he suspected that I'd had that beach photograph deliberately taken. I added that there wasn't any hurry. As soon as George heard from the Yard, then we'd know why Peckenham hadn't been keen on having his photograph in the wrong hands. I did add that maybe Peckenham had tried merely to knock me out so that he could search my room in comfort. That was pretty puerile, I know, and no wonder George's lips were pursed in contempt.

But what he didn't guess was that I'd got involved in what was called a web of deceit. I'd begun by keeping things from George for my own specious reasons, and now I couldn't summon the moral courage to admit the fact. I should have told him about that early morning black market delivery, and myself in the lavatory, and Peckenham trying the door. But that would have had to lead to other disclosures, or to the creation of a wholly new set of extemporisations by way of excuse, and at the moment I wasn't feeling like extemporising. And by luck the taxi arrived.

"Know a pub with any beer in it?" George asked the driver, and it wasn't the one who'd driven me to the doctor.

The driver did and we were taken to a small pub on the outskirts of the town. George was in a generous mood and had the taxi wait. He even stood the driver a drink. When we finally got back to the Hotel, it was just after ten o'clock. Rowse happened to be coming across the lawn from the garage.

"Mr. Peckenham about?" I asked him. "I rather wanted to see him for a moment."

"He's gone, old boy," he said. "Went just before dinner."

"You mean he's left the Hotel?" I thought perhaps I was being too enquiring. "I mean, I rather gathered he was staying at least another week."

"Something to do with his wife," he said. "He told me at lunch he was expecting serious news. About six o'clock there was a telephone message to say she was dead. Died under an operation, so I gathered. Mr. Peckenham came in shortly afterwards and he left almost at once."

"Sorry to hear that," I said. "But he'll be coming back after the funeral?"

"He didn't think so," Rowse told me. "He naturally paid for his room, but he didn't think he'd be back."

George and I went upstairs and it appeared we were both thinking the same thing. Peckenham was the perfect bachelor and that yarn about a wife was more than phoney. We both thought he'd rung the Hotel in an assumed voice just after the attack on me. Maybe he had thought I was about finished for, as I should have been but for that acacia tree.

But there was just one little discrepancy in that line of reasoning.

"If I was done in, why should he bolt?" I asked George. "If I'd been only badly smashed up, then there'd be an enquiry by the police. Nothing could look worse for Peckenham than doing a sudden bolt."

"There's wheels within wheels, if you ask me," George said, and sparring for time.

He was in my room, solicitous over getting me to bed. Then suddenly he was asking me if I'd be all right, and out he went. And I thought I knew where he was going, and that was out to the telephone kiosk on the front. He'd be trying to get hold of Fry to suggest enquiries at the railway station. Peckenham was conspicuous enough and it shouldn't be too hard to find out what ticket he'd taken, or if he had a return, to question the man who'd punched that ticket at the barrier.

I got gingerly into bed and as soon as the muscles were relaxed, the ribs began to hurt. When at last I did get comfortable, I daren't stir, and I was wondering if I'd ever get to sleep. I'm a late bird in any case, and after what had happened, my brain was far too active. Before many minutes had passed thoughts were going round and round in my mind.

I was thinking how easy it had been to follow me from the Hotel, for even if I'd turned and seen Peckenham, the meeting would have been the most natural thing in the world. In the crowds of the High Street he might have been only a yard or two behind me, while in the chine itself he could have followed twenty yards behind, and even if I had looked back, the winding, corkscrewed paths and steps and the intervening trees would have kept him from sight. And then I was realising how lucky I'd been—far, far luckier than I'd thought. But for the chance of taking what I'd absent-mindedly thought a side path and then presenting a sitting-target from the seat above, I knew now that before I'd got far down the chine I'd have had a bullet in me. The sound of the shot would have echoed among the trees and might have been taken for anything, and in the flash of an eye the killer would have been away through the undergrowth. Maybe if I had spotted Peckenham in the chine and he had joined me, then at some convenient moment he'd have had a knife in my ribs.

Melodramatic as that might sound to you, it didn't sound like it to me. I shouldn't have been a pretty sight, for instance, if that rock had caught me clean on the skull, or if the second rock had got me as I lay by the bush. And then I was wondering just why Peckenham should want to kill me. That it had been Peckenham I was fairly sure, for I had never been happy about George's theory that Huffe was still alive. Why should Peckenham so want me out of the way that he was prepared to murder me?—that was what I kept asking, and when I found answers, they were only Aunt Sallys to be knocked over at the first shot.

Was Peckenham wanted by the law, and had he recognised me as being in some way connected with the Yard? But if so, why hadn't he recognised Wharton who was infinitely more of a public figure? Did he think I was in that lavatory for the purpose of spying? If so, why give himself away by trying to open the door? And why should he want to be in the lavatory when he had a good enough view of that old Daimler from his own bedroom windows?

And there was the riddle of the man himself. He must at some time have been in the Church, and how could he have come down to the general nastiness of the black market? And, above all, why had he bolted? He hadn't even waited to see if I was dead. Perhaps he had been too sure. After all, he had warned Rowse that he was likely to be leaving, which meant in other words that he'd expected to settle my hash before the day was out. Then he'd searched my room for the photographs, and had gone. But why? If I'd been found dead, surely that abrupt departure would only have called attention to himself? Unless, again, the manner of my killing made death by accident the only possible verdict at the inquest. And that, as I remembered, was what Fry had said about the death of Huffe.

That was how my thoughts ran on and on, till at last the very monotony of their circling must have sent me to sleep.

George had insisted overnight that he would get *The Times*, and before he left he looked in to see how I was. I told him I'd had an infinitely better night than I'd expected, though the stiffness was worse and I was aching in every muscle and bone. But when he'd gone and I'd taken a turn or two round the room, the stiffness wasn't so bad after all. If I was careful how I moved and breathed, I was almost as sound as ever.

That put me in good fettle—that and the glorious morning. As I smoked a first cigarette I was finding ample justification for not telling George all I knew and suspected. I was an ordinary private citizen, and no more. When a policeman's on holiday, he's on holiday. He doesn't keep his eyes perpetually skinned for transgressions of the law. If he came up against something serious, then he'd know what his duty was, but—as I assured myself—there hadn't been anything really serious, at least till that attack on me the previous night. Up till then all that had happened was that I had become far too curious and had allowed curiosity to take too close and personal an interest in my fellow guests. And I had discovered nothing of which I was absolutely sure—nothing, that is, to have brought either Huffe or Peckenham within the law.

Also, out of friendliness to Fry, and as a good citizen, I had passed on the little I surmised. But if, immediately on his arrival, I had blurted out those surmises to George, I might have spoilt both his holiday and my own. George's conscience might be flexible but just how flexible I didn't know. He might have thought it his duty to do something that would have brought us into conflict with both Rowse and our fellow guests, and a delightful holiday would have become an exceedingly unpleasant business.

No more busman's holiday work for me, I was telling myself. As soon as I'd cleared up any loose ends for my own satisfaction, the Huffe affair and the black market and the rest of it could go to the devil. If George liked to busy himself with this and that, and probably make himself a nuisance to Fry, then that was his affair. But there was one thing I was definitely not going to drop. Peckenham had done his best to kill me, and had nearly got away with it, and in my own way I was going to get even with Peckenham. And I thought I knew a way to begin.

I dressed myself with no great inconvenience except that infernal stiffness, and as soon as I was downstairs, I went to Rowse's office.

"Sorry to be a nuisance," I said, "but I particularly want to get in touch with Mr. Peckenham. Did he leave any address for letters to be forwarded?"

"Sorry, old boy, but he didn't," Rowse told me. "I've got the address he wrote from to here, if that's any good to you."

He flicked over the cards in the filing cabinet.

"Here we are, old boy. Laguna Hotel, Fife Street, Bayswater. Like to take it down?"

That was that and I made my way out to the lawn. George was in a deck chair and he put away *The Times* when he saw me coming.

"I've thought of something you might do," he said. "Why not get Peckenham's address from Rowse? It might tell us something."

I told him, modestly, I hope, that I'd thought of that myself.

"A Bayswater hotel," George said with a sniff. "He hasn't gone back there, or my name's Robinson." He kept the piece of paper nevertheless. "Won't do any harm, though, for Fry to make enquiries."

Then he was adding belligerently that whoever had made that attack on me wasn't going to get away with it. It was so paternal and touching that I couldn't think of a flippancy in return. And if George needed solicitude for me as an excuse for his busman's holiday, who was I to protest?

CHAPTER X

PEGGY, WHERE ART THOU?

AFTER BREAKFAST there was a registered letter for me, and I guessed rightly that it was the report from Bill Ellice. If Huffe hadn't been dead I'd have been pretty excited; as it was I was interested and little more.

Bill said he was sending the report earlier than he'd anticipated because there seemed scant chance of finding out anything further. That scandal about Huffe's leaving Cambridge, for instance. There had certainly been some swindling of a fellow member of the college, but the facts were hard to come by. The Yard could, of course, get them privately from the authorities, but as it might cost me a considerable sum for expenses, Ellice thought it best to hear how deeply I was interested before enlarging the scope of his enquiries.

The other question I had put—Huffe's connection with Howlett and Holmes—had been easy. Huffe had joined the publishing firm thanks to the influence of one of the directors, who was a friend of the uncle who had brought Huffe up after the death of his parents in the last air-raid on London in the last war. There had been some vestige of truth then, as I saw, in the tale that Huffe had told to Barbara Channard. It was obvious too that at the time of his parents' death, Huffe could have been only a toddler.

Huffe had done well with those publishers. He had been promoted ultimately to the publicity department, and someone who had known him there mentioned his push and go and how he was a good mixer. Then the uncle died and Huffe came into a fairish sum of money. Ellice thought it was about six to eight thousand pounds. Huffe left the firm very soon afterwards and opened a kind of literary agency, doing the thing on the grand scale and being lavish in his advertising.

His personal spending must have been heavy according to the company that Ellice's man had gathered he had kept, and then came the embezzling of monies belonging to clients.

The report added that my instructions had been exceeded to what Bill had taken on himself to consider a necessary amount. Huffe had been discharged in the October after war broke out. He at once joined up. Someone who had known him in the Commandos had been contacted. His rank was genuine and he had been wounded rather badly. The informant had said that Huffe was a tricky, flashy, reckless sort of customer, but the value of that assessment couldn't be checked.

I wrote a quick letter of thanks to Bill Ellice and said I'd settle his account as soon as I got back to town. Then I realised I had no stamps so I thought I'd stroll as far as the post-office and get a book. Wharton wasn't anywhere around and I guessed he was getting into touch with Fry and passing on Peckenham's last known address. That suited me all right. I'd intended ringing Bill Ellice and giving him the job, and now I was having it done for me at the tax-payer's expense.

When I came out of the post-office I saw a man selling newspapers. I thought I might as well try to get a *Telegraph* as an extra to our *Times*, but he turned out to be selling the local paper—the *Sandbeach Signal*—hot from the night's press. I love local papers, so I invested twopence, and on the way back halted at a handy seat and had a quick look through. The front page was all advertisements but bang in the middle of the centre page was a photograph of Worne.

UNFORTUNATE TRAGEDY
HOLIDAY-MAKER DROWNED AT THE MOUTH
FAMOUS AUTHOR'S GALLANT ATTEMPT AT RESCUE

Those were the headlines. The letterpress, obviously censored by Fry, said a great deal without telling anything at all. In fact there was far more about Worne than Huffe.

The photograph was a beach one—Worne sitting under a sun umbrella, wearing that sombrero affair and writing on a pad held on his crossed knees. It was in profile and it didn't look to me as if he'd deliberately posed for it; it was far too natural a pose for that. The chit-chat about him said he was spending the season at Sandbeach and that Sandbeach was duly honoured. It also gave the names of Worne's three books and added something I didn't know—that negotiations for the film rights of *Scarlet May* were in progress and Sandbeach was already looking forward to seeing the film.

I went on to the Hotel and then thought I'd also do some writing on the beach—if only belated letters to certain friends. When I'd made my careful way down the steps, the first person I saw whom I knew was Barbara Channard. She was in the water, and with a new partner,—a good-looking young fellow who'd arrived at the Hotel the previous evening. Maybe I smirked and treated myself to a lift of the eyebrows. Not only was Barbara far from inconsolable but also it wasn't I who was doing the consoling.

Worne and I caught sight of each other at the same time and he actually gave me a wave of the hand. He had on the same lounge suit and was simply taking his ease beneath the sun umbrella.

"What happened to you this morning?" he asked me. "Didn't see you out for your usual walk?"

"My friend Wharton volunteered to fetch a paper," I told him, "so I thought I'd take it easy for once. And how're you feeling? Pretty fit again?"

"Quite fit," he said. "I just don't happen to feel like bathing, that's all. That Huffe business has rather put me off it. Silly, I know, but there we are."

"Who's the chap bathing with the fair Barbara?" I asked him.

He gave a nasty little smile, not that mine hadn't been a nasty little question.

"Another Major. Youngs, I believe, is the name. Married, too."

"Really?"

"Wife's having a baby some time or other, which is why she isn't in too. Older than Youngs, by the look of her. Funny how quickly gossip gets round in a place like this."

I said hypocritically that it was.

"Mrs. Youngs probably knows her own business best," Worne went on, "but she's taking a risk, if you ask me, in letting a husband cavort with our Barbara." Then he was looking up at me. "You not swimming either?"

"I had a slight accident and gave my ribs a bit of a twist," I said. "I ought to be swimming again next week."

Then I remembered the *Sandbeach Signal* under my arm, and handed it to him.

"Have you seen this? Take a look at the middle page-"

I judged at once that he hadn't seen it. His brows knit at the first sight of himself and he was biting his lower lip as he read. Then he was crumpling the paper in a fist and smashing it down.

"This is damnable! Who the hell gave them permission to publish a thing like that!"

He had fairly shouted and people were looking round at us, and I told him so.

"Sorry," he said, and then was straightening the paper out. "But it *is* damnable. GALLANT ATTEMPT—blasted nonsense! It's that chap Salt whose photograph ought to be in the paper, if you can call such a bloody rag a paper."

"Why protest so much?" I asked him mildly. "You did a good job of work and you're entitled to the publicity."

"Not that kind of publicity," he told me furiously, and I remembered he'd said something of the sort before. "It isn't fair to that chap Salt. Not a word about him—"

"But there is," I pointed out.

"Just a couple of lines," he told me contemptuously. "And just because he doesn't happen to be a ruddy author." Then suddenly he was opening the paper again.

"Where'd that photograph come from?"

"The bloke who works the beach here," I said. "He snapped me and old Peckenham the other day before we knew it. Peckenham was damnably annoyed."

"And so am I," he said, and was getting to his feet. "I've been pestered by that chap before. About time I had a word with one or two people."

He gave me no more than a nod and was striding off towards the steps. "Much ado about precious little," I told myself and then took his chair, and stretched out my legs beyond the shade of the umbrella. Worne was badly peeved, I was thinking, because the *Signal* people hadn't consulted him about the whole thing. His pride had had a puncture and now he was off to raise a little hell or two.

Barbara and the new Major were leaving the water and making for my direction. Then they went a bit left and joined a woman who was sitting on the outside of the three chairs a little way short of the steps. The two went within a few yards of me and I had another good look at the Major. Then I saw Wharton coming, and ready for bathing. I gave him a wave of the newspaper and looked round for another chair. George grabbed one for himself.

"Doing the heavy, aren't you?" he said with a glance at the sun umbrella.

I told him I'd taken over from Worne and then I showed him the *Sandbeach Signal*.

"I passed him just now at the head of the steps," George said. "Wondered what he was looking so het-up about. But it's funny, isn't it? A chap like him kicking up a fuss about a little local publicity?"

"Ordinary common-sense old codgers like you and me, George, can't always understand the eccentricities of genius," I told him. "But what about Peckenham? Did you get anything from Fry?"

"Who said I'd seen Fry?"

"Never mind that, George. You tell me if there's any news."

He gave a grunt or two and then said it was a bit too early. Fry had made enquiries at the railway station and had been given a variant of the war-time retort about a war being on. This time it was whether he knew there were holidays on. Hundreds of people used the booking office and went through the barriers.

"Now he's trying to get in touch with that Bayswater hotel," George said. "It's got to be done tactfully, of course, so it may take time."

"What about Huffe's hotel?" I wondered if I'd dropped a brick. "I seem to remember Fry talking about making enquiries. Or was it you told me?"

"Huffe was there all right," George said, "but he didn't leave a thing behind when he came down here. He told the management he might be coming back and he might not. If they let his room it wouldn't matter."

"Any other ideas from them?"

"None at all. He slept in the place and that's about all."

"Not much help," I said. "If he's alive, it looks as if he's not risking going back there. Perhaps he made up his mind to disappear before he left."

George got up and began discarding his bathrobe.

"Just one other little thing before I forget it," I said. "Fry had the idea that there might be deliveries of black market stuff at certain local hotels Huffe had called on. If so they're a long time coming, aren't they?"

"Fry's been wasting his time having a man on that job," George said, and snorted. "What'd he expect? A four-in-hand to drive up. This is nineteen-forty-six, that's what I told him. A guest—who isn't a guest—rolls up in broad daylight with a car full of luggage, and the luggage is full of the devil knows what. That's what I'd do if I was in the game. Off goes the guest again and who's to check up?"

He gave a parting snort and off he went, and I was thinking he was right and I hadn't had the sense to work it out. Then I was damning the black market and remembering how I'd made up my mind to concentrate on Peckenham, so I found a comfortable position in my chair and got ready to write a letter or two. But it wasn't the spot for that. It was far too good a morning and there was far too much to see. A couple of youngsters were solemnly engrossed in building a sand castle almost in front of me, and all sorts of fun was being had in the sea not fifty yards ahead. Through gaps between the chairs I would catch sight of and envy George, and every now and again I would take a squint round at the three on the chairs to my left. George seemed to be having a longer bathe than usual, and on a sudden impulse I manoeuvred myself out of my chair and took a casual stroll.

Major Youngs and Barbara were chatting away like old friends. Mrs. Youngs was knitting, and that was all I could see from behind. When I came back I passed right in front of the three. Barbara called to me as I was passing, and at once I was being introduced.

Youngs seemed a social cut above his wife and he was definitely younger. I didn't like the look of her at all, maybe because her make-up was a bit lavish. Perhaps women in pregnancy need plenty of make-up: I wasn't the one to know. Her accent was a kind of precious Cockney, which again is something that I abominate. As far as I was concerned she was definitely devoid of S.A., and she hadn't the saving grace of personality.

A few pleasant trivialities and I moved on, and I wondered what Barbara would be telling them about me. With me she had been quite charming, and I wondered—once more maliciously— if she was taking that way of asking me not to mention Huffe. Then I got back to my chair and George was coming along. We sat in the sun for a bit and I suggested that the petrol would run to a trip somewhere that afternoon, and was there anywhere in particular he'd like to go.

When we were nearing the Hotel, I turned off to the garage to have a look at the car. Rowse came dashing in. He hailed me like a lost brother.

"I suppose you haven't seen anything of Peggy—the chambermaid who does your room?"

"I haven't," I said.

"The bitch has walked out on me. Ought to have been back at nine this morning and hasn't turned up."

"She sleeps out?"

"No, old boy, she sleeps in," he told me impatiently. "Friday night's her night off. She went off yesterday afternoon just before tea and that's the last they've seen of her."

"Did she take her belongings with her?"

"That's where she slipped up," he told me with a nasty-looking smile. "She's left a bag and some things behind. You know the idea. Probably got herself a job at more money and thought she'd slip along some time and collect when I was out of the way."

"When was she paid?"

"Yesterday. Friday's settling day here for staff and everybody. That's how I know she's skipped it." The nasty smile came again. "I'm just slipping along to Carbury to tell m'lady where she gets off. This sort of thing has dam'-well got to be stopped."

"You don't happen to be going to Carbury now?" I said.

"Just where I am going," he told me. "Hop in, old boy, if you want a lift."

I hopped in as well as the ribs would let me. Why, I didn't quite know. That curiosity of mine for one thing, and because I'd nothing special to do. Also I'd never seen Carbury, except the modern part near the beach and chine, not that there was much of it to see.

Rowse talked all the time he was driving, chiefly about the present-day attitude of the sons and daughters of toil as they hail themselves in the *Red Flag*. He was particularly blasphemous about Peggy, and her standing wage of fifty shillings a week plus her keep and her share of tips, and most afternoons as good as off. On her regular afternoons out she'd been allowed to sleep at home and turn up for duty at nine the next morning.

"Something may be wrong at her home," I said.

"Then why didn't she ring me up? There're telephones all over the place. She's rung up once or twice before."

In less than no time we were past the chine and in sight of Carbury proper. All there seemed to be of it was one terrace of Victorian houses and behind that was the usual eruption of bungalows, railway carriages and ultimately shacks, with here and there a house of a once better class that had reached the stage of shabbiest genteel. The straggling suburb wasn't even colourful in the morning sun. Asbestos walls and salmon-pink roofs don't look too well against the subtle grey background of distant downs.

Rowse halted the car on the far outskirts at what looked like a small chicken-farm run to seed. He preened himself in the driving mirror.

"I shouldn't be a couple of ticks, old boy," he told me. "I don't know if there's anywhere in particular you want to go, if so I could pick you up."

I said I'd come principally for the drive and to see Carbury proper for the first time.

"Hope to God you liked it," he told me ironically, and off he went. If Peggy was at home, I thought, there might be fireworks. She looked a tough customer herself and Rowse was bursting for a scrap. But the bungalow, I saw regretfully, was too far from the road for anything less than a stand-up fight to get as far as myself.

Ten minutes went by and Rowse was still invisible. Another five minutes had almost gone and then I heard his voice, though I didn't catch what was said. An elderly woman was with him and half-way to the gate the two stopped. A last word and he was shaking hands, and then his progress to the car wasn't as brisk as his going had been. He gave a little grunt as he took the driving seat.

"What's up?" I said. "Is she ill?"

His hand had gone to the gear lever, but he drew it back.

"There's something dam'-funny, old boy. She got home here yesterday afternoon about half-four and said she was going out to the pictures. She dolled herself up and went out about an hour or so later. That'd be well in time for the first house at Sandbeach. Before she went she said she mightn't be in till late, so the old girl you saw just now—that's her mother—went off to bed at the usual time. When she got up this morning, Peggy wasn't there. Her bed hadn't been slept in either. What she thought—God knows why—was that she'd had to go back to the Hotel for some reason or other. That's why she wasn't worrying too much." He gave a sideways shake of the head. "She's got the wind up properly now."

He moved the car on, reversed at an unfinished concrete road, and headed for home.

"What's your own idea, old boy?" he suddenly asked me.

I told him I hadn't an idea. I didn't know Peggy, for one thing. He leaned slightly my way.

"A bit of a tail-swisher, on the quiet. She wouldn't look so bad, you know, in a dim light. I wouldn't be surprised if she'd gone with some bloke or other. Had a hangover this morning and thought she'd sleep it off." Suddenly he was cheering up. "Wouldn't be surprised if she's turned up while we've been away."

But she hadn't turned up. Mrs. Rowse was in the office when we got back, and waiting for news. Rowse looked flabbergasted.

"Something ought to be done, oughtn't it?"

"She may turn up this afternoon," his wife said hopefully.

"I don't like it," Rowse said. "What do you think, old boy?"

"I think I'd wait till tomorrow morning," was my advice. "If she hasn't turned up then, I'd see the police. What was the name of that Inspector chap who was here asking about Major Huffe?"

"Fry?"

"That's the chap," I said. "On second thoughts I think I'd have a quiet word with him yourself after lunch. If everything's all right, well and good. If it isn't, then you'll have done everything anyone could expect."

Mrs. Rowse thought the suggestion excellent. Rowse was good enough to say that there was one thing about us Civil Servants—we certainly could use our headpieces.

It was not till we were on our way home from our trip that I mentioned Peggy to George. The trip had been interesting and the whole affair had slipped my mind. We'd had tea at the county town and seen the various sights and it looked like being well after six when we'd be back.

"Peggy?" George said. "Isn't that the one you warned me about? As far as I know she's never fingered anything of mine."

"But what about this disappearing business?"

"Well, what about it?"

I told him there'd been far too many missing women lately. He gave a grunt.

"Rowse is getting hot and bothered about nothing. He's that kind. And for God's sake don't do any more talking while you're driving this hell-wagon."

George's pace when driving his own car is the middle twenties. I once knew him do nearly forty and it scared him out of his wits, but that was downhill when he trod on the accelerator instead of the brake.

As we were nearing Sandbeach he asked if we'd time to call on Fry. I drew the car up in the lane behind the station and we went in by the back way. A station-sergeant was on duty and Wharton had apparently seen him before.

Fry wasn't in, but there was a message. It looked like something important for the sergeant had it in the safe. Wharton ripped open the envelope. His eyebrows began to lift. His eyes bulged and then he was staring at me.

"Peckenham," he said. "Who do you think he is?"

I shrugged my shoulders.

"The Deacon!"

I could only shrug my shoulders again. George went on reading. He read the whole thing through twice, and then, instead of handing it to me, he was saying we'd have to be getting along. You can't talk when you drive through Sandbeach and it was not till we were in the Hotel that I was handed that letter.

DEAR SUPER,

Chief Inspector Fodman rang here at 3.30 and asked for you. As the message was about Peckenham I told him I could take it. He only got your letter by the early post this afternoon and thought he'd better attend to it himself. A fuller, official report will be sent later if desired.

PICKFORD CHARLES PERCIVAL. "The Deacon." *Alias* Cuthbert Pugh; *alias* Rev. Claude Pugh; *alias* Conway Peck, etc., etc. Confidence trickster and card-sharper. Born Sydney, Australia 1875. Studied for Church but never ordained. 2 yrs. 1900 for fraud. Deported by Dutch authorities from Batavia 1906. Worked Shimaru-Matso boats and believed held by Japanese authorities 1910. Arrived England 1922. 3 yrs. Old Bailey 1923. 2 yrs. French 1928. Believed connected with Harris affair, Brighton, 1935. No record since.

I am sending this round by special messenger to your hotel with instructions to return if you are not in. The Haven, by the way, seems to be getting too much in the news. Havelock-Rowse has just come in with a story of a missing chambermaid.

Yours,

D.F.

"So Peckenham was a con. man," I said lamely.

"He was a super con. man," George told me. "I never actually saw him or his photograph, which is why I didn't spot him here. The Deacon—that's what everybody knew him by." He gave a sideways reminiscent nod. "That Harris swindle was a masterpiece. A hard-headed furniture manufacturer, and done out of something like twelve thousand quid. And The Deacon got clear."

Then he was giving me a look as if there was no time for frivolities.

"What was Peckenham doing down here? Not the old con. game?" He didn't give me time to answer. "No record for ten years. What's he been doing all that time?"

"Going straight," I said.

"Maybe," he said. "He was one of the best men at the game and one with the fewest convictions. All the same he never went ten years before without making a slip."

Then he was giving me a glare.

"If he's been going straight, why did he have to make that attack on you?"

Then the dinner gong went and I didn't have to answer. I doubt if I could have found anything like an answer in any case.

CHAPTER XI

PEGGY COMES HOME

WHEN I WOKE on the Sunday morning it was with a curious uneasiness at the back of my mind. At first I wondered if it were the weather, for a sea-mist was like a fog in the air. For the last three or four evenings there had been a mist. Out to the south you would see what looked like a line of black cloud against the horizon and almost imperceptibly it would be nearer and nearer. Towards sunset you would see tiny wisps of vapour in the air, and then the street lights would be hazy from a bedroom window. But the very earliest sun would disperse the haze and this was the first morning when it had still been thick till as late as seven o'clock.

But it wasn't long before I traced the uneasiness to its proper source. It was Peckenham who was worrying me, and George's challenging question of the previous evening. Why should Peckenham make an attack on me—that had been the question. For a con. man to resort to violence was a fantastic idea. A con. man has to live and be the part he plays, and that part is always the pleasantly genial. On occasions he can turn nasty and be an exceedingly unpleasant individual, but murder?—never on your life. No risk of long sentences for the con. man. If he makes a false step the fault is his, or the luck of the game, and he takes what's coming to him, and that's usually not a quarter of what he'd have got for, say, robbery with violence. When he comes out, he shifts his ground and perhaps his identity and begins again, and from the vantage point of a lesson learned. That in a way had been Peckenham's history.

But I didn't let it worry me. I had a good breakfast and could chuckle to myself at the way George ladled in the sugar and spread the butter and marmalade without a reference to the black market. Then we lounged for a bit and I went with him down to the beach. Barbara Channard and the Youngs, husband and wife, were there, the wife still knitting. Worne was just going in. He was all wrapped up in a bath towel as if it were still misty—which it wasn't.

"Making another start?" I said.

"Couldn't keep away from it long," he told me affably.

"How'd the fight go yesterday? Did you knock hell out of everybody?"

"To some extent—yes," he said, and gave himself a congratulatory nod. "I don't think that sort of thing's going to happen again."

He moved off then and I turned back to where Wharton had brought our two chairs. I did catch a glimpse of Worne from time to time, and he didn't seem in the mind for fancy tricks but was swimming out in the deep as if making for France. I couldn't help noticing too that he was getting browned up. So was I, for that matter, especially about the legs. George was only emerging from the pink stage.

"A curious mixture, that chap Worne," George told me. "First he kicks up hell about what he calls the wrong kind of publicity. He even goes off swimming by himself as he is now, and then he'll come back and be posing in his chair for people's admiration."

"He hasn't done so much of that lately," I said. "Worne's not a bad kind of chap, once you make allowances."

George went in. Major Youngs and Barbara went in and soon the three were together. Ten minutes went by and Worne came out, but he didn't come near my chair. The next time I looked round, who should I see talking to him but Fry. In about five minutes Fry was coming my way. So was George. I thought it best to make a rather showy introduction of George in public. Another chair was fetched and the three of us sat down.

"Parker just came in by the ten-thirty," Fry told us. "He's got some more news about Peckenham."

To me and George it was surprising news. The Laguna Hotel in Bayswater was a small and select one, and Peckenham had been there for two months. Everyone liked him and he was always liberal with his tips.

Why he had gone to the Laguna was this, according to Parker's information. His wife had been for some time in a nursing home at Folkestone and the home and furniture had been sold. He would occasionally run down to see her, though his visits were said to do more harm than good. The couple had apparently been warmly attached and her illness—he had come to know that her chances of recovery were remote—had tired him out. The Sandbeach holiday, in fact, had been a necessary one.

The Laguna, by the way, hadn't heard of the wife's death. They supposed Peckenham was still in Sandbeach. They were also expecting him back when his fortnight was up. Since he wasn't at Sandbeach, it was a certainty that he was in Folkestone.

*"If the yarn is true," Fry added significantly, and for a moment or two nobody had a comment to make.

"No one at the Laguna has seen his wife?" asked Wharton.

"No one. But he used to get letters regularly from Folkestone. I know that's no proof."

Wharton grunted.

"And what are you proposing to do?"

"Send Parker to Folkestone at once," Fry said. "In fact he'll be on his way now. If Peckenham's there he ought to locate him."

George approved. I asked about the missing Peggy.

"What was her full name?"

"Lafford," Fry said. "Margaret Lafford. The father's dead, and she was in service in Reading. She came home from there two years ago and had an illegitimate child. Died at birth, lucky for her. The mother's not a bad sort but the father was a pretty bad egg."

"Any news of her?"

"Devil a bit," Fry said. "If she did go to the pictures that night, then nobody saw her. By the way, we've made a search of the two chines."

Wharton raised enquiring eyebrows.

"You daren't take chances," Fry said. "We combed both chines at daybreak this morning. The only suggestive thing was in Sandbeach Chine. A young tree there was all smashed about. No real sign of a struggle, though."

George and I said never a word, unless it was to ask what would be Fry's next move. Fry said there were so many moves that he didn't know where to begin first. Maybe she'd changed her mind about the pictures and had gone to the theatre or the Pavilion. If she'd picked up a man, the two might have called in at a late café. If nothing came of that, he might have to try a broadcast appeal. Her mother had been seen and he knew the exact clothes she'd been wearing.

"On top of all that, there's one other little difficulty," Wharton said. "She may never have set foot in Sandbeach at all that night."

"I know," Fry said. "It's the very devil. We can't even get a starting point to pick her up from. Best part of ten thousand visitors in Sandbeach, and who was to notice anybody in particular."

No sooner had he gone than Wharton was harking back to Peckenham.

"All this Folkestone business must be a pack of lies. As for going back to that Laguna Hotel, he'd be the biggest fool in the world if he did. He'll know we're on his tail."

"This whole business is getting a bit too involved for me," I said. "The more it links up, the more it doesn't. But it can't be all chance, George."

"What can't?"

"That all these happenings are connected with our hotel. Huffe gets drowned, or doesn't, in a remarkably queer way. This chambermaid's missing. I'm attacked. Peckenham turns out to be a con. man. The mathematical odds against those four things being unconnected must be colossal."

"And if they *are connected?"

"Then there's a central something holding them together. Four moths round the same candle, it you like, and Fry's got to find the candle."

"Well, it's his headache," George said piously, and added that he thought he'd be jogging back to the hotel.

I didn't even suspect it at the time or have the least premonition, but the crisis was very near at hand. It was like a warm spell in midsummer when for days the little clouds have rested harmlessly along the horizon, and then suddenly, towards a late afternoon perhaps, they move and coalesce. The air is heavy and more humid and then comes the first rumble of thunder, and in a matter of minutes the lightning's flashing and the rain is lashing down.

That Sunday afternoon it wasn't easy to think about anything, unless it were finding a spot of cool shade. It was the hottest day we had had, and the only sensible place would have been the sea, or lying in a bathing costume beneath a sun umbrella. I made my unhurried way down to the deserted lawn to make up my mind what precisely I should do, and I could see George having a nap in a chair he had brought out to the bedroom verandah. Perhaps I didn't make it clear that the first and second floors of the Hotel had verandahs. Each bedroom, in fact, had its own verandah, separated from its neighbours by a kind of railing partition. But those on the first floor were infinitely better than those above, for the simple reason that the lower ones were shaded by those of the second floor.

The lawn was not wholly deserted, for Mrs. Youngs was asleep in a deck chair in the shade of a tree. She was a tall, Amazonian kind of woman, and she wasn't a handsome sight as she slept, for her mouth was open and her pink face was wet with perspiration. Her knitting had fallen from her lap but I thought it best not to replace it. My own chair I took to a lawn verge by the back path where the tall shrubs made a good shade. I settled myself comfortably and stretched out my legs, and then I happened to glance up at George again.

At once I was thinking back to the night when I had seen Huffe entering Barbara Channard's room. Huffe had been a fool to risk the stairs and corridor, I thought. All he had to do was to hang from the floor of his verandah and his feet would easily reach the rail of the verandahs of the first floor. If Barbara Channard's verandah door had been left ajar, then everything would have been easy. And just as quickly, I knew that I might be wrong. Where Huffe's bedroom had exactly been I didn't know, but unless it was directly above hers, then things wouldn't have been so easy. People—myself for example—slept sometimes with their verandah doors open. Huffe would have had to pass them, and he would have had to get over the partitions that separated verandah from verandah.

The thoughts ran lazily on. If Huffe had been seen in his progress along the verandahs, he could have made a quick enough getaway. In a flash he could have been standing on the verandah front, his hands would catch the floor of the verandah above him and he would be up in a moment. For an ex-Commando like him, that would have been child's-play. Or he could have gone downwards, and my eye was judging the distance from where Wharton was sleeping. A vault over the verandah to the gravel drive wouldn't have been too much for a chap like Huffe. Nor would the re-ascent be hard. In two or three places there were supporting posts from the ground to the floor of the verandah. Then my thoughts shifted to cat burglars. The Hotel was a burglar's dream. It was almost as if a series of ladders were placed against open bedroom doors. Not that I was worrying. I'd done as advised in the Hotel brochure—handed in my surplus cash, cheque book and petrol coupons to Rowse.

Then a rather staggering thought was making me wriggle in my chair. Barbara Channard and Brian Huffe. Wharton's theory that Huffe was still alive. Had she become aware of it?

Had she even known the drowning was a fake before it actually happened? Was that why she hadn't accompanied Huffe that morning in the boat? Was that why she'd been far from inconsolable at the news of his death? If one could tamper with her correspondence or even follow her about the town or beyond, could one get in touch with Huffe or discover his whereabouts?

It was a startling train of thought. For a moment I was thinking of putting it up to Fry, and then I was aware that Fry would have his own methods of following up Wharton's theory—provided he had in it sufficient faith. Maybe by this time Huffe's description had been circulated in the *Police Gazette* and all over the country there would be men with their eyes open. Huffe's hair alone, unless he had dyed it, would be enough to give him away.

Then I was wriggling in my chair again, but at something very different. Why the devil was I worrying my wits about all these happenings. Either it was my job of work or I was no more than an onlooker. Would an actor on holiday, passing a leisure evening at a pierrot show, suddenly dash on the stage and suggest this and that or show how a bit of acting should be done? Devil a bit of it—if he had any sense.

And if it came to that, what did the happenings at the Haven amount to? Nothing but surmise. I couldn't even prove—and Fry couldn't either—that Huffe had been connected with the black market. Even those silk stockings might have been acquired in at least a semi-legitimate way. Even Huffe's death *might* have been an accident, and we weren't even sure if he was dead or not. And take old Peckenham. I'd accepted him at first at his face value, and then found him something else. Now he'd turned out to be something even more different. If his own stories at the Laguna were to be believed, then heaven alone knew *what* he was. It might not have been he after all who had made that attack on me. And then the last happening—the disappearance of Peggy Lafford; even that might have its explanation. Surmise—that's what everything was and always had been. And why then wasn't I having the sense to realise that I was having a holiday. If anything was really wrong, then Fry was more than capable of handling it. Then I treated myself to a little ironical smirk. Fry—with Wharton jogging his elbow.

Within a minute or two of that rather smug thought, I was asleep. Even in my shadow there was a languorous warmth, and all I remembered for the next three-quarters of an hour was a shake of the head or a twitching of a muscle to disturb a chance fly. When I woke it was because of a baby crying, and there was a nannie entering the drive with a pram. I looked at my watch and it was ten minutes to four.

Mrs. Youngs had picked up her knitting. Now she picked up her bag and took a quick look at herself in the mirror. More people were trooping back from the beach, and all at once she was getting to her feet and making her way hurriedly ahead of them to the main door. I glanced up at the verandah and caught sight of Wharton at his dressing-table mirror, and he seemed to be adjusting his tie. My eye went to my own room and past it, and I saw Mrs. Youngs closing her verandah door. That was when I first knew that she and her husband were occupying the twin-bedded room vacated by the Brigadier.

There is no tea gong at the Haven. If one goes to the dining-room at four o'clock sharp, everything is ready on the tables, and only one waitress is there, standing by in case anything should be wanted. I was prompt to a second that afternoon, as

I hadn't felt equal to a wash. By the time I'd poured out my tea, George was joining me.

"Just what I can do with," he said, and poured himself a cup. Then he was peering out at something that went across the lawn. It was Mrs. Youngs, and she didn't interest him. But she certainly interested me.

All the time George and I were chatting about nothing in particular, I was taking a surreptitious peep at her. She would glance at her wrist-watch and once she gave an angry shake of the head. Then she fairly flopped down in a chair, and I couldn't see her very well as she was facing the entrance gates.

Five minutes went by and then Youngs appeared and Barbara Channard with him. They'd evidently been walking at a rare pace for they were still keeping it up as they came through the gates. They were joking about it too, for I heard Barbara's laugh. I rather fancy the laugh came to a sudden end. Mrs. Youngs was on her feet and I could almost see the angry flush on her cheeks. What she said I didn't know—the three were best part of fifty yards from me—but it pulled Barbara up with a jerk. Youngs seemed to be protesting. His wife snapped a final something and stalked angrily towards the Hotel.

George had finished his tea and was moving restlessly on his chair. He doesn't care a lot for cigarettes, and pipes like his are strongly discouraged in a dining-room. When he wanted to know if I'd any programme for the time till dinner, I said I hadn't. I told him he wasn't to wait for me, so off he went and his pipe was in his hand before he got to the door. I sat on and awaited developments. What had happened hitherto was fairly plain. Mrs. Youngs had preferred to spend the afternoon on the lawn. Her husband had said he would go for a stroll or down to the beach, and probably he'd promised to be back well in time for tea. Then by chance or design he'd encountered Barbara Channard, and that was that.

It was Barbara who appeared first in the dining-room, and in spite of the make-up, the angry glow was still on her cheeks. A couple of minutes and Youngs appeared, and he wasn't looking too self-possessed. He poured himself a cup of tea and waited.

Almost another five minutes went by and then he was leaving the room. I guessed his wife was having a fit of the sulks, and he was going to try to induce her to come down. So I stubbed out my cigarette and made my way out too.

At the front door I saw Worne. He mentioned the heat and, as he was on the move, I fell into step.

"Quite a little domestic scene just now," he said in that rather querulous voice of his. "The lady isn't prepared to lose a husband without putting up a fight."

I said I didn't quite get him. Then I was nudging him violently in the ribs and moving quickly on. The fool had been talking right against the dining-room window and Barbara Channard must have heard every word he had said.

"You'll be getting into trouble one of these days," I told him tartly. I was feeling very annoyed. As I told him, I didn't want to get into the bad books of anyone in the Hotel.

"You're too sensitive, my dear Travers," he told me, and in so superior a tone that I could have kicked him in the pants. Then Wharton came towards us and he sheered off.

George and I took a couple of seats and began discussing how we'd pass the time till dinner. I favoured a walk and he was keener on a visit to the Pier. We decided on the Pier.

I went up to do a bit of quick tidying and as I went to the mid-corridor lavatory I heard voices coming from the Youngs' room. I shot quickly into the lavatory and I couldn't help thinking of the comedian's gag. "When we were engaged, I talked and she listened. Soon as we were married, she talked and I listened. Now we both talk and the neighbours listen." When I came out of the lavatory they were still at it, and I wondered what Barbara Channard was thinking if she were in her room.

Mrs. Rowse and I met on the stairs.

"Just looking for you, Mr. Travers," she said. "You're wanted on the telephone."

I took the call and when I came out she was still at the end of the corridor.

"Where's the Great White Chief?" I said flippantly. "Out enjoying himself?"

"Gone to see a friend in the country," she said. "Tomatoes," she told me with a confidential smile.

I gave a smile to show that I understood and approved. Out on the lawn Wharton was still sucking away at the same wheezy pipe.

"Don't look alarmed, George," I said, "but Fry's just rung up. He'd like us to go round at once."

"Anything the matter?" He was already hoisting himself to his feet.

"A bit too much," I told him. "They've found that chambermaid's body."

PART III

Chapter XII
THE MISSING LINK

A recently demobbed soldier named East, with his wife and two small sons—one aged six and the other eight—were staying with relatives at Carbury. That Sunday morning they decided to have a picnic lunch on the moorland to the north of Sandbeach, and, as so often happens, had been unable to make up their minds just where to stop. The spot they finally and belatedly chose was under a clump of silver birches not a hundred yards from where one of the tracks leading from the town passed under a sunken way beneath the railway embankment and became merely a path.

After the meal the two boys wanted to gather a bunch of honeysuckle of which there was plenty trailing over the innumerable thickets of the scrubby downland. Their mother warned them to remain within call, but after they'd been only some ten minutes away, the elder boy came running with the younger not far behind, and he was yelling excitedly and frightenedly that they'd seen a dead woman.

"Must be someone gone to sleep," their mother said, and then wondered if they'd made the story up.

The two insisted that it was true, and it was plain that they'd been badly scared. They had put up a rabbit, the elder said, and as they were running after it, they saw a pair of legs protruding from a clump of bracken. When they came close up they saw what they described as a dead woman. At that stage of the story the younger boy began crying. While his mother soothed him, the father took the elder boy to make an investigation. It took them a longish time to find the spot again although it was only a yard or two from a side path.

A few minutes later he was making his way hurriedly to the town, the nearest houses of which were only some two hundred yards away. As he couldn't see a policeman he went on to the police-station. A police car, and Fry in it, took him back. In the tall bracken that grew round a thicket of thorn was the body of Margaret Lafford. The bracken had been roughly folded across it and only the legs were plainly visible. That, very briefly, was the evidence given at the subsequent inquest.

Wharton and I knew nothing of that. The police car had taken the East family back to Carbury, with the strict injunction not to divulge, until permitted, the happenings of the early afternoon. But that, as Fry was to tell us, was more than human nature could be expected to stand, and he was concluding his own examination of the murder site before a crowd of sightseers almost certainly appeared. The same police car was waiting at the station when Wharton and I arrived.

Wharton and I looked down at the body from which the bracken had now been folded back. I didn't look very long. To Wharton corpses are five a penny, but to me there is always something horrible and unbearably depressing about such a violent and tawdry death. What interested me was the spot itself. The silver birches and thickets were densest southwards towards the first houses of the town and the low embankment of the railway, and from where we stood only an occasional house was even visible. When one looked north and forgot Sandbeach, one might have been miles from a human habitation. There the country was lonely and with a subtly colourful beauty, and beyond where the thicker undergrowth ended, the uplands showed the chalky flecks of the open downs.

Wharton turned to the doctor who was at his elbow.

"Manual strangulation?"

"Every sign of it."

"No signs of a struggle, though."

Fry stole Wharton's thunder.

"Ten to one she wasn't killed here. Probably killed somewhere handy along the path there, and then dumped in here."

Wharton looked round him. As far as I could see there was no crushed bracken to show the track the murderer had taken. But strong bracken, as Fry said, is resilient, and everywhere were little gaps where he could have set his feet. And, as he recalled, the night of the probable killing had been misty and moonlight, which had meant good visibility for at least a few yards.

Photographs had been taken and the ambulance was standing by. Two of Fry's men lent a hand and the body was carefully raised and laid aside in an open space. Fry and Wharton began looking among the bracken. I had another look at the body.

She was wearing a cheap-looking tweed costume and an imitation felt hat. The hat was askew and the hair only slightly disordered. The imitation silk stockings looked untorn. The only marks of a struggle were the bulging eyes and the patchy redness of the skin of the neck.

"No sign of a handbag," Wharton was saying. "You've had a good look round?"

"It'll take hours to search properly," Fry told him. "I think the bag was taken when she was killed. Perhaps she was killed for the sake of what she had on her."

"And how much was that?"

Fry said the mother didn't know. Peggy Lafford was always very secretive about her affairs.

"If robbery was the motive, murder wasn't necessary," Wharton pointed out. "A man could have knocked her down and been away and gone among this bracken and she'd never even have seen him in the mist."

"That wouldn't have been any good to him if she knew who he was," Fry told him quietly, and Wharton was protesting that he was only throwing out feelers. Then he was turning to the doctor.

"Know what her last meal at home was?"

"Half a tin of salmon with lettuce and tomato and bread and butter and tea," Fry said.

"Shouldn't be any difficulty about stomach content," Wharton said. "But I'd be very careful about her finger-nails in case she did any scratching. Any facilities for a scientific examination of her clothes?"

Wharton wasn't being too helpful. My idea was that he was telling Fry in a guarded way that the sooner the Yard was called in, the better. The doctor got to his feet again. He'd been kneeling by the body and gently feeling the head.

"There's a swelling just there and a bit of an abrasion. Looks to me as if she might have been knocked out first and strangled afterwards."

"When you've made your report, we'll know a good deal more," Wharton told him. "You got any ideas before they take her away, Mr. Travers?"

I said I hadn't. A quarter of an hour later we were on our way back to the station. Fry had rung his Chief Constable and he was asking us to make two at a quick conference.

"Let us suppose something," Wharton said. "Suppose she picked up a man and he killed her for what she'd got on her. That wouldn't need much of a conference, would it?"

Fry supposed it wouldn't. But he obviously didn't see what Wharton was driving at.

"You wouldn't think I was taking too much on myself if I handled things along those lines?" Wharton went on.

Fry said he'd be happy to fall in with whatever Wharton decided on.

"You're the one who's going to have the credit in this case," Wharton told him largely. "You just leave the Old Gent to handle things in his own way. What's your Chief like, by the way? A Colonel Something-or-other, isn't he?"

There was a world of meaning in that last phrase. Fry's reply was tactfulness itself. Colonel Demaire was quite a good Chief to work under, if only because he let a man get on with his job.

"That's all I want to know," said Wharton enigmatically, and I wondered if Fry knew just what he meant.

Wharton and I had met Chief Constables like Colonel De-maire, though they're rarer now than they were. Ex-Army men mostly, with considerable County influence; looking for cushy, well-paid jobs on retirement and being deftly wangled into Police appointments over the heads of those who've forgotten more than they're ever likely to acquire. Generally beautifully mannered, mind you, and capable of putting up a good public show when well coached beforehand, and always available for writing a signature on a dotted line.

Demaire was just that type. He was very impressed by Wharton and quite charming to my far less important self. He apologised handsomely for his late appearance and added that he had known everything would be in Fry's highly competent hands. Wharton was soon twisting him round a little finger, and giving Fry a tremendous boost at the same time.

In under half an hour everything was settled. The question of calling in the Yard might stand over for a few hours, Wharton said, and in the meanwhile the finger-nail contents and the clothes might be rushed to town. He himself would get on the telephone to the Yard.

Demaire said he'd like to have a look at the actual spot, though he wouldn't disturb Fry or the men who were searching the cordoned area. He added that he had a rather special engagement at seven o'clock and wouldn't be coming back. If anything important happened, perhaps Fry would give him a ring at his house. Wharton and Fry accompanied him to his car.

Wharton came back rubbing his hands.

"That's that," he said. "Now we can get on with the really important business."

First he rang the Hotel to say we might be as much as an hour late for dinner. Rowse told him something cold would be left for us in the dining-room, and it would be no trouble at all.

"As soon as Mr. Travers and I leave here, you can get hold of him," George told Fry. "There might be a question or two arising out of what we're talking about now. We shall see."

He stoked his pipe and made himself comfortable. His very first words made Fry's eyes open wide.

"I haven't mentioned this to Travers, here, but we two have got a confession to make. Something we'd decided to keep to ourselves."

It was that attack on me that he meant. I told Fry what had happened and how—as police, so to speak, we'd thought it as well to settle our own affairs by ourselves and in our own way.

"Now it has gone too far," Wharton cut in. "Your Chief just put it in a nutshell when he said that after the Huffe drowning affair, this new business would give the town a pretty bad name—among what he called the right people.

For once he didn't claim his theory as his absolute own.

"What we've been thinking is this: various things happen and they're all connected with the Haven Hotel. There's the Huffe drowning, the attack on Travers and now the murder of this girl. There's the presence of an old crook like Peckenham, and what we've been asking ourselves is whether or not everything's connected up. In our judgment there's a link somewhere. Something that holds everything together. Something around which everything revolves."

"What's wrong with the black market?" Fry was asking at once.

Wharton gave a dubious shake of the head.

"I don't like it. It doesn't satisfy me, if you get what I mean."

"Mind if I give a personal view?" I said. "And a few explanations at the same time?"

For an extempore speech it was one of my best efforts. Wharton hardly shot me more than one upbraiding or painful glance as I explained why I'd kept things to myself and seen no necessity to butt in. Hitherto, as I pointed out, everything had been surmise, but now it was a matter of murder and a vastly different business. That was why I was putting every possible card on the table.

There was nothing that I kept back. I gave an account of the Huffe-Channard *affaire* and even added the wrong interpretation that Worne had placed on what he had thought a quarrel between the pair. I put George on the spot by telling all I suspected about Rowse and the black market. For George's benefit I went over the events of that early morning when the old Daimler had brought a load of something to the Hotel and I had spied from the lavatory. I mentioned the mystery of Peckenham and the lavatory door. The last thing I remembered was Peckenham's bribing of Gerald.

"That's all I know that seems to have the least bearing," I said. "The rest of the happenings are what I might call common property. Huffe's calling on certain hotels, for instance, and Peckenham following him up. Peckenham with that horrible-looking Sporelli at the Regal, and so on. And just one other thing that occurs to me—that Barbara Channard, as Wharton knows, isn't in very deep mourning for Huffe."

"That isn't unnatural," Fry said. "If she let him into her room at night, she wouldn't like to show any grief, so to speak. Something might come out if she drew too much attention to herself."

"About that boy Gerald," Wharton said. "Didn't you rather jump to conclusions in imagining that Peckenham was bribing him to open his mouth and own up about the plug? Why shouldn't Peckenham have been bribing him not to open his mouth but to keep it shut?"

"You mean that the boy had seen Peckenham tampering with the plug?"

Wharton shrugged his shoulders.

"That, or something else that Peckenham didn't want to have known."

We thought that over for a minute, then Fry was saying we might leave Peckenham out of things for a bit. After all, in a very few hours we might know his whereabouts, then he could be held for questioning. There were plenty of reasons. His identity card and ration book, for instance, had the name Peckenham. Had he legally acquired the name or was he illegally using it?

"Take the three events that come or might come under the heading of murder," Fry went on. "There's the Huffe drowning, the attack on Mr. Travers and now this Lafford murder. I still think the connecting link is the black market. Huffe was in it up to the neck, even if we mayn't now be able to prove it. Mr. Travers happened to give away the fact that he suspected what was going on, and therefore someone tried to eliminate him. This Lafford woman was a Nosey Parker. Probably she discovered something and gave herself away too."

"Leave out the missing link business altogether," Wharton suggested. "Let's deal with the Peggy case by itself. All she told her mother was that she was going to the pictures and she might be late home. I repeat that. *Might be late home.* Sounds as if we've got something there, don't you think? But have we? Did it necessarily mean that she had a previous appointment? I claim it's wishful thinking to place that interpretation on the remark. She *might* have been late home for a variety of reasons. Because she intended to go to the dance hall after the pictures, for instance, or because she was hoping to pick up some man. All we can be reasonably sure of is this. *If* she didn't have an appointment that night, then she was murdered. If she did have an appointment, then it was a murder of quite a different kind; not a chance, opportunist murder, but a planned murder. A murder planned by the man who killed her."

"And planned," I said, "for the spot where she was actually murdered."

"Exactly. And planned so as to look like a pick-up murder. The bag taken to suggest robbery, and so on."

We talked and talked till it was after eight o'clock. Fry had urgent things to attend to so we adjourned till something new should happen. But as soon as we were back at the Hotel, Fry was getting hold of Rowse. And he would question the Hotel staff in case Peggy Lafford had mentioned the evening's appointment. Later he'd go through her belongings and have another talk with her mother.

Wharton and I came out of the station by the back way. That was when I thought of something. Instead of cutting through to the High Street I kept along the back road. George soon spotted that we weren't taking the usual way.

"Just as quick this way," I told him, and when we got to the Memorial, I halted.

"Isn't this the way we came to the heath?" he was wanting to know.

I said it was. There was the narrow lane between two houses and beyond it would be the very track along which was the path and the thicket where the body had been found.

We moved on again and I told him what I'd thought. That Memorial was a definite landmark, erected after the last war. At the T-head was an obelisk, and below it a drinking fountain, the whole surrounded by lawn intersected by beds of flowers. What would have been an easier place to mention for an appointment? Peggy Lafford might have waited there in the dusk or dark after her visit to the cinema. Fry could certainly do no harm in making enquiries.

"Let's get down to brass tacks," George said. "If she met somebody by appointment, who was it? If this idea of ours is going to hold together, then it was someone connected with the Hotel. Fry keeps on harping on the black market, so suppose he's right. Who, connected with the black market, could have killed her if it wasn't Huffe?"

"Then there's more in everything than meets the eye," I said. "I can't think of a thing connected with the black market that would have made Huffe commit murder. And what about that attack on me? Did Huffe do that too? If so he was in a mighty desperate hole. The black market doesn't explain it."

"You said Huffe talked to you pretty freely?"

"Maybe he did," I said, "but nothing he could possibly have said would have made him want to murder me."

"You can't call yours murder," objected George. "To heave a lump of rock at someone you'd rather see out of the way—well, that's hardly murder. It's too much on the spur of the moment."

"Spur of the moment be damned!" I said. "Whoever tried to kill me must have followed me. It's too much of a coincidence that he should have been sitting innocently on the seat above and suddenly seen my head and shoulders underneath. And if you'd been at the receiving end of that second rock, you wouldn't be talking so cheerfully about the spur of the moment."

"There's still Peckenham," he said.

"If it comes to that, there's Rowse," I told him. "He's mixed up with the black market, too. He might have thought I was wise to him. And he has the virtue of being someone we haven't considered up to now."

The argument petered out. We were back at the Hotel in any case and it didn't take us long to get to the dining-room. Nobody was there but we didn't want help to tackle that meal. Then we went out to the lawn and lounged in the late evening cool. The air was heavy as if there might be thunder.

"Don't drowned men come to the surface after thunder?" I asked George.

"An old wives' tale," he told me with a snort. "And if it's Huffe you're thinking about, I'm still open to bet he never was drowned."

There was the sound of a car braking.

"That's Rowse," I said. "Let's go and have a look at my car and meet him by chance."

Rowse was closing the garage doors when we got there. I said he needn't keep them open for me. My car could wait till the morning. Then he burst out with what he'd been itching to tell us.

"Murdered!" we said together, and Wharton was adding that it was incredible.

"I'm not all that surprised," Rowse told us. "She was a bitch, and I told Mr. Travers so. Picked up some man or other and that's what it did for her."

"She hadn't a man of her own?" Wharton asked.

"If so, she'd never mentioned him to her mother," Rowse said, "nor to the staff. And you bet your life she'd have boasted about him if she'd had one."

"Any idea when the murder took place?"

"Must have been on her night off," Rowse said. "A rather peculiar thing happened, by the way. My wife nosed it out when she was making enquiries. They've got their own room downstairs, the staff have, and Peggy came in that afternoon all dolled up ready to go out. Someone pulled her leg about having a chap. Instead of getting on her high horse, she gave a knowing sort of smile. The you-can-laugh sort of business and just-you-wait-and-see."

"Wait and see what?"

"Something about having a boarding-house—boarding-house mind you—of her own before very long. Just hot air, that's all my wife thought it was. But I've been thinking. I've just been to see that Inspector Fry and he agrees with me."

His voice lowered impressively.

"Whoever she met that night she'd met before, and he'd filled her up with a nice lot of hot air. You know: about having a hotel or boarding-house of her own. Said he was a widower probably. Wouldn't be surprised if he kidded her into bringing some money with her. You know: making out he didn't believe she had any."

"You're probably right," Wharton told him, Rowse turned the key in the garage lock and said he'd better be breaking the news to his wife. The Huffe business was bad enough but this business was the very hell of a thing to happen to the Haven. Not that he'd care so much if they caught the man who'd done it.

Wharton and I moved on to the cliff path.

"Well, what do you think of it all?" I asked George.

George muttered something about still more hot air and then began stoking his pipe.

CHAPTER XIII
HUFFE COMES HOME

THERE WAS THUNDER in the night but only enough to rouse me for a moment or two from sleep. When I finally woke in the morning I saw that there'd been a heavy shower of rain, and no more. But it had been enough to clear the air and, what was better, we looked like being in for as fine a day as we'd had.

George had talked of seeing Fry early and when I looked in his room he had already gone. Perhaps it was the exhilarating air of that morning that made me feel almost like trying a swim again. When I wriggled my body to test the ribs, there was hardly any pain at all. What made me decide to put it off were the array of bruises and scratches that a bathing costume could never cover. But I felt in fine fettle for a walk, and just before what had been my usual time I was in the queue at the newspaper shop.

I hadn't been there a minute before I knew that the murder of Peggy Lafford had got out. Then I was straining my ears for the gossip, and all I could catch was very little more. A man just behind me was saying with all the aplomb of the uninformed that the police knew who the murderer was—an escaped lunatic who'd once been in Broadmoor. Then the queue began to move on and in a couple of minutes I had my paper.

I set off towards Carbury Chine and just as I was turning off the High Street I saw Worne coming towards me. He was very excited and wanted to know if I had heard the news. I thought it best to say I had, and from Rowse. He said he'd just heard it from a man on the beach.

"What about going along and having a look at the spot?" he asked me. "They say it's just behind the Memorial."

I didn't see how I could very well avoid it, but I did say that I'd thought murders were well out of his line.

"This is something different," he said. "It's almost like one of your own household being murdered. Besides, there was that queer business you told me about. You remember; how she was listening one night at my keyhole."

When we reached the Memorial there was no need to ask where the scene of the murder was, for men with newspapers under their arms were making for the narrow lane.

"Getting in a quick look before breakfast," I said, "and going home and telling their wives all about it."

We walked through to the track but all we could see was a rope drawn across where the track became a sunken way, and a policeman on duty. My curiosities are all personal and private and I hate to be one of a morbid crowd. Besides I was suddenly realising that Wharton might be somewhere around with Fry, and it would take some skilful lying to explain him away.

"Doesn't seem much to see here," I said. "Might as well push on back."

"This is the kind of thing that interests me," he said. "Not the murder. That's nothing, if you know what I mean. But this extraordinary curiosity that's inherent in the British public." He waved what was meant to be an explanatory hand. "A fine background for any sort of episode—this sort of thing. You never know when it might turn out useful."

He lingered exasperatingly on for a minute or two, peering about him and nodding to himself as if he were taking a series of mental photographs. Then at last he moved off.

"You mightn't think so," he said, "but one of these days I might want a scene like this. It saves all bother if you've got something handy in your mind that won't need too much distortion." Then came a harking back to something I'd forgotten. He gave a little titter as he said it.

"I was forgetting you were an author yourself. What's your particular line, by the way?"

Social economics in my very early days, I told him. I didn't mention one or two books on bygone murders and apparently he had never heard of them. I was pretty sure of that because I turned the conversation to Peggy Lafford, and he still didn't seem to be connecting me in any way with crime.

"There was something curious about that woman in what I might call a rather sordid way," he said. "After you mentioned that snooping business, I kept an eye on her. Not as a precaution, of course, but as a type. That's my job. I like to make my own analyses of people and docket them for possible future use."

I said I quite understood.

"I look at it from the point of view of the average man-in-the-street," I went on. "I'd like to know who murdered her, and why."

"Simple enough, my dear fellow," he told me airily. "She picked up some man and had the bad luck to get hold of a wrong 'un. Murder doesn't interest me but I wouldn't mind wagering a small sum that I'm right."

We were back at the Haven and there we left things. In five minutes the gong was going. Wharton was a minute or two late and we didn't talk about Peggy Lafford—except to agree that the news had got out—till we were up in his room. In any case he had very little to report.

The search of the ground had so far revealed nothing, he said, and the post-mortem was merely a confirmation of what had already been guessed. The stomach content had shown that the murder had taken place at about ten o'clock. The blow on the back of the skull was the one really revealing thing.

"She was definitely knocked out first," Wharton said, "and then deliberately strangled. That eliminates the idea of a pick-up, or so I think. A pick-up might have knocked her unconscious but then he'd simply have gone off with her bag. He wouldn't even have worried about moving her."

That seemed clear enough to need no argument. In any case argument couldn't have got us anywhere. What was needed was some definite clue.

"Those houses round the Memorial are being questioned," George said, "Fry isn't very hopeful on account of the mist."

"What about calling in the Yard?"

"Demaire's getting into touch this morning," George said. "I told him I was here on the spot and the best thing was for me to take over privately and go on working with Fry. If it got out who

I was and what I was doing, we'd lose more than we gained. See what I mean?"

I said I did. If we were right in thinking that mere coincidence couldn't be playing a part in the various happenings connected with the Haven, then the Haven was George's real headquarters and vantage ground.

"Any news about Peckenham?" I wanted to know.

George said that Fry's man Parker had sent a somewhat cryptic message to the effect that he was on to something, and there might be news from Folkestone during the day.

"And no more about Huffe?"

"Very little," George said. The Yard were lending a hand at the London end but the only thing of interest was that Huffe had a balance of nearly two thousand pounds at his bank. His gratuity might account for a bit of it, but, as George put it, he'd certainly been in the money. Fodman was very hopeful of getting a black market lead. George himself was even more of the opinion that Huffe was very much alive. It was probably a question of rival gangs. Huffe, he thought, had done some double-crossing and had thought it best to stage a disappearance rather than risk, at the very best, a razor slash or two across that handsome face of his.

I went down to the beach with George. No sooner had he gone for his dip than Worne was coming towards me. I was rather annoyed. I'd had enough of him for one morning, and that morning he'd been at his most pretentious.

"I've just solved a mystery," he said, and I was relieved when he refused to take Wharton's chair. "Remember I was saying this morning that that Peggy woman had rather puzzled me? Well, I just happened to have a word with Rowse, and he gave me the very clue I wanted. What do you think it was? "

I said I hadn't the foggiest notion. His voice lowered impressively.

"She'd had an illegitimate child!"

I raised my eyebrows.

"Now do you see it?" he asked me triumphantly.

I said I did and I didn't.

"No one knew it but Rowse," he told me patiently. "She told him when he engaged her. Not a soul on the staff knew it. Now do you see it! That's what I couldn't understand about her. She had it on her mind. Always wondering if anyone had found out after all. Perhaps that's what made her a snooper. Wondering what people were saying about her, and all that."

I said that was undoubtedly it. I even added that it was remarkably brainy of him to have worked it out like that. A modest disclaimer or two and off he went, and I was thinking that his must be a remarkably small mind to have made a mountain out of that psychological mole-hill.

That afternoon there was to be another affair in which Worne was to be involved. I saw the whole thing and from very close quarters, and as it was to have a considerable bearing on yet another strange happening, I'd like you to see the event as I saw it myself.

It took place on the lawn soon after two o'clock that afternoon. In the morning I'd noticed that Major Youngs was bathing alone, his wife in a deck chair and at her usual knitting. There had been no sign of Barbara Channard.

It was just after two o'clock, as I said. The beach parade had moved off. I was doing my crossword and keeping an eye out for Wharton. Mrs. Youngs was in a deck chair about two yards from me and obviously waiting for her husband, for every now and again she would look impatiently up at the window. She closed her book with a snap and let it lie on her lap. Behind her, under the same tree, was Worne, knees crossed and writing a letter.

Something moved by the front gates and I looked up to see Barbara Channard coming in, and I thought how remarkably smart she was looking in the red frock. Her progress along the drive was going to bring her within a yard or so of Mrs. Youngs, but just as she was nearing her, that lady gave a malevolent stare and got ostentatiously to her feet. So obsessed was she with her pose that she forgot the book and it fell to the ground. Barbara gave quite a pleasant smile as she picked it up, but Mrs. Youngs was already on the move.

"Isn't this your book, Mrs. Youngs?"

The lady turned. Her cheeks flared angrily and then she snatched the book from the other's hand, and turned on her heel and was off to the door again with never a word. Barbara Channard stared after her.

"Well!" she said. "Did you ever see such manners in all your life!"

She was talking to me. Her face was an angry scarlet.

"Did you see it? Wasn't it abominable?"

I smiled consolingly. Mrs. Youngs had disappeared and I drew her chair in.

"I shouldn't worry," I told her.

"I think that woman's disgusting." She was seething with rage and I was wondering how to keep out of things. And then Worne was suddenly with us. I looked up to see him looking ironically down.

"My dear lady, doesn't it occur to you that your very charms may have made the lady rude?"

If that was meant to be a compliment, then, I was thinking, it was a double-edged one. Barbara's cheeks flared again, and then all at once she was on her feet and facing him. The ironical smile was still on his face for all that.

"You dislike me, Mr. Worne, don't you?"

Worne shrugged his shoulders. The drawling voice was an insult in itself.

"Dislike you, my dear lady? Quite the opposite, I assure you."

She had been biting her lip. Now the torrent was let loose.

"This isn't the first time you've made insulting remarks about me. I've got ears, and I'm not a fool. And let me tell you this. Other people can talk besides you, and tell the truth too, and not a pack of lies. You dare to interfere with me or my affairs again and you'll be sorry for yourself. Very sorry indeed."

Worne's eyes had narrowed. There was something he was trying to say but the right words wouldn't come. She gave him a sneer to match his own, tossed her head angrily, and then sat down with an assumption of indifference. When I looked back at Worne, he had turned too, and was making his way across the lawn.

"Well," said Barbara again. "What do you think of that? Of all the insufferable creatures!"

"Don't take it too seriously," I told her. "Life's far too short."

"But it's damnable!"

"Now, now, now," I said soothingly, and then I was producing my most charming smile. "Why not get your own back. Let's talk scandal about Worne—"

"He's not worth talking about."

"Of course he is," I said. "You just ease your mind and tell me all the things you told him you could say about him."

"That wouldn't be hard," she told me with another toss of the head. "He's just a poser—that's all he is. Jeffrey Worne the famous author! Nothing but a mass of affectations. Look at the way he smirks into the dining-room at meals. Thinks he's making a royal progress. All he does is make everybody positively sick. Everybody with any sense, that is."

"Bravo!" I said, though it was plain that she'd thought out much of that speech before. "Feeling better now?"

"Much," she said tersely, and then she caught my eye and had to smile.

"Sometimes you can be very nice," she told me, and then luckily Wharton appeared, and that was that.

When I told George about it, he didn't appear too interested. What we did agree was that Worne was being so hostile to Barbara Channard, and so insufferably rude, because she had at some time wounded his vanity. It wasn't improbable that before our arrival he'd made eyes at her or had had reasons for thinking his advances wouldn't meet with disfavour. If so he'd certainly been wrong.

I have said that I hate loose ends. That afternoon when George and I got back from our little trip along the coast, I happened to see old Mrs. Smyth in the lounge. She was one of those women whom one describes—a bit too hastily perhaps—as a motherly old soul, but I'd soon come to know that there was very little that escaped her eyes and few happenings at the Haven that escaped her tongue. That afternoon, then, it was childishly easy to get to the subject of Barbara Channard. It was far less easy to get away from her when four o'clock came and tea was on the table.

We'd reviewed the short affair with Major Huffe and touched on the Youngs affair. Mrs. Smyth, by the way, was on the side of Barbara Channard, which rather surprised me. At any rate I was able to put my question.

"Am I wrong, or did someone tell me that Jeffrey Worne was rather smitten with Mrs. Channard?"

"Very definitely he was," she told me, and seemed to revel in the new twist to the topic. At once she was relating this and that, and she was even giving me her confidential opinion of Worne; a vastly different one, I may tell you, from the one I'd imagined.

I don't suppose I shall ever forget the events of that Monday night. Wharton and I had booked for the second house at the cinema, and but for our running into Rowse, some of the happenings would never have taken place. We met him as we were leaving the Hotel.

"Kicking your heels up tonight?" he said.

"Not quite," I told him. "Second house at the cinema, that's all."

He said he'd been told it was pretty good, and that was all that happened. We got to the cinema in good time and had to wait a few moments till the first house had gone. Half an hour later the first stop-gap picture had almost run its boring course when I saw the usherette showing her light on the seats just ahead of me. Wharton was at the end gangway seat, by the way, and almost at once the light was flashing on him. Then it was off, and I saw a man stooping down and whispering. Wharton gave me a nudge, and before I could gather what was meant, he was on his feet and making his way out with me at his heels.

The first dusk was in the sky when we came outside. With us was one of Fry's men.

"This way, sir," he told Wharton, and we circled round and in a minute or so emerged at the west end of the High Street. Fry was standing by the open door of his car.

"Sorry I had to disturb you," he told us. "I wouldn't have known where you were if Rowse hadn't remembered." Then he was smiling lamely. "Just heard that Huffe's body's been found. I thought you'd like to come along and see it."

Wharton's eyes opened wide. They fell accusingly on me, as if the faked drowning had been my theory. He was shaking his head as the car moved off, and we'd gone quite a way before he spoke.

"Well, I suppose I've made as many mistakes as most people in my time, but I'd have bet I was right about Huffe. Something's wrong somewhere. Looks as if we've got to find a whole lot of new ideas."

Fry had nothing to tell us except that the body had been washed up on a sandbank at low tide near a little place called Holby, ten miles beyond Whitesands, where previous bodies had come ashore. The local policeman had sent the messages and Fry had asked for a doctor to be waiting for us. Meanwhile the body was not to be touched. Apparently it had been brought to a shed near the shore.

The road was winding and often narrow. Fry drove fairly fast but it was dark, except for the afterglow, by the time we were at the village. It seemed hardly that. Just a few houses back from a shelving, pebbly shore and a fisherman's hut or two in the shelter of the low cliffs. A boat or two was drawn up and fishing nets were festooned on the huts. Inside the hut that we entered was a strong tang of fish and tar.

Huffe's body was on a rough table and after those days of immersion it wasn't a pretty sight. I was glad that the light wasn't strong, but Wharton picked up the oil lamp and held it close to the face. Everything was eerie and Rembrandtesque. Beyond the faint light was deep shadow against which was the face of the local doctor as he peered by Wharton's shoulder. Behind them the constable and the fisherman were almost invisible.

Wharton set the lamp down and turned to the doctor.

"You've noticed nothing unusual?"

"Well—no." The doctor seemed taken aback.

"A silly question, perhaps, but no sign of a wound?"

"Nothing at all."

"In fact it's just an ordinary case of death by drowning."

"Well—yes." He gave a little titter. "Naturally I haven't made a detailed examination."

"Of course you haven't," Wharton told him placatingly. "What I'm going to ask you is to make a quick one now." He gave an ersatz chuckle. "They say there's no fool like an old fool, so just do something to humour me. Make sure he wasn't shot before he got in the water. And have a good look at the head."

The constable had found another lantern. Wharton left the doctor to it and turned to the old fisherman. We heard how the body had been seen and brought ashore. The constable reported what action had been taken as soon as he'd got the news. Wharton handed out commendations and both tails were wagging. The fisherman was allowed to go home and Wharton went across to the body.

"Well, how's it going?"

"No sign of any bullet wound," the doctor told him. "There's this old wound in the chest—"

"A war wound," cut in Fry.

"Exactly. Shrapnel, by the look of it. But there's a nasty abrasion on the skull." He drew back as Wharton leaned forward. "The immersion's made examination a bit tricky. I doubt if you'll see much."

Wharton had a look for all that. He even borrowed Fry's glass while the doctor manipulated the lamp. Then Fry had a good look.

"As you say—a bit tricky," Wharton said, and pursed his lips. "But let's put it another way. Our information is that the boat was waterlogged and sinking. I expect you've read all about the case yourself. This Major Huffe was getting out in a hurry—that's only natural—and he slipped and caught his skull a crack on the side of the boat. This is all I want you to tell us. Is this abrasion consonant with what I described? Or is it too severe?"

The doctor gave a wry shake of the head.

"That's going to be a bit of a problem. It depends on how he fell. And exactly what he struck."

"Well, do your best," Wharton told him. "No man ought to be asked to do more. And don't forget it isn't official. This is just a little idea of my own."

Then he was asking if there was the chance of a cup of tea. A minute or two later we were in the constable's house and his wife was brewing us a pot. Wharton wrote a telephone message for the Haven, and the constable went to the back room to send it.

"What did you think of that abrasion?" Wharton quietly asked Fry.

"I didn't like it at all," Fry said. "If it was done when he fell, then he must have given himself the very devil of a wallop, and against something pretty ragged."

"The face was in bad shape," Wharton said. "I'm wondering if fishes or crabs or something could have got at that abrasion. Still, we'll hear what that doctor has to say and leave it at that. Tomorrow you can get the body back to Sandbeach and your own man can have a real go at it."

We made our way back to the hut. The doctor had finished and was protesting that he was no wiser than before. He also mentioned fishes—the mackerel season was in full swing—and added somewhat vigorously that by daylight and under better conditions he could give a more reliable opinion. Wharton did some more placating and he and the doctor were almost two cronies when ten minutes later the car moved off.

There wasn't much talking on the way back to Sandbeach. Wharton did put one interesting point.

"That attack on Mr. Travers," he said to Fry. "Someone heaved a lump of rock at him. And take that Lafford woman. She was hit on the skull and then strangled. Huffe had a crack on the skull. Is all that coincidence?"

Fry said diffidently that it mightn't be. Then he was pointing out that the circumstances were different. I hadn't actually been hit on the skull by that lump of rock. Peggy Lafford hadn't been hit by a lump of rock but by some unknown blunt instrument.

Huffe—ostensibly at least—hadn't been hit at all, and definitely not by a rock.

Wharton gave an impatient grunt and I knew he was thinking that Fry was begging the question.

"Who says he wasn't?"

Fry gave a quick, amazed look back.

"Well, he just wasn't."

"That's something that's got to be proved," Wharton told him. "Just look in your mind's eye at the scene of the supposed accident. You're standing on the edge of the cliff at Carbury Chine on the Sandbeach side. The Mouth is right below you. Why shouldn't a lump of rock have been dropped from there right on to Huffe's skull? It'd have fallen at the devil of a lick. Neither of your two best witnesses—Worne and Salt—would have seen it." He gave a satisfied smirk. "And doesn't that tie up with the little matter of a rock that was thrown at Mr. Travers?"

"If it was the same thrower, then he was damnable erratic," I said. "He hits Huffe from the very hell of a way up and he misses me at a few feet."

"Well, think it over," Wharton told us, never a bit nonplussed. "Tomorrow we might make a test."

If we went on thinking it over it was because there wasn't much else to do. Practically nothing could be seen from the car except the road in the headlights and by the time we reached the first houses of Sandbeach, it was as if the journey had taken hours. We called at the station on our way to the Hotel and it was still not midnight.

"Anything been happening?" Fry asked the man on duty.

That was the moment when a new and extraordinary day was dawning for me.

CHAPTER XIV

PECKENHAM TELLS THE TRUTH

ONE O'CLOCK that morning found me in what we used to call a night mail—a train that would get into London in the small hours—and the reason had been a message that had come from Fry's man Parker, and a very few minutes after we had left for Holby.

Parker, it appeared, must have got on the trail of Peckenham earlier if Folkestone had been Folkestone, so to speak. But the nursing home had been at a place called Gadsford, a kind of suburb village, and Parker had only just discovered that the funeral was to be on the Tuesday at two o'clock. Peckenham himself was staying in Folkestone—at the Phoenix in Hope Street—and Parker had also discovered that he would be leaving the hotel the same day. In other words, if we wanted to be dead sure of interviewing him, it would have to be well before the funeral or immediately after. And that put us at Sandbeach in rather a hole. A morning train could never get to Folkestone in time, and if one went by car, then it would mean a start in the early hours.

I was the one who had to make the decision. As soon as we'd realised that Peckenham would have to be seen at once, unless he was to slip through our fingers again, I volunteered to make the trip. Peckenham, I said, was my pigeon. To my relief there was no competition. Wharton and Fry seemed indeed only too glad to give the job to me.

We went back to the Haven and Wharton was giving me copious advice. In his eyes I'm often the neophyte of twenty years or so ago, but it gives him pleasure to scatter advice around and it doesn't hurt me to listen, and in any case I knew I should do precisely as I pleased. Not that I was anticipating the Peckenham interview with the zest that would have been mine a day or two earlier. That Peckenham really had a wife, and that there was really going to be a funeral, were facts that cast considerable doubt on previous theories. It was true that it made even more inexplicable the part that Peckenham had been playing at Sandbeach, and yet somehow I didn't like it. Peckenham had *not* bolted from Sandbeach, for instance. Therefore he might not have made that attack on me. Nor—and it was a theory we hadn't disregarded—had he been concerned in the death of Peggy Lafford.

I had a first class compartment to myself and made no bones about lying at full length. Under the circumstances I slept quite well, and in spite of the innumerable stops. When the sun came streaming in and finally woke me just before five o'clock, I had a quick wash and by the time we were in the first suburbs, I was feeling remarkably hungry. It was half-past seven when I got to my flat. There I removed the strapping from my ribs and had a bath and a service breakfast. Charing Cross is practically on my doorstep and I didn't have to hurry to catch the nine o'clock. Parker was on the station at Folkestone and we adjourned to the refreshment room for a talk. What he had to tell me didn't please me a bit. Either Peckenham was the biggest fool in the world or else a reasonably innocent citizen, and unless my judgment had been utterly wrong, then he certainly wasn't a fool.

Take Peckenham's wife, for instance. She was a Folkestone woman, or near enough: the daughter of a local parson, long since dead. That was why she had gone to the nursing home at Gadsford. Parker had been given to understand, by the way, that in addition to being seriously ill, she had become rather mental, which was why Peckenham had visited her very rarely. In fact, the story Peckenham had told the management of the Laguna Hotel seemed perfectly true, and it seemed to me that I should have to be remarkably careful in my approach.

But finger-prints, as Parker and I agreed, don't tell lies. Peckenham was the Charles Percival Pickford who'd served various stretches for fraud. At Sandbeach his conduct had been guileful, to say the least, and that business of tailing Huffe had been more than suspicious if Huffe was what we almost knew he was.

"Where's the actual funeral to be?" I asked Parker.

He thought he'd made that clear. It was at Gadsford, where Mrs. Peckenham's father had once been rector.

"I suppose you haven't any idea of her age?" I said.

But he had. She was about five years older than her husband, which made her about seventy-six. That cheered me up, even if Parker wasn't too happy about it. Anything that made Peckenham less of a desperate criminal was something of a cold douche for Parker.

"No record of him for ten years," I said. "He himself was intended for the Church. She was a daughter of the Church, so to speak, and older than he was. Had she money, by the way?"

"Very comfortably off, so they say."

"The wedding was in Gadsford?"

He said it wasn't. Mrs. Peckenham had been away from the district for years. An old lady whom he had been able to question had thought she had been living in Guildford.

"I think I'm beginning to get it. Or some of it," I said. "You see daylight yourself?"

Parker didn't, unless it was that Peckenham seemed to have done pretty well for himself. I left it at that, if only because it was the right answer, and we began making our plans for that afternoon.

Just before two o'clock we were in Gadsford churchyard. It is sprinkled with abundant yews and there was no difficulty about a handy spot from which to watch. The nursing home was about a mile away and prompt to time the hearse and one car appeared at the lychgate. One or two elderly people had already entered the church and when at last the coffin was carried to the grave, there were about ten people straggling behind the rector and the chief mourner, Peckenham. A man who looked like the undertaker was carrying two handsome wreaths.

Peckenham was in black and if he'd been wearing a clerical collar he'd have been more of a parson than the rector himself, vestments and all. Unconventional as I am, there are still a few conventions, not to say decencies, which I would never dream of breaking, and yet I felt no twinges of conscience at spying on Peckenham's grief. For, unless he had tears on tap and at will, he *was* grieved; there wasn't a doubt about that. When everything was over and the rector shook him by the hand, he turned away as if the grief were still too deep and close.

"Let's get away," I told Parker. "You follow him up from here and I'll be at the hotel. Don't stir from the hotel till I give you the sign."

At the hotel bureau—a quiet, select hotel, by the way—I asked for Peckenham and at once was having the circumstances explained. I insisted that I had to see him on a very urgent matter, even if I had to wait till night. The receptionist said I might wait in the lounge and she'd tell Mr. Peckenham as soon as he arrived. The name I'd given was a fictitious one.

Parker and I had seen no reason why Peckenham should linger at Gadsford and we were right. I was in that lounge only about twenty minutes and then I heard Peckenham's familiar voice in the lobby. Another minute he was entering the lounge. The room faced north and it wasn't too light. He peered at me as if he were looking over the tops of invisible spectacles. Then I got to my feet and he recognised me. His eyes opened wide and for a moment he couldn't speak. I gave what I hoped was an ironical smile.

"I happened to be this way," I said, "and I thought I'd give myself the pleasure of a call."

"Of course," he said. He gave me another peering look and moistened his lips. Then he cleared his throat. "You heard perhaps of my sad misfortune?"

The voice had something of the old unctuousness, but it still wasn't just right.

Yes," I said, and nodded heavily. "That was why I came to see you, in a way. I wonder if there's anywhere we might talk?"

He suggested his room and led the way up. Confidence was partly coming back and he was mentioning the weather and even when we were in his room and he'd indicated the comfortable chair, he was asking about Sandbeach. But his looks were wary and I knew he must be working that agile brain of his far harder than he'd done for some months.

"Mind if I smoke?" I said.

"My dear sir, please do." He beamed, if with the same wary benevolence. "I myself have long since given up the weed—"

He broke off, and perhaps because I was giving an audible sniff. For a bedroom, that room smelt uncommonly strong of tobacco.

"We are over the smoke room," he said, and waved at the old-fashioned grate. "Had I been aware beforehand I should have asked for another room. Not that one can expect everything."

"It's a very charming room," I said, and began looking through my wallet. "By the way, I have a confession to make. I'm here on what one might call false pretences."

He raised his eyebrows, and again as he took the Warrant Card. I don't think he could have spoken even if I'd have given him time, but I went straight on. "There've been some very serious happenings at the Haven Hotel. We may have to ask you to return to Sandbeach as a material witness."

I reached across and took the card from his none too steady hand. I don't know why, but all at once I felt a real liking for the man. If he'd blustered or lied—then I don't know. But there he was. He—Peckenham of all people—absolutely deflated. In his eyes was something very like a hurt, and in some extraordinary way I was feeling almost shabby.

"Let's have a friendly talk," I said, and got to my feet. "Just as man to man. Business, if any, can come later."

"Yes," he said slowly. "Perhaps that would be as well. I take it you have—er—certain information about . . . well, about myself?"

I told him exactly what his record had been. That seemed to ease his mind. It was as if he knew the worst. He began to nod in asseveration and by the time I'd finished, his hands were folded in the old familiar attitude across his paunch.

"Unhappily what you have said is true," he told me heavily. "Regrettably true. In my youth I fell into bad company—the company of men who were older than myself. Evil courses, my dear sir—"

"Just a moment," I said. "This is a friendly talk. Suppose we take that record as read. Let the dead past bury the dead, so to speak." Then I couldn't forbear a sly dig. "All that is *consule Planco,* shall we say?"

"I didn't catch the phrase," he said.

"*Consule Planco,*" I told him. "When Plancus was consul. When we were young, in other words."

"Of course," he said. "My Latin is somewhat rusty. But you were saying?"

"Only that we'll wash out that record. What I'd like you to tell me is what happened to you after—shall we say?—1935—"

He repeated the date. For a moment his pudgy fingers caressed his chin.

"I wonder if you still understand me," I told him. "This is a confidential talk. I want the truth and nothing but the truth. Either you trust me, or you don't. But I ought to warn you that if I don't implicitly believe whatever it is that you tell me, then I shall have to ask you to come with me to Sandbeach."

He had drawn himself up with an assumption of dignity, but that last warning shook him a bit.

"Surely we can assume that we are both gentlemen? I can assure you—"

"That's all the assurance I want," I told him. "You go on from 1935 and tell me in your own way."

That was the year he returned to Australia, he said, and I'd like you to imagine him as he talked. The cultivated mannerisms of a lifetime were soon too much for him and his plump hands were soon folded across his ample paunch again. The voice had its careful, fruity intonation and the vocabulary its Biblical garnishings. But for the wary looks he would occasionally shoot at me, I might have been a first-year man and he an amiable if somewhat tedious old don.

He had gone to Australia, but not to his old haunts. Western Australia was his choice and he had made up his mind—thanks to being in funds—to go straight. He had changed his name to Peckenham and then his money had begun to run short. Then he had seen nothing for it but to work the boats again and then— he instanced Saul of Tarsus—a miracle had happened. While he was getting his bearings on the boat he had been of service to a certain lady. The two became more closely acquainted. On the voyage he didn't touch a card. Two months after landing in England, he was married. "To the lady, sir, whom I buried today."

I murmured a quick, if lame, condolence, but he was going on. His wife had been a woman of deep religious convictions. He had married her as an ex-missionary and it was a pretence that he was forced to keep up. But deeply though it hurt her at times, he had to insist on the genuineness of those supposed principles of his.

"There are circumstances, sir, under which it is hard to be a hypocrite. I ask you to understand me. At this very moment she perhaps understands me herself."

"I do understand," I said hastily. I said I now understood why it was that he had done his smoking in the seclusion of Sandbeach Chine.

For the first time for minutes he looked a trifle ashamed. But it was a foolish subterfuge, as he said. The old Adam would be too strong for him and though he would fortify himself by announcing that he didn't smoke, the urge would often be too much and he would succumb.

"Just a personal question," I said. "You mentioned subterfuge. Did that include your feelings towards your wife?"

He drew himself up with a real dignity. From the very first he had had more than a warm regard for her. Some might think it was on account of her money but that was only what he called a fortuitous adjunct. That his wife trusted him implicitly was shown by the fact that she had left him all she had, and, as he hastened to add, by a will dated long before her faculties became clouded.

"Well, if it isn't in too bad taste, I congratulate you," I said. "And I'd like to thank you for the frank way you've told me all this. And now let's get to Sandbeach. You were there when that unfortunate accident happened to Major Huffe?"

"But, of course," he said. "I remember telling you about that abominable child Gerald. Naturally at the time I didn't suspect that you had any—what shall I say?—personal interest."

Was it imagination or did his tone convey a slight reprimand? I didn't know. What I did want to know was what he knew about

Gerald and the plug. And his answer rang true enough. He had seen Gerald hammering at something in the bottom of that boat. After the tragedy he recalled the fact, and that was why he had questioned the boy. In spite of the bestowal of the sixpence, the information elicited hadn't been too satisfactory. Gerald admitted it was the plug at which he'd been hammering, but he'd said he hadn't actually dislodged it.

"That brings us to something far more important," I said. "In strict confidence I may tell you that we suspect that Huffe wasn't drowned by accident. He may have been murdered."

His eyebrows raised and he was watching me closely.

"Let's not beat about the bush," I said. "You were interested in Huffe. At this moment you probably know that we must have known it." I sat down again and drew my chair in close to his. "I wonder if you'd like to tell me exactly why?"

"Ha!" he said. "Why I was interested in Huffe." He let out a breath. "I wonder if you'll believe me."

"Why not?" I said. "All I ask is your implicit assurance that what you tell me is true."

"Yes," he said, as if to himself. And then his face lightened. He was hoisting himself from his chair.

"Fortunately I happen to be in possession of certain evidence. You will pardon me a moment?"

Through my mind flashed the sudden idea that he was about to make his escape. But it wasn't a subterfuge. He went no further than the couple of yards to the chest of drawers. He unlocked the bottom drawer and took out an attaché case. He unlocked that too, and I could see that it was filled with writing materials and official-looking papers. From underneath them he took a book. With a queer look from over those invisible spectacles, he handed it to me. I read the title:

CONFESSIONS OF A CON MAN

I looked at him, then back at the book. The author was a Martin Clarke and the publishers were Tufford and Hughes. I looked at him again. A minute later and I was hearing a strange, if credible story. Credible only because I thought I was beginning to know Peckenham.

Time at Guildford had begun to hang heavy on his hands, if only because his new life had become a re-orientation and a series of repressions. Then one day he had the idea of writing an autobiography. It had come to him after reading the confessions of an English crook, but what troubled him was the problem of his wife. Then he had found a solution, though one, as he frankly confessed, of which he had every reason to be ashamed. What he did was to mention a fictitious trickster with whom his missionary work had brought him into contact. This trickster, after turning over a new leaf, had at various times related his life history to Peckenham and now Peckenham was thinking that it might be a good idea, with the story still comparatively fresh in his mind, to get that story down on paper and possibly published. It would be a valuable deterrent, as he pointed out, to any young man who might be tempted to leave the narrow path for the broader and far more pleasantly seeming way that leads to destruction.

She was wholly in favour, even if he could never induce her—I gathered from a long look he gave me that he'd never tried overmuch—to read what he'd written. Even if she had, she could never have suspected the truth. Peckenham claimed he had made far too good a job of that autobiography, and he admitted that truth was concealed behind an excellent screen of the imaginary. In time then, the book was finished and the problem was a publisher.

Then he saw an advertisement of a Literary Agency and he sent the manuscript along. While he considered the book as good as the one that had first fired his imagination, he was far from sanguine about its acceptance, so imagine his excitement when the agency informed him that there should be no difficulty in placing the book. They also asked for an immediate interview.

But there was the snag. Peckenham was still in none too safe a position. He might be running a hundred risks in going to London.* The agent might even want to have a publicity photograph. Innumerable fears went through his guilty brain, and then he found another solution—a plea of temporary ill-health. So a young lady from the agency came to Guildford and Peckenham signed a contract. Thanks to his being able to arrange the interview to coincide with a visit of his wife to town, he was able to preserve his incognito of Martin Clarke.

Two months elapsed and then he heard that Tufford and Hughes wanted to publish the book. But, as the agency pointed out, it was a first book and there would be many expenses in connection with its publication. Tufford and Hughes could therefore offer only a token advance of twenty pounds and no royalties on the first fifteen hundred sales, but thereafter the royalty rate was quite good. Naturally on a subsequent book—the contract gave Tufford and Hughes an option—there would be fewer preliminary expenses and royalties would begin at once.

"And you fell for all that?" I said.

"I did," he told me ruefully. That mention of fifteen hundred copies was a good enough bait and at once he was thinking of sales of thousands and handsome royalties, and he made no bones about signing the contract that the agency sent him.

In due course he received six copies and had the thrills of the parent of a first offspring. He also received his twenty pounds, less commission. Then months went by and nothing happened, so he wrote to the agency, and the damper he received by return he was never to forget. According to the figures supplied, the book had sold just over nine hundred. The agency did add that it might suddenly take fire—as they put it—and begin selling like hot cakes, but they advised him not to be too sanguine. Meanwhile, if it was ready, might they see the second manuscript.

But Peckenham still didn't dream that he'd been in any way swindled. There was the agency's handsome notepaper and the remembrance of the charming lady who had seen him at Guildford. And it was not till he saw one day a mention of the agency and the various swindles of the B. Huffe who was its managing director, that his eyes were really open. Although it was too late, he paid a visit to Tufford and Hughes. That contract he'd signed had been a fake and his signature had been forged on the firm's copy. Huffe had been paid fifty pounds advance and royalties at ten per cent on all sales up to the first two thousand. The total sales had been just over fourteen hundred. As the book had sold at ten shillings, Huffe had made somewhere about fifty pounds. Not a large sum, but if every client of Huffe's had been swindled every year to the same extent, then Huffe had done remarkably well.

"I bore him no offence," Peckenham told me, just a bit piously. "But it rankled. I oughtn't to own up to such weakness but it hurt my pride." He smiled apologetically. "I almost said my professional pride. Naturally I didn't want the matter to go any further. I couldn't possibly have appeared at any trial. But what you must imagine, my dear sir, was my arrival, quite fortuitously, at the Haven Hotel, Sandbeach, and finding this man Huffe. And to realise—if I may put it that way—that he didn't know me from Adam." I had to smile. It must have been an intriguing situation. "Ah! but there was something else," he said, and wagged a pudgy finger at me. "Or rather, there was a someone else. That Mrs. Channard. Who do you think she was?"

"Heaven knows," I said.

"The young lady who'd come to see me at Guildford!"

CHAPTER XV
GLIMMER OF LIGHT

"MY GOD, what a fool!" I said. I had to smile at his start of surprise. "Not you. It's myself I'm talking about. That very first night at the Haven, I heard her and Huffe coming home. He was calling her darling and they were kissing each other good night. All I thought was that he was a remarkably fast worker."

"That first night in the lounge there," he said and nodded reminiscently to himself. "I must confess it gave me an ironical satisfaction. That pretence, my dear sir, of the two being strangers. That was why I thrust myself on the three of you."

Then he was peering curiously again.

"You won't be annoyed if I mention something?"

"Go ahead," I told him.

"Well, as I'd recognised two of them, I was highly suspicious of yourself. I thought you might wonder now why I'd—what shall I say?—cultivated your acquaintance."

"To be perfectly frank," I said, "I thought it was being the other way about. But tell me something. Why didn't the Channard woman recognise you? "

"I was expecting you to ask that," he said. "But in those days I wore a beard. And if you remember, I was practising a little innocent deception. I was a semi-invalid, just for the occasion."

"Of course," I said. "I was forgetting that. But one other thing before we go on. You spoke of cultivating my acquaintance. What about hers? Did you get her to talk at all?"

"Yes," he said. "I admit I did. I think perhaps—you'll pardon the apparent boastfulness, but I think sometimes I must have a way with me. She told me a considerable deal about herself. She'd been a confidential secretary, she said, and she'd married her employer. Quite a well-to-do man, I imagine. A Territorial officer too—so I understood. He was certainly killed in Normandy."

"But you couldn't induce her to talk about Huffe?"

"My boy"—it was rather amusing to hear the old phrase again—"I didn't try. In vain is the net spread in the sight of the bird."

"You should know," I said. "But what about Huffe? Did he do any talking to you?"

"I made no real attempt," he said. "Spiritually we were in no way akin, if you understand me. I preferred to keep him under observation."

"That's what I've been waiting for," I told him. "Just why did you keep him under observation?"

His fingers fidgeted and he screwed up his eyes in thought.

"Let's put it this way," he said. "I've had to be a judge of character. I studied that young man's face. There was a little matter of a gold cigarette case and a gold lighter. There was—if you will pardon a vulgarism—the whole set-up: the woman being there and that pretence of being strangers. In fact it seemed to me that the holiday wasn't only a holiday. There was also that old business of my own that rankled, as they say."

"You suspected some connection with the black market?"

"At first—no. But very soon—yes. That was why I made it my business to call on various hotels where he had called himself." He anticipated my questioning look. "A little harmless deception had to be employed. For the occasion I had to assume the role of a private detective. Just the preparation of a little harmless document, if you follow me."

"And what happened?"

"The hand must have lost its cunning," he told me ruefully. "On two occasions I was requested, more or less politely, to leave. At one hotel—the Regal—I was received more sympathetically. Perhaps because the manager there happened to be a foreigner. Naturalised, of course. An Italian of the name of Sporelli, I think—indeed I know—that he was very grateful for the warning I gave him."

"Anything else suspicious did you discover?"

Well—yes," he said slowly. "Something that's given me considerable thought." His head went sideways and I thought he was listening for something. "I wonder if you could throw any light on the matter."

Huffe, it appeared, had gone into that quite good bookshop in the High Street. Peckenham was fairly close on his tail and naturally, after that experience of his own, he wondered why Huffe should again be interested in books. All he could do was suspect some new swindle, and as there was no reason for him to conceal himself, he too entered the shop. Huffe was talking to a lady assistant. Peckenham began looking at the books on a tall central stand, with the two in earshot and himself concealed. Huffe was asking if they'd any books by a man named Lionel Bright. The girl said they had, and he bought the book she produced. Then he looked inside the cover and almost at once he was asking if she knew any other books that Bright had written. She thought for a moment and said she didn't. She knew he wrote detective novels and a lot of people liked them, and that was all. Then she said he might find some more names in the catalogue, and the usual trade list was produced and Huffe had a look. Then he was thanking her and saying he wouldn't have bothered if he hadn't been fond of Bright's books and anxious to get hold of any he hadn't read.

"That seems reasonable enough," I told Peckenham. "I've done the same kind of thing myself. And Huffe was the sort of chap that might read detective novels and thrillers and nothing else."

He hoisted himself out of the chair again and unlocked that attaché case.

"I still think there was more in it than that. In fact, I proceeded to the railway station and managed to purchase an example of this Lionel Bright's work. They said it was his latest."

He passed me the book, which was still in its colourful jacket.

"*Death in the Dairy*," I said. "Published by Glowers."

I had a look inside.

"Here's one of his I think I've read. *Death and the Diver*. Quite good if I remember rightly."

I was handing the book back.

"I wish you'd keep it," he said. "Perhaps something will occur to you. I wouldn't ask you," he added, "but something tells me there's more in that book than appears on the surface. Perhaps some swindle was being contemplated on this Lionel Bright."

I still wouldn't have taken it if I hadn't thought of something. A new book by a Lionel Bright had definitely not been among Huffe's belongings. And if he had read it and no longer wanted it, then he hadn't left it in the lounge, which was the usual thing to do. If he *had* left it there, then someone must have snaffled it pretty quickly. But I was thinking he hadn't had time to read it. In fact I'd never seen Huffe with his nose in any book.

"Well, if anything occurs to me, I'll certainly let you know," I said. "But to hark back to something: Huffe and the black market. This, by the way, is most confidential. Perhaps I'd better put it in question form. Didn't you think of beginning at home—at the Haven—when you started watching Huffe?"

"A pertinent question," he said approvingly. "A very pertinent question. But you're not a fool, my boy. You're most definitely not a fool. It was obvious, Huffe or no Huffe, that our friend Havelock-Rowse must have dealings with the black market." He raised a hand to check the unspoken question. "There's a rule that I've always found it paid to follow. Never by any chance foul your own nest."

I had to smile, but I don't think he noticed it. There, I was realising, was a remarkably good excuse for the non-interference of Wharton and myself.

"Still in the very strictest confidence," I said, "I was pretty sure Huffe and Rowse had got together."

That brought me to the question I'd been wanting to ask—why Peckenham had tried the lavatory door on the night of the Daimler delivery. At first he didn't recall the happening. When he did, everything was natural enough. He hadn't been aware of anything going on below his window. All he'd woke up with was the knowledge that he had to go to the lavatory. When he got to it he was surprised, at that hour of the morning, to find it occupied.

I had a look at my watch. In twenty minutes there was a train I could catch for town. There seemed to be nothing else that Peckenham could tell me, and heaven knows he had told me enough.

"Just an official word," I said. "You're going back this evening to the Laguna. You undertake to stay there in case we want you? And to notify immediately any change of address?"

He was only too ready to guarantee anything.

"Here's the Sandbeach number," I said. "If anything else occurs to you, don't hesitate about ringing at once. You play ball with us and you won't have to worry about going into a witness box. I won't say that you mayn't be asked at some time or other to make a highly confidential statement but that needn't worry you. You keep in with us and we'll look after you. In case you should need it, this is my private address and telephone number."

He insisted on going downstairs with me, even if he did show me out the back way through the tea garden.

"Just a little personal question," I said. "The little matter of an autographed photograph of an archbishop—"

I didn't need to push the question. His stare and the look of perturbation was enough.

"And just one other little matter, strictly between ourselves. Were you ever at Bikini?"

That caught him for the second time clean in the wind. But I hadn't reckoned with his old resiliency. We were at the gate and I was holding out a farewell hand. His hand went to my shoulder instead and he was giving me an avuncular pat. On his face was an expression partly whimsical, partly shy.

"You were asking about a certain photograph. And—er—Bikini." The smile became definitely roguish. "Mayn't we consider that as being—shall we say—*consule Planco*?"

That was the last I saw of Peckenham. With regard to Parker, Othello's occupation, as Wharton might have put it, was gone, and he and I caught that train for town. I spent most of the time writing a full report for Wharton and Fry, and Parker—who was going straight on to Sandbeach—would deliver it. Then in the few minutes I had left I read a chapter or two of *Death in the Dairy*. I found it quite good; in fact I was sorry to leave it. For one thing it was pretty well written.

I had dinner at my flat and then rang the Yard again. Fodman wasn't in but they expected him, and they repeated that they'd give me a ring. Soon after nine o'clock there was a ring at my door, and there was Fodman himself. He said he thought it might save my time if he just looked in.

I gave him a confidential outline of what had happened at Sandbeach. Then I was asking about Huffe.

"We've got him absolutely figured out," he said.

Huffe, it appeared, had been operating in the Liverpool area until quite recently. Fodman asked if I hadn't read about that big haul that the police there had made, and I had to own that I hadn't. Huffe, he said, had been one that the police had had their eyes on, and immediately after that haul he had disappeared. At Liverpool he'd called himself Colonel Brian but at the Aldgate hotel and at Sandbeach he'd apparently taken his own name again. People in the know like him could get identity cards and ration books for any name under the sun.

Fodman was on his way home and he didn't stay long. When he'd gone I began thinking of Huffe in the new light of what he'd told me, and everything, including Huffe himself, seemed to fit.

Huffe hadn't thought it careless to revert to his own name. He was an ex-Commando; a dare-devil who was in the black market game as much for the adventure as for what he was making out of it. After his war experiences, the pre-war age, and even that prison sentence he had served, must have seemed very remote. In himself he had an unlimited confidence. Maybe he had liked me in some peculiar way and had used me as a safety valve. The swaggerers and the overconfident can't live without safety valves: they simply have to talk and let off a certain amount of steam. Huffe admittedly had talked guardedly, but talked he had.

I read a few more chapters of *Death in the Dairy* and then felt like turning in on the chesterfield which I'd made up as a bed. Then I began thinking about Peckenham, and I wished he'd given me that faked autobiography instead of the detective novel. But perhaps I could get a copy, and I made a mental note to ring my bookshop bright and early. I was still thinking of Peckenham as I dropped off to sleep, and when I woke in the morning, he was the first thing that came to my mind. I reached for my glasses, looked at the time and eased myself off the chesterfield. Then suddenly I found myself with my glasses in my hand, and I was giving them a polish on the jacket of the pyjamas.

What the train of thought had been didn't at that moment matter. What did matter was what I suddenly thought I knew. Peckenham could be discarded as a strange happening. What was left was the drowning of Huffe, the attack on myself and the murder of Peggy Lafford. If our theory had been right, then Wharton and I were looking for the connecting link. Everything had to revolve round something or somebody apparently out-side the three happenings and yet with a subtle connection. And why shouldn't Barbara Channard be that connection?

A few moments later and I was discarding it. What had I to go on except that she had come to the Haven by arrangement with Huffe, and that she had made a sort of dead set at myself. She might somehow have fixed the drowning of Huffe and heaved those rocks downhill at myself, but she couldn't have strangled Peggy Lafford. And yet the idea kept teasing me. It made me forget to ring the bookshop for a chance copy of *Confessions of a Con. Man*: it made me wriggle more than once on my seat in the train, and it was with me when I got out at Sandbeach. But it was when I caught sight of George waiting there for me that I suddenly decided to keep the whole thing to myself.

I had only an attaché case and there was ample time before lunch so we decided to walk. Wharton didn't say much about that report of mine except to wonder if Peckenham had been too glib-tongued for me. When I offered to bet him ten bob to two that my judgment had been right, he dropped the subject like a hot brick. I was wanting to know what had been happening at his end.

He said there wasn't any new development. The doctors were very dubious about that crack on the skull. A small area of bone had actually been crushed, and it would have taken a remarkably heavy fall to have lacerated both skin and bone. Worne had been called in to describe the fall. According to him Huffe's head had struck the side of the boat, which should have made the cut deeper and narrower and more elongated. Salt said he had seen Huffe fall but hadn't seen the head actually strike.

"What about that theory of a rock thrown from the cliff?" I asked.

"No go," George said bluntly. "We tried it and it's a hundred to one against. What we're wondering now is if it was a shot after all. A glancing blow on the back of the skull might possibly have had the same effect. How fast was Huffe rowing that morning when you saw him?"

"Just rowing, and no more," I said. "He wasn't going at anything like a racing speed. How could he be? The boat sank only a minute or two afterwards."

I'd missed the formal inquest on Peggy Lafford, as he said. Nothing new had come out except that a witness was prepared to state that she'd seen her near the Memorial just before ten o'clock. But it had been established that she'd gone to the cinema for she was seen leaving at about a quarter to ten. That meant that she'd probably gone out where she went in, for a quarter past ten was the middle of the big picture. On the other hand, if she had had an appointment at the Memorial at ten o'clock, then she'd probably seen the whole programme through and after that was merely sitting on till the time for the appointment came. Then George was adding that Fry wasn't worrying too much over the Peggy Lafford murder. He had heard that the Bournemouth murderer might be arrested at any moment, and he was hoping for a tie-up.

As we entered the Hotel gates a taxi was coming out, and we drew aside to let it pass.

"Wasn't that the Youngs couple?" I said, and I looked back to see the luggage on the taxi top.

George frowned for me to say nothing. A few people were on the lawn, waiting for the gong. George made for Mrs. Smyth's chair.

"The Youngses gone away?"

She nodded and frowned suggestively. George grimaced in return.

"What's it all about?" I was wanting to know. George gave another mysterious nod and led the way upstairs.

"Something fishy happened last night," he told me as soon as we were in my room. "It's more or less secret. Rowse doesn't want it talked about—not after what's been happening. He swears the reputation of the place is pretty well ruined as it is. And he thinks Mrs. Channard is a liar. Especially when she asked him not to call in the police."

George, it appeared, had had a front seat for the show. It was at exactly a quarter past one and he was awakened by a perfectly horrible screaming. He scrambled half-awake out of bed and without waiting to grab a dressing-gown had merely tightened the cord of the pyjamas round his middle and had rushed out to the corridor. Other doors were opening. The two girls in Peckenham's old room were there, and Mrs. Smyth, and then Worne. One of the girls was pointing frightenedly to the door of Mrs. Channard's room. Wharton gave a sharp rap and then listened. As he opened the door, Barbara Channard literally fell into his arms. The reading light above her bed was on and she had managed to get into a dressing-gown and make her way to the door.

Worne and Wharton carried her to the bed. Mrs. Smyth produced a bottle of smelling salts. Almost at once Barbara Channard was opening her eyes and looking frightenedly around.

"What is it, Mrs. Channard?" Rowse said. "Weren't you well?"

"It was a man," she said, and then she began crying. "There was a man in the room."

"A man?" Wharton said. "Did you recognise him?"

Mrs. Smyth had taken charge and was motioning him to be quiet.

"There, dear," she said. "You'll be all right in a moment. Then you can tell us all about it."

She whispered to Rowse to fetch a glass of water. On the small bedside table had been a glass of orangeade, and somehow it had been knocked over. One of the girls picked the glass up and went off with it. When she came back Barbara Channard said she didn't want any water, and she was feeling all right.

All the same it took another five minutes to get her story out of her. She had had a slightly relaxed throat and had gone to bed early. At dinner she had asked for a glass of orangeade for the bedroom to ease the throat in the night, and she had also taken three aspirins to make her sleep.

Then something woke her. There had seemed to be a flash of light as from a torch. Then a dark shape was moving towards the bed and at once she was paralysed with fear. It came nearer and by a superhuman effort she managed to make some sort of sound. It was that loosening of the throat, as Wharton put it, that made her able to scream. In a flash the dark shape had disappeared.

The verandah door was ajar and Wharton had a quick look round. Rowse meanwhile was shooing the guests back to bed, and Mrs. Smyth was saying she would stay the rest of the night in the room and share the double bed. Outside in the corridor there was a quick conference. Youngs was there and Worne and a couple of other men. Worne said the intruder must have been a burglar and the others agreed. Rowse was inclined for his own reasons to put the whole thing down to a nightmare. Then Wharton put his foot in it.

"All she said she saw was a dark shape?"

"Well?" asked Rowse belligerently.

"A dark shape needn't have been a man. It might have been a woman."

Wharton had had nothing special in his mind. All he was trying to do was to tackle everything logically. What he didn't know was that the conference was going on outside Youngs's room and that the door was ajar. And he didn't realise that the Mrs. Youngs-Channard affair was common knowledge. He did realise the brick he'd dropped when he saw the look on the faces of his listeners. Another moment and he was pooh-poohing his own idea and suggesting bed, and a calling in of the police in the morning when Mrs. Channard should be in a better condition to talk.

The lunch gong went but I had to hear the rest of it.

"You mean that's why the Youngses have gone?" I said.

"Never a doubt of it," George said.

"But surely—"

"Of course not," George said, and took the words out of my mouth. "Mrs. Youngs hated the other one like hell, but she'd never have been such a lunatic as to go into that bedroom in the middle of the night. Besides, she and her husband occupy twin beds. That screaming must have woke Youngs up and he'd have seen his wife's bed was vacant. And if she *was* in that bedroom, what was she there for? To strangle the other one, or what?" He gave a snort or two. "But that didn't stop Mrs. Youngs from guessing what some of the cats in this Hotel might be thinking. You bet your life that's why she's left."

"What happened when the police got here?" I wanted to know.

George was impatient for his lunch and said he'd tell me later. But I did whisper to him at lunch that Barbara Channard wasn't in the dining-room.

Chapter XVI
THE LIGHT SHINES

As we were leaving the dining-room I caught sight of Rowse. I gave Wharton the tip and hurried after him.

"Have a nice trip?" Rowse asked me, and then was ushering me into the office.

He didn't wait for me to answer his question.

"The devil of a bitch-up here, old boy. One more ruddy day like this and I might as well pack up."

"Something about a burglar in Mrs. Channard's room, wasn't it?"

"Burglar, my ruddy foot!" he told me. "The damn woman wasn't well and all she had was a nightmare. The police came round this morning and couldn't find a thing. Now Major Youngs and his wife have gone." His lip curled. "Good riddance in some ways. You're not one of the gossiping chaps, old boy?"

"That sort of thing is not in my line," I told him severely. He was good enough to say that naturally it wouldn't be. But doubtless I'd noticed things myself about Mrs. Youngs. A trouble maker if ever there was one.

"What excuse did she give you for going?" I asked him. "Some cock-and-bull story about not having been well down here, and having to go and see her own doctor."

"They paid for their rooms?"

"The whole fortnight, old boy," he assured me. "Inclined to haggle a bit, but I wasn't having any."

"And how's Mrs. Channard?"

"Right as rain, if you ask me. Says she'll be getting up this afternoon."

That was the gist of what I gleaned from Rowse and very soon afterwards I was repeating it to Wharton. Naturally, too, I asked him—what I'd not had time to ask before—if he hadn't been staggered about that connection between Barbara Channard and Huffe. He admitted he'd been surprised but he didn't see where the new knowledge was going to get us.

"Let me put something to you, George," I said. "Don't start snorting about my theorising. Just listen. There'll be plenty of time to pull the theory to pieces.

"This business of a man in Barbara Channard's room," I went on. "Let's begin at dinner last night when she mentioned a sore throat and asked the waitress to see that a glass of orangeade or something was taken to her bedroom. Did you hear anything of that?"

He gave me a look, then said he might have heard something. In fact he remembered that old Mrs. Smyth had suggested honey and vinegar or some such concoction, but that Barbara Channard had said the orangeade would do, plus some aspirins.

"Right," I said. "Then it was fairly common property that the glass of Orangeade would be by the bed. If I'd happened to be upstairs at the right time, I might even have seen the chambermaid or the waitress taking it into the room. If I'd waited upstairs by design, I could have been dead sure it *was* in the room."

"What's the idea? What're you getting at?"

"I'm planning how to murder Barbara Channard," I said. "I know that I have a bottle of sleeping tablets, so I make a solution of enough of them to send her to sleep for ever. I wait at night till a convenient time and then I enter her room. I've made sure the verandah door is unlocked or even open. What I'm intending to do is simply pour my solution into the glass of orangeade and hope for the best. I'm also going to leave the almost empty bottle of tablets—veronal or what you will—on the bedside table. That's all I have to do. In the morning Barbara Channard ought to be found dead, and there'll be an obvious verdict at the inquest. Meanwhile I have a torch and I flash it on the bedside table to make sure there's orangeade still in the glass. It's not my fault that the light catches her face and wakes her up."

The look of scorn on George's face came and went.

"That glass of orangeade was upset!"

"I know," I said. "That's all part of the theory. The vital question is, who upset it."

"Who upset it," he said, and was frowning away in thought. "Damned if I know," he told me at last. "I didn't even hear the glass fall on the carpet. Everybody was crowding round the bed till Mrs. Smyth took charge."

Then he was thinking of something.

"Wait a minute. We were saying Mrs. Youngs couldn't have been in that room. Putting that dope in the orangeade was the sort of thing a woman might do."

Then he was making excuses for himself. If he'd dismissed the idea of Mrs. Youngs it was because he'd had strangling or smothering in mind. Now he wasn't so sure. Suppose she had done it. Suppose Youngs had woke up and found his wife's bed empty. Mightn't that explain the couple's hasty getaway from the Haven? As for motive, wasn't there plenty? Maybe the lady had long become aware that she wasn't too sure of her husband's affections. Already she had taken the Channard affair far too seriously. A baby was coming and at all costs she had to make sure of her husband.

I told him I was glad he thought there was something in the theory. Then I asked him point blank if he was prepared to risk being thought something of a fool by Fry.

"Where does Fry come into it?" he wanted to know.

"Like this," I said. "Get Fry to come round here and make some excuse to scrape off enough of that carpet to send to the Yard. If Barbara Channard's had lunch in the room, then the room won't have been tidied. The damp will still be on the carpet where the orangeade spilled. The Yard will tell us if there was anything in it."

George's lips pursed out till the moustache was brushing his nose. Then he said he'd see Fry at once.

"Just one other thing, George," I said. "We've got a tremendous hold over Barbara Channard, thanks to Peckenham. Rowse says she's getting up this afternoon. Suppose I lie in wait here and have a highly tactful heart to heart talk with her when she does come down. I needn't be afraid of telling her precisely who I am. She'll keep her mouth shut, knowing what I know. And she ought to tell us a few things we don't know about Huffe."

"Yes," George said slowly, and I could see the thoughts as they ran through his mind. Like Bottom the Weaver, George wanted to play all the parts. He was seeing himself questioning Barbara Channard.

"You're different, George," I told him quickly. "I don't think she ought to be told under any circumstances who you are. I don't matter."

"Perhaps you're right," he told me reluctantly, and off he went to find Fry. At least he got as far as the door.

"One thing Fry might ask, George, is where the intruder went after Mrs. Channard spotted him."

"And where did he go?"

"Don't forget my room was vacant," I said, "and everyone knew it. He or she could have hidden in there and then popped out in the general confusion."

"But that would have meant getting over the dividing rail."

"Why not?" I said. "Those rails are only about three feet high. Even Mrs. Youngs could have nipped over. She might have slipped back into her room. Her husband would have been only half-awake and she could have said she'd heard something outside."

George said I was rushing too far ahead. It didn't matter a tinker's cuss, at the moment, who'd done it. What did matter was whether or not that orangeade theory was correct.

I watched from my bedroom window. Much sooner than I expected, Barbara Channard appeared, and Mrs. Rowse was with her. The lawn was deserted but for those two, and Mrs. Rowse was only there to see the lady made comfortable, and in a minute or two she was going back to the Hotel. Barbara Channard had her back to me and her chair was under the chestnut-tree in the far corner of the lawn. I saw a curl of cigarette smoke and guessed that the throat must be easier.

She didn't hear me coming across the lawn but my shadow betrayed me and she looked round. Her smile was just a bit wan.

"I've been hearing about your horrible experience," I said.

"Dreadful, wasn't it," she said.

"Lucky for you it didn't turn out any worse," I said. "And how're you feeling now?"

"Just a bit shaken. You know how it is."

"And the throat?"

"That's very much better."

"Good," I said. "I'm glad of that because I want to have a little confidential talk."

"Really?" The smile was more flirtatious than alarmed.

I gave her my Warrant Card. She had a look at it but it didn't seem to convey anything at first. I had to explain.

"You mean you're a detective!"

I've told you that in the sacred cause of justice I'm prepared to lie with the utmost fluency.

"In a way, yes," I said. "I was sent down here to keep an eye on that unfortunate Major Huffe."

She coloured to the very eyebrows. I drew my chair in more closely.

"You and I are going to have a talk," I said. "If anybody comes, then we'll switch the conversation to the normal."

"But talk about what?"

"About certain discoveries I've made concerning Huffe and yourself. Don't think me unfeeling, but I don't want denials and I don't want tears. All I shall want when the time comes, is the truth. Now you listen to me."

I suppose it took about five minutes to say what I had to say. In the first minute she was scared. Half-way through she was relieved. By the time I'd ended, she was bursting to talk.

"One thing I should have mentioned," I said, "because it makes things easier. This is a confidential talk. As far as I'm concerned, nothing's ever going to get out. Provided, of course, that what you're going to tell me now is the absolute truth."

"It *is* the truth," she said. "I never did think Brian Huffe was guilty of what he was sent to prison for. Well, not as guilty as they made out. I think he'd just let things get into a muddle. I'm sure he'd have paid every penny back if he'd been given the chance."

"Maybe," I said. "You weren't a witness yourself?"

"I was far too insignificant," she said. "I was sort of part secretary and part any old thing. I admit the police questioned me, but they admitted I hadn't anything to do with anything."

"That was reasonably obvious," I said. "But what did you do when your job had gone?"

Her version to me and what she'd told Peckenham tallied to a nicety. She told me her husband's regiment and the amount of her pension, and admitted that in any case she'd been left more than comfortably off. She told me the restaurant at which she'd run into Huffe again, only three weeks before coming to Sandbeach. She admitted that they'd met after that and gone places but she insisted that Huffe's coming to Sandbeach was by his own arrangement. Her room had been booked weeks before, and it was he who said he needed a holiday and would try to get fixed up at the Haven too. Then she had to admit that they'd agreed to pretend to be strangers. She had thought the idea rather fun.

"That was originally *his* idea—about your being strangers?"

She said it was, and she was repeating that she'd fallen in with it because it seemed an amusing thing to do.

"Well, it's nice to be able to see the amusing side of things," I told her. "But it turned out a pretty poor joke for Huffe. It might have turned out just as bad a one for you if you'd been murdered last night."

"You're joking!" she said, but I knew I'd shaken her.

Huffe told you he was working for a firm of importers," I went on. "You believed that?"

"But of course!"

"Then I'm afraid you were very credulous," I told her.

Huffe was a black market lad. He may have been combining business with pleasure, but he was in Sandbeach to get orders for black market stuff—and I don't mean little oddments like those silk stockings he got for you."

That shook her again.

"And in spite of the relationship between you and Huffe, you tell me that you thought he had an honest job and was down here simply for a holiday?"

"I do," she said. "I'd swear it anywhere."

"I'll take your word," I told her. "But tell me this. Did he ever boast to you about having done any business at all down here?"

That rang a distant bell. She frowned for a moment or two.

"Well, there *was* something he did say. I think it was a day or two after we got here. You see, we'd agreed to pay our own shares of expenses. . . ."

She hesitated, but already the brick had been dropped.

"You mean that he'd wanted to pay for everything."

"Yes," she said. "Naturally I couldn't agree to that and we arranged that each should pay their own. Then he began doing all the paying.

"I remember," she said, and her face lighted. "We'd been having cocktails and you know how expensive they are nowadays. That was the second time he'd paid and I insisted it was my turn. Then he said he'd . . . No, that wasn't it. It was something about having found a little gold-mine, and he could pay for everything and still be better off than when we came."

Fry went along the drive but her back was to him and she didn't turn.

"Well, that's about all," I said, and knew the time had come to turn the screw. "I'll do my best to keep you out of the witness box."

Her eyes opened in horror.

"If you haven't told me the absolute truth, that's what it may come to. Or, for instance, if you mention to a soul in this Hotel or anywhere else a single word of who I am or what we've been talking about."

"I'd never dream of it," she told me.

"Splendid," I said. "Then your name might be kept out of everything, provided you're prepared to go on telling the truth."

"But there's nothing else I can tell you."

"Perhaps not," I said. "There may be one or two things which you might admit—to me only, and in the strictest confidence. Your holiday here with Huffe. It wasn't planned as strictly platonic?"

For the second time her face went a fiery red. I could see the indignant protest flashing through her mind. Then she was moistening her lips.

"Well?" I said.

"Need it have been strictly platonic?"

"A purely personal matter," I said, "and nothing to do with the law."

I got to my feet. To answer the next question would be easier if she hadn't to see my face.

"I saw Huffe go to your room," I told her quietly. "That's why I knew you were telling the truth. But just one last thing. You were on—well, intimate terms with him when you worked with him before the war?"

"Not at first."

"But that's how it ended?"

"Well—yes."

"That's all right," I said. "No need for you to worry. Never a word will ever get out. You keep quiet about me and I keep quiet about you."

I moved away and through the back path to the cliff gardens. It was a grand afternoon and the beaches below me were more crowded than ever, and for a moment I was tempted to go back to the Hotel and dress for a swim. *Swim*. That, as they say, was the operative word. That's what started me off on a train of thought. People who swam and people who didn't. People who wore glasses and people who didn't.

People who courted publicity and people like Peckenham and Barbara Channard who had good reason to fear it. People like Worne who liked some kinds of publicity and didn't care so much for other kinds.

There was a deserted seat well back in the shade and there I sat for best part of half an hour. What I first knew was that when I'd thought of Barbara Channard as the connecting link, I'd been wide of the mark, and yet far nearer than I ought to have hoped. And about Barbara Channard I could tell myself that I'd been more than lucky. If I hadn't questioned her that afternoon and, frankly, put her on the spot, then I'd never have been in a position to force her to do the things that I now had in mind.

But that's rushing too far ahead, or else not far enough. What I thought I knew at the end of that half-hour was startling enough. At the moment I had a dozen pieces of possible evidence, not one of which had passed a thorough test. But the mere fact that I had so many pieces of evidence was something. It was true I couldn't as yet go to George Wharton and say, "George, I've found that connecting link we've been looking for!" I couldn't do that. But what I could do was make one rather elaborate test. If that came off, then at once I'd go to George. Even then, as I knew, things would sound pretty fantastic, but he wouldn't be able to get away from what he couldn't deny—the overwhelming suggestiveness of my one piece of proof.

I didn't go back to Barbara Channard, if only because I was sure of her. When I got up from that seat I made my way to the post-office and put a call through to Bill Ellice's office. I had to wait some time, but when I did hear his voice at the end of the line, it sounded as if he'd been roused from a nap.

"Things none too busy with you, Bill?"

He admitted there wasn't a lot doing.

"Could you send a couple of men down here?"

He said it might be managed. When did I want them?

"They've got to be here at Sandbeach not later than ten to-morrow morning," I said. "An early train actually gets in at ten. I'll meet them at the station."

"And how long do you want them for?"

"Just the one day—I hope. And thanks for not asking questions, Bill. I'll spill all the beans when I see you."

That was that, and I now stood committed. It was well on the way to four o'clock and when I was back in my room I was hurriedly concocting a note for Barbara Channard. What I wrote was this.

> *Very urgent and confidential.* Slip out after tea and meet me at the Pier entrance. When you see me, don't recognise me. Simply follow me. I repeat, *most urgent.*
>
> L. TRAVERS.

I looked in George's room and we went down to tea together. He'd fixed up that little business, he said, and I ushered him through the dining-room door. As we passed Barbara Channard's table I slipped her the note.

With George I had to be very specious. I said I hadn't had much chance of a talk with the lady but I'd arranged for one after tea. That might mean that I shouldn't see much of him before dinner, but I reminded him that we were due at the theatre that night. I was rather surprised to find he didn't mind in the least having the period till dinner on his hands. So smooth, in fact, was he about it all that I was wondering if he'd discovered something for himself and was hoping to make a few enquiries.

After tea I watched from my room. George departed in the direction of the town. Then Barbara Channard appeared, and in the company of Mrs. Smyth. I could see she was having a job to shake the old lady off but at last she did. Mrs. Smyth anchored herself in a chair on the lawn, and in a minute or two one of the nannies and a couple of small children joined her. I nipped quickly through by the garage.

Barbara Channard was nearing the Pier when I overtook her. I went through the entrance and past the tea-room to where a row of sheltered seats faced out to sea. It was tea hour for the non-elect, and I found a seat to ourselves. As soon as I looked at her and she at me, there was something different about the pair of us, and we each knew it. She was thinking that I now knew the precise relationship between herself and Huffe. I don't say it made for an intimacy, but it made for something very like it.

"We're still good friends?" I said.

"Why not?" she told me. The answering smile had done its best to be provocative.

"That's good," I said. "I'm going to be a good friend to you. I may even be going to save your life."

That made her stare.

"I'll explain in a minute or two," I went on. "But as soon as you get back to the Hotel—I'll follow you and see that you get back safely—you're to attach yourself to Mrs. Smyth or somebody. She's sleeping in your room tonight?"

"She wasn't, but I could ask her."

"Then ask her," I said. "If she can't, then let me know and I'll arrange something else. First thing in the morning you're leaving the Hotel."

She stared again.

"Not for good," I said. "You'll be coming back at the right moment. Which may be very soon. Anywhere you can."

She said she could go to her flat in town. Near St. John's Wood, and overlooking Regent's Park.

"Couldn't be better," I said. "I'll arrange everything with Rowse. All you'll have to do is have your things packed ready to leave by the eight o'clock in the morning."

Her hand went to my arm, then drew back.

"Can't you explain all this? It's frightening me."

"The explanation's just coming," I said. "In fact you'll see it yourself as soon as you've written a certain letter."

It was not till half an hour later that she left and I followed at a safe distance. When I went in by the garage way old Mrs. Smyth was still there, gossiping this time with a couple of young mothers. I went in search of Rowse and found him in the office.

Now I'd definitely committed myself there was no point in deceiving Rowse. His face was a study when he saw my Warrant Card. Inside five minutes I had him just where I wanted him. The police knew when to keep a blind eye, I said. If he, for instance, liked to buy stuff on the quiet, that was his business—*on certain conditions*. When he tried an indignant protest I had to mention the old Daimler and that quietened him down. By the time I left him I could say that the Haven Hotel was more than living up to its boast of super-service.

So to dinner and, at eight o'clock, to the theatre. The place was packed to the roof and the show itself was much better than *Ginger for Pluck*. I don't say it was first class, but it didn't make me wince and wriggle in my seat. George seemed to enjoy it even if in the two intervals he commented on the acting. Maybe he had the idea he could do much better himself. Then when it was all over we had the usual disadvantage of being plumb in the middle of the stalls. George and I got separated in the crush. When I got back he was all by himself in the Hotel lounge.

"What happened to you?" I asked him accusingly. Attack is always the best defence against George.

Then I was saying I was devilish sleepy, and up the stairs we went. When he wanted to know more about what had happened in my interview with Barbara Channard, I told him the morning was time enough.

CHAPTER XVII
DAYLIGHT

I'd asked George overnight if he'd mind fetching *The Times*. As soon as he'd gone that morning, I had a look in Barbara Channard's room. The door was wide open in any case and she and Mrs. Smyth were putting the finishing touches to the packing.

"What's happening here?" I asked jocularly, and was suitably surprised to hear of the immediate departure. Then I also managed to hand her a letter with some last-minute instructions. It was a risky game she had to play and nothing could be left to chance.

By the time Wharton was back with the newspaper, Barbara Channard had gone. After breakfast it was easy to give him the slip and make my way to the railway station. I knew both the men Bill Ellice had sent and they knew me, and that made things easier. Our conference took only a few minutes.

I went back to the Hotel and when I came down the steps to the beach I saw that George was already in the water. I don't quite know why that should have relieved my mind but it did. A minute or two and I was joining him. As he made no mention of Barbara Channard I was pretty sure he was unaware that she had gone. Then it appeared that he had had his usual time in the water. I naturally had to hang on for my usual paddle and just as I was coming out, I saw him talking to Mrs. Smyth. My conscience was troubling me at once. Would she tell him that I at least had known Barbara Channard had gone?

But she hadn't. As soon as I joined him, George was giving me the news and asking what it meant. I said I thought it was a perfectly natural procedure. She'd had a bad scare and she couldn't go on asking someone to sleep in her room. Also she must have been glad to get away from Sandbeach and any possible questioning about Huffe. The fact that she'd been innocent of any complicity in that pre-war swindle didn't alter the fact that it would be far from nice to have her name mentioned in connection with Huffe's if ever that swindle came to the fore again. George said he still didn't like that hurried departure, and I didn't ask him exactly why.

After he'd dressed he said he thought he'd drop in and see Fry, not that there'd be any news, till later in the day, of the results of the analysis of the spilt orangeade. As he wasn't pressing, to say the least of it, about my accompanying him, I was able to get on with something of my own, and as soon as he'd gone I went to that book-shop in the High Street. The young lady assistant said they hadn't anything of Lionel Bright's but if I left an order she might be able to get his latest. Then she added a most peculiar thing.

"We've had two or three people lately interested in Lionel Bright."

"Really?" I said. "I expect one was a friend of mine, enquiring on my behalf. A biggish man, was he, with a drooping moustache?"

I left the shop with the knowledge that Wharton had been interested in Lionel Bright. It gave me an uneasy feeling, and then I knew that he had done a perfectly natural thing. Huffe had been interested in Bright and Wharton was interested in Huffe. And, I could tell myself, if George had discovered anything important, he would have come hot-foot to me. Or would he? If he had discovered a tenuous clue, wouldn't he wait till the clue led somewhere definite?

But it was unsettling all the same, if only for the reason that I couldn't make head or tail of the Lionel Bright business. I could see no possible connection between a writer of detective novels and the events that had taken place at Sandbeach. Huffe's interest in Lionel Bright and his subsequent enquiries at the book-shop had been perfectly normal happenings. Huffe liked

Bright's books, and that was that. And probably by now, I could tell myself, Wharton must have come to the same conclusion.

The departure of Barbara Channard had been a minor sensation at the Hotel, as I gathered from the chatter on the lawn before lunch. But after lunch there was a far bigger sensation. Wharton was called to the telephone. It was at the very end of the meal and all at once I became aware that Worne was making the round of the tables. My ears were cocked when he came to Mrs. Smyth.

"You're not actually leaving us, Mr. Worne!"

"Yes," he said. "Almost at once. Most important business in town."

"In connection with that film of yours?" she said, and he didn't deny it. He was approaching my table and I was suitably surprised when he held out his hand.

"You're not going?"

"Indeed I am," he said. "Something highly important has turned up and I just can't afford to disregard it."

"Good-bye, then," I said. "Perhaps we shall run up against each other one day in town."

He said he hoped so and off he went. No sooner had he gone than Wharton came back and he was suggesting a little chat up in my room. But he couldn't wait till we were there.

"That was Fry ringing up," he said, "and what do you think? Worne told him just now he had to go to London and mightn't be back. He'd let Fry have an address in case he might be wanted at an inquest. The resumed inquest on Huffe."

I told him what had happened in the dining-room.

"Something's funny somewhere," George said. "I can understand the Channard business but it's this coming on top of it that puzzles me. The Youngses go and Barbara Channard goes and now this chap Worne goes. What do you think? Is there any connection, or isn't there?"

I said it might be the old, old story. When we were on a job and looking frantically for clues, the most unimportant or explicable things could be viewed in a wrong light. I admitted that there was the other side to the matter: that the highly important could often be dismissed as trivial.

"Well, I've been doing some heavy thinking," George said, and waved me impatiently to a chair. He took a long time lighting his pipe.

"Perhaps I ought to have mentioned it before," he said, "but I've been interested in Worne. When that report of yours said that Huffe was suddenly interested in books, I couldn't help wondering. In fact, I'm beginning to have a theory."

"No need to be apologetic, George," I said. "You don't sound very hopeful, but just what is it?"

"That connecting link we've been looking for. The pivot round which everything revolves. Don't you think it might be Worne?"

That was one in the solar plexus for me. *It was the theory at which I'd arrived myself.* A moment and I was stoking my own pipe and thinking of the things I couldn't understand, and wondering if George might have some of the answers.

"Yes," I said. "You've got something there. It's a lead if it's nothing else. Mind if we go into it?"

George said, far too humbly, that that was the very thing he was wanting to do.

"Take Huffe first," I said. "Why should Worne want to kill Huffe?"

George didn't know. What he said was that it was a far more important thing to know how Worne could have had a hand in Huffe's death, other than by tampering with the plug. And that tampering with the plug we'd discussed before. It couldn't conceivably have been the main cause of Huffe's death.

"But suppose Huffe was hit a glancing blow by a bullet," he said. "Remember how Worne claimed to have been in the water *after* that man Salt? All he had to do was hide the gun quickly and then dive in."

"You've got to get an expert opinion on that skull wound," I said.

"As a matter of fact Fry's getting one," Wharton said, and mentioned a famous Yard pathologist who was due at Sandbeach that afternoon.

"Then why not leave it temporarily like that?" I said. "When you hear his report, then there can be a conference. All the same, the more I think of that theory of yours, the more I like it. If Worne killed Huffe, then he might have tried to get me out of the way because he thought I knew too much. The same with that snooping Lafford woman. The same with Barbara Channard. And even if it's right, we're still left with the main question. What absolute hell of a hole must Worne have been in to have gone in for murder?"

"Plenty of time to go into that," George said. "Pin one murder on him and the rest follows. How often have we run up against the same thing. A man hangs for one murder. After that it doesn't matter a damn to him if he commits a dozen more, provided always he's of the opinion that it'll clear him of the original murder. He's due for hanging and he can only hang once."

"Look, George," I said. "You be on hand to get that skull abrasion report. I'd like to try an experiment on my own account."

"Why not?" he said. "Try anything you like, provided it's going to help."

There was a sound outside the window. It was a taxi departing and we had been so engrossed that we had not heard it arrive.

"There goes Worne," I said. "What I'm going to do is find out just where he's gone."

"But how're you going to do that?"

"You leave that to me," I told him hurriedly and was making for the stairs.

But there had been of necessity, as I saw it, a certain amount of duplicity, and there would have to be more. I would do nothing till that private experiment of mine had produced either some definite results or a complete lack. If there were results, then I would go at once to Wharton. If there weren't, then all I could do was to keep my mouth shut and offer to lend a hand to George or Fry in their own enquiries. In the meanwhile, as I said, there would have to be more duplicity. George would be thinking that I was off to the railway station to get on Worne's tail. If there wasn't a message from me till late that night, he wouldn't be unduly disturbed. Besides, I could always fake a message through Rowse.

What I was guessing was that Worne had gone to London. If so it would be hours before I should get a report, and meanwhile I had an afternoon on my hands. So as soon as George had gone I hurried to the depot behind the railway station. Inside five minutes I was one of a motor-coach load of trippers off for a circular tour. We had tea at a country pub and it was after five o'clock when we got back. I sneaked into the Haven by the staff entrance and so to Rowse's office.

"Anything happened?" I said.

"Nothing at all, old boy." Since that discovery of my identity he'd become even more affable.

I told him to bring in some sort of a meal later, as we'd arranged, and then he gave me a spare key to lock myself in. If I wanted him I could use the extension.

As to what did happen, I'd prefer you to hear the report I made to Wharton. All I will say is this. Sooner than I'd expected—at half-past six to be exact—a call came from one of Bill Ellice's men. What he said was startling enough but I told him to make some further enquiries. Next Rowse brought me a meal on a tray and I told him to tell Wharton that a message had come from me and I'd asked that he should stay in the Hotel till he'd seen me. Then just before eight o'clock a call came from Barbara Channard, but I still sat on. Within half an hour a second message came from Bill's man. It was so startling and inexplicable that I felt I had to see George at once. Rowse took over the telephone. Wharton, he said, was in the lounge.

George was with two or three more people, including Mrs. Smyth, listening to the wireless. He hopped up at once at the sight of me and out we went to the cliff gardens and a handy seat. He was wanting to know where the devil I'd been. I told him I'd been in touch with Bill Ellice and Worne had been picked up in town.

"Where is he?"

"At Lexham Street, just off Long Acre," I said. "He's at a flat above a wholesale stationer's premises. He went straight to it."

That conveyed little, but he nodded to me to go on.

"Within half an hour of his getting there he went out and did some telephoning. Whom do you think he telephoned?"

George didn't know.

"He telephoned Barbara Channard," I said. "I'd already got hold of her and asked her to ring me urgently if anything happened." Then I had to hand off his question. "Wait a minute, George. There's more to come. The next thing that happened was another message from Ellice's man. I'd asked for further enquiries and he'd made them. That flat where Worne is, is not his own. Whom do you think it belongs to?"

Again George didn't know.

"It belongs," I said, "to a writer of detective novels. A chap named Lionel Bright!"

Half an hour later George and I were in my car and on the way to London. Rowse had been seen and a hurried message sent to Fry, and the reason for all the haste was this.

Take first what George had to tell. The expert opinion of Huffe had been that he had been struck a tremendous blow on the skull and had been knocked unconscious. Death had been caused, in layman's language, by drowning. As for the analysis of the spilled orangeade, it had been proved beyond question that there'd been a veronal content enough to cause death. That, as I told George, I should always consider about the luckiest guess of my life.

Then there was what I had to tell George. The time had come, in fact, to make a full confession, and George had been graciously pleased to admit that my devious means had been justified by the ends. Among other things I told him was the scene where Barbara Channard and Worne had had a showdown on the lawn. She had told him to keep his mouth shut unless he wanted her to open her own. If she did open it, she had said, it would be to some effect. That had scared Worne stiff. He hadn't known that all she could open her mouth about was his posturing and posing, and the supposed opinion of him that was held by the sensible residents at the Hotel.

Worne had made that attack on her and it had failed. Then she had left the Hotel and she'd left a note for him. It strongly advised him not to talk any more scandal about herself and hinted that the consequences would be serious. Huffe's name was adroitly brought in. If Worne had had anything to do with Huffe's death, then he'd read between the lines that it had been Huffe who'd told Barbara Channard what she knew.

And that, I said, was just about what Worne did read into that letter, and at once he knew that he had to follow Barbara Channard to town and either get the truth from her or close her mouth. The letter had conveniently given her address and the telephone number. As soon then as he'd reached town, he'd telephoned that number and asked for a meeting. She had agreed to think things over and let him know.

George had worried about her being in danger. I told him I'd arranged about that. And I'd arranged for Worne to be kept under observation. But I certainly agreed with George that the sooner we got to town ourselves, the better. It was for him to take charge and say how things were to be handled from then on.

He had a corner in the back of the car and had talked about getting some sleep. I knew he wouldn't sleep; he was always far too nervous in that hell-wagon of mine, as he called it. But I didn't drive particularly fast, even if driving by a clear night is infinitely easier than driving by day. It was just after two in the morning when I drew up at the all-night garage, and a very few minutes after that we were making up a couple of scratch beds in my flat. I found the kitchen alarm-clock and set it for six o'clock.

George was actually up and shaved before the alarm went off. There wouldn't be a service breakfast till seven o'clock, and then only by request, so we had a quick conference. Both of us had managed to get in some thinking before sleep and we began talking about Huffe, and Worne's motives, but before we'd hardly mentioned the names, George was suggesting something else.

"There's an idea I'd like to try out," he said. "After breakfast I'll see Bill Ellice and get the latest and then I'd rather like to pay a call. You go and see Mrs. Channard."

He was asking what I was proposing to do when I got there. I said I didn't quite know, but we ought to arrange an interview between her and Worne and manage to overhear what was said. That would mean that she would have to be elaborately and carefully coached. The difficulty was, just what could she tell him that would make him give himself away. All I could suggest were various bluffs: that Huffe had told her he was afraid of Worne, for instance, or that Peggy Lafford had told her she was meeting Worne at the Memorial, or that she'd actually seen Worne following me that afternoon into Sandbeach Chine. George didn't like any of them. If the bluffs were called, where should we be?

"Leave it like this," he said. "I've got an idea or two in my head, and I'll pay that little call. You slip round to Mrs. Channard's flat and we'll meet here again at eleven o'clock."

At half-past seven he had gone. I was in no hurry so I got my pipe going and settled down to a bit of concentrated thought. There were things I could have told George if he'd had the patience to listen and not have turned the talk aside to hide some scheme that had suddenly come to his mind. I could have told him, for instance, why I had lost him after our visit to the theatre. I could even have gone on from there and given my theory of how Huffe had been killed. But there it was. George hadn't given me the chance.

What I did do was to take the things I knew and to work outwards from them. Worne, I could tell myself, simply had to be that missing pivot. I had thought I'd met him before but it turned out to be a Long Acre cousin I'd met. Because I'd claimed to have met Worne, I'd been attacked. Then there was Huffe who'd told me he was sure he'd met Worne somewhere before. Afterwards he said he'd been mistaken but that didn't prevent his murder. Barbara Channard had told Worne that she knew things about him—dangerous things, as he'd thought—and Barbara Channard had had a narrow escape. Worne had caught Peggy Lafford snooping in his room, and Peggy Lafford had gone the same way as Huffe.

But that Long Acre cousin puzzled me, if only because the explanation might be so simple. Worne had said he was no longer the occupier of that flat. Yet Worne had gone direct to that flat. Was it he then who had taken it over when the cousin had given it up? If so, why hadn't he acknowledged the fact? Why should he have made so trivial a thing a secret and, now I remembered, why should he have been so perturbed when I mentioned my sister-in-law and how I was intending to hunt through that district for a vacant flat? And above all, what was the connection with the Lionel Bright who now had that flat?

It was beyond me at the moment and the time was getting on, so I finished my toilet and walked down to the Strand to get a Regent's Park bus. At the flats they rang to see if Barbara Channard was visible and I was asked to wait. When I did go up I found that breakfast for two was in the dainty lounge. She was also dressed to kill and I couldn't help feeling vaguely flattered. She said she hadn't slept too well and she'd dreamed of what she called that dreadful man.

"What about communicating with him?" I asked her. "Did he give you a number or anything?"

"He didn't," she said. "All he said was that he'd ring me again."

I claimed a recent breakfast and confined myself to coffee. There didn't seem anything to talk about except Sandbeach and that was somewhat sticky going. She said she'd heard I was married and I said my wife was in Switzerland at the moment. Then we began talking about things in general and we were on at least our third cigarettes when the telephone bell shrilled.

"It's him," she said. "I'm frightened!"

"Rubbish!" I said. "You've only got to hear what he has to say. Remember what I told you in the letter."

She picked up the receiver and was giving a diffident hallo. Then she was frowning at me to show that it was Worne. I didn't catch what he might be saying and then she was looking meaningly at me again.

"I'm almost sure I'm engaged for tonight. If you wait a moment I'll look at my engagement book."

She slipped noiselessly across the carpet and was whispering to me.

"He wants to meet me tonight. Half-past nine. In the Park. Just behind the lake."

"Tell him yes."

She picked up the receiver again and her voice was a bit shaky. When she finally rang off she was looking scared.

"Why did you make me do it?" she was saying to me. "He wants to murder me—that's what he wants to do. The same as he did that Peggy Lafford."

"No, no, no!" I told her and I didn't loosen the hand that was clutching my arm. "Nothing on earth can happen to you. We'll see to all that. It's our job."

"I won't do it, I tell you. I won't do it!"

"Of course you'll do it," I told her wheedlingly.

"I'm still frightened," she was saying, and her arm was tightening about me. Her face rose slowly to mine and her other arm was suddenly round my neck. In quite a different way I was feeling a bit frightened too.

As I let myself into my flat I realised that I was wearing an expression that might be described as devil-may-care. But Wharton didn't turn up till after another quarter of an hour, and he was looking pleased with himself. So bursting was he with his news that he forgot to dissimulate.

"Just heard the latest from Ellice's men," he said. "Worne slipped out at about ten o'clock and did some telephoning."

"I know," I said. "He was ringing Barbara Channard. It's fixed up that he meets her tonight in Regent's Park. Behind the lake."

His eyes narrowed.

"Behind the lake, eh? Well, that shouldn't worry us. But I was telling you something. When he came out of that flat he wasn't wearing glasses. He'd shaved off those little side whiskers and when he came back he'd had a hair cut. He didn't look like the same chap, so Potter said."

"Wait a minute, George," I said, and was suddenly fumbling for my glasses. "Worne's hair was dyed when he was at Sand-beach."

My eyes opened wider.

"I've got it, George. Worne *is* Lionel Bright. They're one and the same person."

"I know," he said. "That's what I was going to tell you." Things began flashing back to me and yet they didn't quite explain.

"Yes," I said. "But why should he want to kill Huffe?"

"If you'll let me get a word in edgeways," George told me huffily, "I'll tell you that too."

CHAPTER XVIII
THE REASON WHY

IT WAS three o'clock when I saw George again, and then only for a matter of minutes. He was still on good terms with himself. The latest news of Worne was that he'd gone to a Covent Garden bank where he had an account in the name of Lionel Bright, and had drawn out a hundred pounds in small notes.

"What about his other account?" I said. "If we're right—and we must be right—he'll have one in the name of Worne."

"You're always in too much of a hurry," George told me. "Wait till you hear the rest. Worne's got that dye off his head. He's fairish haired with just a touch or two of grey."

He was telling me the name of the dope Worne could have used to remove the dye, but I wasn't interested in that. If he was drawing out cash, then he was prepared to bolt, and if he was going to bolt, why hadn't he drawn out some Worne money too?

"Dense all of a sudden, aren't you?" George said. "He's now got himself back to the Lionel Bright identity. He couldn't go to the bank till he'd done that. Then how could he go to the other bank where they know him as Worne?"

He was right, and that I'd been a bit dense. It was that embarrassing episode with Barbara Channard, I could tell myself, that had blunted my wits—not that I had found it too embarrassing, except perhaps in the remembering.

"Yes, but one other thing," I said. "If Worne's about to bolt, doesn't that look even more dangerous for Mrs. Channard?" Another thought came in the same context. "Or isn't he seeing her after all?"

"What do you mean?"

"If he's now Lionel Bright, how can he see her? She's expecting to see Jeffrey Worne—the man she knew at Sandbeach."

"That's the very reason why she's going to be safe," he told me exasperated, and then he was saying he had a dozen and more things to do, and he'd have to be off. At eight o'clock sharp he'd be back at the flat.

For the life of me I couldn't see what he'd been driving at. If Worne was preparing to bolt—anticipating a possible necessity to bolt, if you wish—then it could only be because of what might happen to Barbara Channard. But if he was no longer Worne, then how could he interview her? If he told her that Worne hadn't been able to come but had sent that fictitious cousin instead, how could he expect her to open her mouth to a stranger?

Then I could tell myself that that was George's headache. My problem was how to spend the evening and I solved it by taking tea out and going to a cinema. It was a good show and for minutes at a time I completely forgot what was to happen a few hours later. Then I had a meal at the flat and well before eight o'clock was ready for Wharton.

"I don't think you're going to see much," were his first words to me. "Sure you want to come?"

I told him I'd been in everything from the beginning, and even if I had to be blindfolded, I was going to Regent's Park. And I did go. Before half-past eight George and I were approaching the lake from the far side. It was an overcast night and later there was to be a thunderstorm as heavy as London had known for years. Maybe that was why that part of the Park was almost deserted.

We had left the path and were among the mountainous clumps of shrubs. George pointed across at an open space.

"That's where Mrs. Channard will wait—on that seat," he said. "You'd better get right in the middle of these bushes. Whatever happens, don't move."

He didn't even say he'd be seeing me later. In fact he'd gone before I was hardly aware. I wriggled my way into the far side of the clump and when I'd broken a twig or two, had something of a view. At least I could just see the seat where George had said Barbara Channard would be. Then I settled down to a long and uncomfortable wait.

Nine o'clock came at last and dusk was in the sky. With each minute the air was more heavy and oppressive. Soon the midges were beginning to bother me and I had an overwhelming urge to light a cigarette. A quarter past nine and I could pass the time by counting seconds and checking on my watch. The minutes slowly went, and then in the deep dusk I saw movement. I polished my glasses and regardless of Wharton's warning, reached out a hand and widened the field of view. But for that I'd never have seen Barbara Channard.

She was walking slowly up and down and once or twice I saw her glance at her wrist-watch. It was now so dark that I could scarcely see my watch and when I had brought it near my face and seen that it was nearly the half-hour, I looked out again and saw that now she was on the seat. But for the light colour of the raincoat I could never have seen her at all. And it was at that very moment that I heard a faint sound from behind.

I slowly turned my head and it seemed that there was a dark shape that moved and was gone. I held my breath and listened but there was no longer any sound. Behind me was the dull hum of traffic, and that was all. But that was no more than a background and the silence seemed now as oppressive as the darkness and the air. Then the moments went slowly on again and I was feeling that at all costs I must move, and see. Now the figure on the seat was barely discernible. Again I polished my glasses and strained to look, and it was then that the silence was broken by a shriek.

There were confused noises. I heard Wharton's voice and then I was shielding my eyes and bursting a way through my shield of bushes. The last branches gave too quickly and I fell. As I rose, a torch flashed ahead of me. There were two torches, and Wharton was calling something. I made my way forward and heavy drops of rain were on my face. A torch shone full on me, and there was Wharton.

"Everything O.K.," he was telling me. "Like to have a look at him before he goes?"

Somehow I didn't, and yet I was too much of a moral coward to refuse. A police car was already drawn up and I could see the three men by the door. Wharton flashed his torch on the face of the middle one and that middle one was trying to cover his face with his handcuffed hands.

He was hatless and I should never have known him, except maybe as the man into whom I'd barged that distant day in a London street. Somehow he was not Worne but a stranger. His eyes were wild and he was still panting from the struggle, and I turned my head away. In some strange way he was only a queer, impersonal episode, born of that long wait and the surrounding dark.

"Take him along," Wharton said curtly, and we watched and listened till the sound of the car had gone. Another car drew up behind us and its headlights made another world.

"How's Mrs. Channard?" I said.

"Mrs. Channard?" Wharton said, and gave a little chuckle. "That wasn't Mrs. Channard. That was one of our own women in her clothes, got up to look like her as near as ninepence."

"But suppose he'd attacked her?"

"Of course he attacked her," he told me. "He couldn't talk to her, could he? He was Lionel Bright. The only thing he could do was attack her. He sneaked up on her from behind and he had his cosh in his hand. That was when we nabbed him. If we hadn't, she'd have been another Peggy Lafford."

He was motioning for me to get in the car. He'd drop me at my flat, he said. But he'd already done some planning ahead. In the morning I ought to go back to Sandbeach and collect our things, and I could bring Fry back with me. At what time was I proposing to start?

"As soon as I can," I said. "Probably at about eight."

"Tell you what you might do with yourself tonight," he said. "Get out a rough report for Fry. Make a couple of copies and I can show one to the Powers-that-Be. In the morning I'll be round at about half-past seven, if that'll suit you."

I said it would suit me fine and I'd have a couple of breakfasts ready. Then I was asking him something that puzzled me. I said I still didn't get all the implications of Worne's getting back to the identity of Lionel Bright.

"He was desperate," George said, "and he still didn't know we were on his tail. But if we did get on his tail or had to question him, then we'd never have found him at all—or that was his idea. Jeffrey Worne would have disappeared. If ever we did run across anybody, it would have been a certain Lionel Bright. If he was never suspected, then he could have reappeared some time as Worne again."

Then I was getting out of the car and he was giving a sudden chuckle.

"A bit of luck for the pair of us, the way things have turned out? That little holiday at Sandbeach ought to go down as expenses."

I'd just got down to that report for Fry when the telephone bell rang. I cursed the interruption, but as soon as I heard the voice I couldn't help smiling. It was Peckenham. He'd rung the Haven but had been told I was in town, so he'd taken a chance on my private address.

"That little book of mine," he said. "I've run another copy to earth and I wondered if you'd care to accept it."

"Delighted," I said. "But what about having lunch with me? Say the day after tomorrow. You might meet me here."

"I don't know, my boy," he began diffidently.

"Rubbish!" I told him bluntly. "It's a hell of a long time ago since Plancus was consul. Besides, I'd like to see you. It'll really be a pleasure."

That was that and I was still smiling as I hung up. Somehow, too, it put me in good heart for writing that report, for I was very soon recognising that if I weren't to spend half the night in getting things in meticulous order, that report would have to be very scrappy indeed. But it could at least be a report on which a more detailed one could later be based. So this is what I finally wrote, and my intention was to hand it to Fry who could read it while I was at the Haven collecting the gear and settling up with Rowse.

"DEAR FRY,

"This is a brief synopsis of the Jeffrey Worne affair. You'll be reading things you never even suspected—nor did we at the time, for that matter—and any further explanations can come later. I am writing from what I might call my own angle, and I hope you will be gratified to learn that even a so-called expert can still miss seeing what is under his nose.

"Let's leave out reasons and begin with the killing of Huffe. Huffe told Mrs. Channard, and he as good as told me, that he'd found a little gold-mine in Sandbeach. That mine was Worne. Either in his days in a publisher's office, or else as a fake literary agent, Huffe had met Lionel Bright. At Sandbeach he spotted Bright who was now Jeffrey Worne, and Huffe was astute enough to arrive at the reason. He must have guessed it and proved it, or he'd never have been able to terrify Worne into murder.

"Briefly, there was a rendezvous in the dark, and probably away on the beach beyond the steps. Worne was a powerful man for all his affectation of limpness and he struck Huffe a murderous blow on the skull. The tide was in, or almost so and he held the head under water. Huffe was wearing flannel bags, a soft shirt and a tie and a light sports coat. Worne took shirt and tie off and put on a swimming vest and pushed the body into the deep water against the rocks. Later he took the shirt and coat to Worne's room.

"That was where he was a fool. The ingenuity of mind that made him quite a good writer of detective novels, prompted him to be over-elaborate. Huffe's body would ultimately be recovered and he thought he had to explain how it was that he came to be drowned, and with that crack on the skull, and in those clothes. He had, in other words, to fake a drowning.

"After the show at the theatre the previous night he had called on the leading man in *Ginger for Pluck* and had contrived to appropriate a wig that could at least be doctored to the colour of Huffe's auburn hair. Once he had that he could get on with the scheme. It involved a visit to the foot of Carbury Chine and the concealing among the undergrowth—after the murder—of a coat and shirt for himself.

"It didn't strike me as strange that Worne should suddenly have begun to take pre-breakfast walks towards Carbury Chine. It was natural therefore—to me at least—that he should have been at the Chine that morning and have witnessed the drowning. It was his own drowning. That morning, after faking Huffe's bed to make it look as if it had been slept in, he sneaked down to the beach and, as Huffe, rowed towards the Chine. He was a magnificent swimmer, remember, and it isn't unreasonable to suppose therefore that he must also have been something of an oarsman. In any case, he was: at least good enough to look like one, and like Huffe. I, for one, took the hair and the flannel bags and swimming vest for granted. I saw Huffe, and never did I have a suspicion to the contrary.

"The plug had been loosened and at the right moment Worne pulled it out. The boat sank and he pretended to fall. Then he swam under water to the overhanging boughs and pulled himself up. He slipped off the swimming vest and hid it and he slipped on the shirt and coat. Then he waited till Salt was in the water and then he swam out under water again and suddenly appeared.

"Why was he so sure somebody would see the drowning? Because of that Sandbeach arrangement of times for meals. At the hotels on the Carbury side, people would be out on the lawns or at their bedroom windows completing a hasty toilet, and listening for breakfast gongs. Carbury Chine and The Mouth were under their eyes, whereas the steepness of the cliffs on the Sandbeach side hid Worne when he pulled himself up among the un-dergrowth, and changed his clothes and hid vest and wig.

"While he and Salt were trying to recover the body, he would be insidiously coaching Salt. Impressing on him how Huffe had struck his skull on the boat and how he, Worne, hadn't been in the water till after Salt. He wanted Salt to be the real hero, for that would draw less attention to himself. That was why he was genuinely furious when the local paper put Salt in the background. That was something I should have wondered more about—why there were certain kinds of publicity that Worne should dislike.

"And there were other things I ought to have remembered. I'd told Worne I'd seen him somewhere before. We were on the beach and he went in to swim without his glasses. I wasn't going in with him but he went right to the water's edge with his glasses on and left them in his shoes. Why? Because he feared I should see him without glasses and be still more certain I'd seen Lionel Bright. But that was only a first panic. Later on he didn't mind my seeing him without the glasses. But I should have known the glasses, huge rims and all, were only a fake. They were supposed to be distance glasses, and yet he could tell me that Barbara Channard—a good hundred yards away—was Barbara Channard. He at once corrected the slip, but that should only have made it worse, especially as I was very soon to discover that his hair was dyed. It was silly of him too, and I think he recognised the fact at the time, to pretend he'd heard Barbara Channard and Huffe quarrelling and her talking about killing. It was a feeble red herring and I'm sure now he was kicking him-self for having tried to draw it across what shouldn't have been a trail at all.

"Two other things occur to me. When Huffe was dead that night, Worne took a certain detective novel from his room but you'll hear more about that later. Then after the supposed drowning, Worne wore a lounge suit. I think it was to conceal his arms and shoulders. He was less tanned than Huffe and proba-bly he'd applied dope to his arms and shoulders before he rowed that boat. When he felt he really had to go swimming a few days later he kept himself to himself and didn't swim near the shore.

"So much for the Huffe affair. But then Worne had a shock. I think that on a certain night when I caught Peggy Lafford listening at Worne's door, Worne and Huffe were in that room and Huffe was putting on the screws. Or maybe she saw him bringing back Huffe's clothes or doctoring the bed or sneaking out to the boat. She must have seen something or heard something and she was just the kind to throw out hints and suggest that a sum of money would keep her mouth shut. Worne decided to shut it in another way.

"As for the attack on me, I honestly think that was made on the spur of the moment. Worne had every reason to wish me out of the way. He had reasons perhaps to suspect that I was taking too great an interest. Perhaps, for all my care, he'd seen me enter the police-station. I don't know. I do know that he must have followed me into the chine and that I gave him an absolutely sitting chance. He took it, but he bungled the job.

"You will have noticed the ingenuity of the detective writer's mind. So far every killing and attack was well-ordered, and when he had a new panic about Mrs. Channard, he had to fake a suicide. Huffe had died by accident; I should have died by accident, and Peggy Lafford was the victim of a sadistic murderer. Never a chance there of any suspicion falling on one so—shall I say famous, as Jeffrey Worne. So the Channard affair was planned as an accident too. Just an overdose of sleeping tablets. And the reason? Loss of sleep on account of the shock to Barbara Channard by the death of Huffe—the man, as Mrs. Smyth would confirm, to whom she'd just become engaged.

"So much for all that. No use crossing the t's and dotting the i's and worrying about omissions. What you're wanting to know is the *reason* for it all. Why did Worne kill Huffe? That's the vital question. All the other happenings are only adjuncts.

"Perhaps you've already guessed the reason. We haven't every detail of evidence and information yet, but we've got quite enough. These are the facts that have so far come to light. Some of them we could have verified at that bookshop in Sandbeach High Street. Easy, isn't it, to be wise after the event.

"We begin with Lionel Bright. For years he'd written detective novels and he'd changed his publisher twice. His output was a book for publication approximately every nine months. His average receipts from those books—including cheap editions— was just over three hundred and fifty pounds a year. On that sum he could just keep the Long Acre flat going and have a reasonably good, if quiet, bachelor time.

"Then, in 1941, he had the idea of writing a book under another name. I'd say that when it was finished he knew it was pretty good. It was so good, in fact, that he was certain he'd find a publisher. And then he began to ask himself a few questions. Trepnich was the name of his agent, and he wondered if Trepnich need know about that book. If he didn't, there'd be a saving of the usual ten per cent. He wondered especially if the Income Tax people need know about that book. If they didn't, then whatever it brought in royalties would be sheer profit. You may or may not know, by the way, that publishers have consistently refused to divulge what they pay to their authors. Agents are different. They have to furnish accounts.

"Well, Bright sent that manuscript to a publisher, and under the name of Jeffrey Worne. Correspondence was conducted through an accommodation address and over the telephone. The book was published and—partly owing to merit and partly to war conditions—it brought Bright over five hundred pounds. By the time the second manuscript had been accepted, he had hit on a further scheme.

"This was the dual personality idea. After years of comparative obscurity, his head was a bit turned. He was now a writer, not of the humble detective novel, but of a serious novel that had been well enough reviewed. And he had money. He could spread his wings and bask in publicity—provided always that that publicity didn't bring him too much to the notice of the Commissioners of Inland Revenue.

"How he worked it is still guess-work, though it won't be so for long. But what he must have done was to plan to spend all the long middle of the year at some good spot. Before he left London he'd dye his hair, grow the side-whiskers and generally assume the personality of Jeffrey Worne. He could have told Trepnich he was going away—to Ireland, shall we say—and Trepnich could carry on with anything that concerned Lionel Bright, and make all decisions till he returned in the late autumn. I needn't labour details. You can see for yourself how things must have been worked.

"That second book sold even better than the first. But for paper restrictions *Scarlet May* would have sold extremely well. As it was, it brought its author best part of a thousand pounds, and it made his name really known. But there was a snag. Look at the way Jeffrey Worne was living. You know what I was paying at the Haven. That sort of expense was going on for Worne month in and month out. No doubt he thought he was getting good value. He was a somebody and he was having a good time. But the fact remains that he was spending a very considerable deal of what he'd earned.

"You see what I'm driving at? You see why he was like a cornered rat when Huffe spotted not only Lionel Bright but also what was behind the dual personality business? At the very best there would have been a heavy fine to pay as well as all the tax owed, and Worne just hadn't the money. Most likely he'd have been given a term of imprisonment, and in any case he'd have been a ruined man. I'd say he'd always been an egoist and just a bit queer, Success had turned his head and got into his blood and made him something of a megalomaniac and the thought of exposure, and prison, must have driven him almost mad.

"That's all then. The only thing about which I might reproach myself, is that I ought to have attached more importance to the fact that Worne always poured such scorn on detective novels. I admit that an author can be capable of intellectual arrogance—especially one of Worne's type—but still I think that there I missed a clue. Maybe I shall think of other things that I missed, not that I'm going to let them worry me now.

"Yours as ever,

L.T."

George Wharton turned up at half-past seven the next morning as we'd arranged. Breakfast was on at once and after it he read that rough report. I didn't give him a chance to give me one or two peculiar looks. I was busy completing preparations for the journey, and if he discovered yet more things that I'd kept to myself, that was his headache. But I wasn't thinking too much about that. I was realising that I hated going back to Sandbeach and seeing again the Haven Hotel. Somehow it would be like revisiting a scene of one's dead youth. Everything would be unreal and different. No Worne, no Barbara Channard, no Huffe and even no Gerald. The thought that I should soon be seeing Peckenham again made no difference, except that I should be going to a Sandbeach that had no Peckenham. Those first few days at Sandbeach had been vivid and alive, and among them I too had felt a peculiar kind of rejuvenation. Now I felt I hardly knew what except that I did know that I somehow hated the Sandbeach I was soon again to see. I think I'd have given quite a deal to have put back the clock or to be realising that everything had been a dream, I even shut my eyes and saw with an inward eye that Hotel again: Peckenham on the lawn as the crowd waited for the gong: the flick of Huffe's thumb as he held that gold lighter for Barbara Channard's cigarette. I could frown at the boisterous Gerald and his fools of parents, or run a surreptitious eye over a pair of sheer silk stockings, or curl an ironic lip when Worne came into the dining-room.

But George was giving me a call. He had finished that brief report and was good enough to say that it wasn't too bad. By the time I was back with Fry, of course, there'd be a lot more to add. His own idea was that Worne was ripe for a confession.

"By the way, old Peckenham rang me last night," I said. "I asked him to lunch with me tomorrow. You'd better join us."

"Me?" George said. "Rather spoil his lunch, wouldn't it?"

"Don't you believe it," I said. "You can't keep a good man down. I'll bet you half a crown that before that meal's over, you and Peckenham'll be like two bugs in a rug."

"I'll take you," snapped George. "And something else before I forget it. I was thinking this morning that you might like to take that Mrs. Channard back with you to Sandbeach. She's supposed to be going back. Mind if I try to get hold of her?"

He helped himself to the telephone and I wandered off to the bathroom again. What to think I hardly knew. Then something flashed to my mind and I gave a little shudder. There was a question I'd have to put to George, and at once.

I waited till he'd finished telephoning and then he wasn't giving me a chance to put my question.

"It's all right," he said. "You needn't wait. She says she isn't going back to Sandbeach after all. She thinks she'd like to stay on in town."

It was not till we were nearing the lift that I could summon the courage to put my question.

"Tell me something, George. When did Mrs. Channard know that she wouldn't have to go personally to Regent's Park to meet Worne?"

"When?" he said, and pursed his lips as he sparred for time. Then he was giving me a playful nudge in the ribs.

"To tell you the truth, she knew yesterday morning. When you were on the way there, I got her on the telephone. Just gave her the tip that whatever you told her, we were fixing it so she definitely wouldn't have to go."

"So that was it," I said, and my fingers went instinctively to my glasses.

"Was what?"

"Oh, nothing," I said off-handedly. "Just something I happened to remember."

But I was doing some remarkably quick thinking. Barbara Channard had staged that frightened business. She'd had designs on me from the very first. Maybe from that night when she'd smiled at me when I'd entered the dining-room at the Haven, and like an idiot I'd smiled back. Like a fool I'd played into her hands and now. . . .

The lift was there and I suppose I must have uttered something like a grunt. That woman, I was telling myself, was staying on in town. She wasn't a man-hunter. She was a man-eater.

"Something still worrying you?" George said as he stepped into the lift.

"Not at all," I said, and my smile must have been even more fatuous than usual. "I just happened to be wondering how soon it would be before my wife was back."

THE END

Lightning Source UK Ltd.
Milton Keynes UK
UKHW041442280319
340081UK00001B/11/P